D0442911

A Head in Cambodia

JENNA MURPHY MYSTERIES

A Head in Cambodia

A Death in Bali (forthcoming)

A HEAD in CAMBODIA

A JENNA MURPHY MYSTERY

Nancy Tingley

Swallow Press | Athens, Ohio

Swallow Press
An imprint of Ohio University Press, Athens, Ohio 45701
ohioswallow.com

To obtain permission to quote, reprint, or otherwise reproduce or
distribute material from Swallow Press / Ohio University Press
publications, please contact our rights and permissions department at
(740) 593-1154 or (740) 593-4536 (fax).

Printed in the United States of America
Swallow Press / Ohio University Press books are printed on
acid-free paper ⊗ ™

27 26 25 24 23 22 21 20 19 18 17   5 4 3 2 1

Library of Congress Cataloging-in-Publication Data

Names: Tingley, Nancy, date– author.
Title: A head in Cambodia : a Jenna Murphy mystery / Nancy Tingley.
Description: Athens, Ohio : Swallow Press, [2017] | Series: Jenna Murphy
    mysteries ; 1
Identifiers: LCCN 2016053680| ISBN 9780804011853 (hardcover : acid-free
    paper) | ISBN 9780804040808 (pdf)
Subjects: LCSH: Women detectives—Fiction. | Museum curators—Fiction. |
    Art—Collectors and collecting—Fiction. | Murder—Investigation—Fiction.
    | Art, Southeast Asian—Fiction. | BISAC: FICTION / General. | FICTION /
    Mystery & Detective / General. | GSAFD: Mystery fiction.
Classification: LCC PS3620.I537 H43 2017 | DDC 813/.6—dc23
LC record available at https://lccn.loc.gov/2016053680

To the best kids ever
Sloan and Jessie

Thanks

Elizabeth Fuller Collins

Nina Schuyler

Eliza Harding Turner

Elizabeth Rieke

Amy Torgeson

Sheila Levine

John Morris

and the staff of Ohio University Press/Swallow Press

A Head in Cambodia

1

The head lay on the table before me, partially covered by a cloth that did nothing to disguise the fact that it had been severed from its body. The eye like a lotus petal torn from the seedpod. The curve of the earlobe like a whorl of sand in the midst of a tornado. A hole where an earring had fitted snugly in place. Hair pulled back in a chignon, each strand clearly articulated. So thick and lush that you knew the hair would spill to her waist if loosened.

I leaned forward, better to see the lips, full and puckered, slightly extended as if reaching, arching, longing for a kiss. Longing, yet partially opened as if taking in breath.

That was what I was missing, that taking in of breath. That link to the living and all that living entails. Breath, consciousness, attachment—not just of head to body, but of the ephemeral to the concrete, soul to body, mind to body. That connection of mind and body that our California gurus encourage us to embrace, to bring to fruition, to cultivate. We are incomplete until we do.

I shook myself, doubting I would be thinking all this if confronted by an arm, a leg, some other body part. Seeing the head gave me a sense of the whole. It had personality. It had wishes and desires that would not exist for me if I had some other piece of her before me.

P.P. handed me gloves.

I put the first on backwards, thumb where the little finger belonged, because I couldn't tear my eyes from this face, the taut smoothness of the skin, the contrasting fine detail of her coif. I pressed my body against the table as I yanked the glove off and put it on correctly.

As I reached to touch that perfect skin, I felt P.P. move closer and heard his sharp intake of breath. "I know her," I said. I hefted the stone, dense and fine-grained, the head dark against the white towel, and held it in my hands, her weighty cheek pressed against my breast.

"Jenna," he exclaimed. "No!" His rotund body slumped against the table and stilled, this man who was always in motion.

"Afraid so. Oh, yes. Radha."

"Radha," he repeated numbly, rubbing his hands together as if the friction would bring him back to life, would animate her. He knew who Radha was: consort to the Hindu god Krishna, a *gopi*, the gorgeous cowgirl who had captured Krishna's heart.

I nodded.

"Female. But how?" he asked.

"How do I know who she is? She's famous, well, famous for those of us who know Khmer sculpture. It's the head from the eleventh-century Krishna and Radha sculpture in the museum in Siem Reap, Cambodia. Detached from the body and stolen five or so years ago." I paused and frowned. "Unless this is a copy."

"No," P.P. said emphatically. P. P. Bhattacharya—a trustee and patron of the Searles Museum, in Marin County—had brought her in to show her to me, Jenna Murphy, curator of Asian art and a friend. "She's going home," I said.

"So beautiful," moaned P.P.

"That's why she's famous," I said. I turned the head around in my hands, pushing aside my niggling doubts about authenticity.

I appreciated each little detail—the braids in her hair; the flowers of her narrow tiara tucked so carefully behind her ears and tied in a bow at the back of her head; the thin, carved outline around her lips that yearned for that kiss; the eyes that stared straight into mine, asking me, begging me, to take her home, back to Cambodia. I knew how P.P. felt. She expanded my heart as she did his, as only a great work of art can.

I said, "The Baphuon—a monstrous temple. You've been." P.P. had spent two weeks in Siem Reap at the ancient capital of the Khmer empire, Angkor, just a few years before. "The French have been restoring it for years. Decades. They began in the early twentieth century, then renewed their efforts after the Pol Pot era, once the genocide had come to an end. That was when they excavated this sculpture."

"Don't want to." A pout spread across his face, and he began to pace.

I watched him, this short round man. "I know. It will be hard to let her go. But when you see her reattached to her body, you'll feel rewarded. You'll love her even more. And you'll be a hero."

"Expensive, Jenna."

I gave him a look. Not because I didn't understand him. I did. I was one of the few people who had decoded his abrupt, abbreviated manner of speaking. I gave him a look because P.P. was one of the wealthiest men in Silicon Valley, and "expensive" wasn't usually in his vocabulary. I knew why it was cropping up now. He'd already become attached to this piece and would use any excuse—even pretending expense was an issue for him—to keep it. His raison d'être was the act of collecting—the search, the discovery, the purchase—the best of all retail therapy. Now that the piece was part of his collection he would do or say anything to protect it.

I turned my attention back to the head. Flawless, I thought as I studied it more closely. Too flawless? No tiny chips around the edge of the ear or the eyelid, no wear to the braids or breakage to the tip of the nose, those hints that denote age. In a sculpture that had tumbled to the ground in a deteriorated temple one expected the wear of rain and wind, or breakage and rough edges caused by falling. I set the head on the table. I'm a small woman, and it was a heavy head.

As I touched those glorious lips, I said, "I know. But the Cambodians will love you when you return this sculpture." Yet, as I spoke, I was tallying up the pros and cons. Real or fake. Old or new. That's always the question with Southeast Asian sculpture, as the number of fakes increases yearly and the quality exponentially. I adjusted my shoulders, as if straightening my five-foot-two frame might help me resolve the question.

"Don't want love," he responded, sounding more like a petulant four-year-old than a man with a string of degrees and an accent that combined his homeland, India, with upper-crust Eton and Oxford. He hated words, superfluous words, though I'd heard him speak eloquently on occasion.

"Well, I'm afraid there's no other option if it is the authentic, original Radha. It would be unethical of me to do anything other than have you—"

"I know." He impatiently picked up the head.

"Gloves, P.P."

"No," he said crossly as his hands caressed the stone surface. As if in a daze, he repeated, "Return her."

I opened my mouth, horrified at the oils that his fingers were imparting to the stone. But I managed to restrain myself before saying more. After all, it was his head. I pulled my gloves off and brushed away the strand of hair that seemed always to be flopping into my eyes. P.P. turned the head over and over, perhaps trying to process, as I had, its lack of apparent wear.

I mentally shook myself. It was so gorgeously carved, the proportions so perfect—everything about it attested it a masterpiece. It was difficult to think that it might be a fake, a modern copy.

"Return what?"

We both jumped.

"Return what?" Arthur Philen, deputy director of the museum, repeated as he stepped through the door of the conservation lab. Arthur was a hoverer. He gave us all turns, popping in when least expected.

"This head that P.P. just purchased. It's the head that was stolen a few years ago from a famous Cambodian sculpture. I'm sorry—it *looks* like the head of that sculpture. That head was broken right off the work while it was still in the museum." I cursed myself and my tendency to speak before thinking. One was always better off saying as little as possible to Arthur, since he had the innate ability to turn the simplest thought, act, moment into a drama.

He sidled into the small space between us. He was a narrow man, physically and intellectually.

"That isn't good. We don't want stolen art in our museum . . ." He began to dither, circling P.P. and the head. P.P.'s jaw locked. So did mine. Philen was impossible.

"I can't be sure it's stolen," I said. "It could be an extremely good copy. I need to do some research, and Tyler should examine it."

"Tyler," P.P. said flatly, as if the excess energy that kept him in motion at all times had been drained from him. He held the head more closely to him.

"Conservator," Arthur said, picking up not only P.P.'s abbreviated style, but also a bit of his lilting accent.

P.P. rolled his eyes. He knew who Tyler was. P.P. practically lived in the museum.

"Yes, once Tyler goes over it and we're certain it's the original, then we can decide what to do." A cramp began to knot my calf, and I pushed up on my toes. I'd been so busy with my upcoming exhibition of Chinese Qing monochrome porcelains, I hadn't found much time to ride my bike.

"Where is Tyler? This is his lab, why isn't he here?" Arthur spun around, looking for the missing Tyler. He would have been a great dancer if he wasn't so uptight. I could see that he was beginning to get his underwear in a knot.

"P.P., you can't bring stolen art into our museum," Arthur said primly, circling around the head and P.P. Though he waved his hands around, he didn't seem interested in touching the head, or admiring its great beauty. Not for the first time, I wondered if Arthur really liked art. He wouldn't be the first art historian who didn't. I couldn't think of anyone else in the museum who thought less about art. Even the guards were always up on current exhibitions and grilled me on what museums I'd visited when I traveled. Our staff parties were permeated with art, with art history charades, more obscure with each passing year, as details of paintings—not just complete paintings—made their way into our charade lexicon.

P.P. glared at him and shifted his body, causing Arthur, in his ever-tightening progress around the room, to run into the worktable. "Didn't know."

"Of course he didn't know," I said. "We don't know. Arthur, please, we need to do some research. If it does turn out to be the original head, P.P. will happily return it to the Cambodian government." I looked meaningfully at P.P. His mouth was set in a harsh line, but he nodded agreement.

"Return it? Without being asked?" Arthur began marching again, gesticulating as he did. "Return it like that famous lintel that was returned to Thailand, or those sculptures to Cambodia a few years ago?"

Arthur's parts made one view him as a two-dimensional fabrication—a mechanical toy with jerky movements and exaggerated physiognomy. Aquiline nose, a slab of a face, limbs extended like Laurel in that old Laurel and Hardy movie when he was stretched on a rack. Right now the gears in the head of that mechanical toy were moving so fast I feared it would suddenly begin to do a full three-sixty spin.

The grinding of gears in Arthur's head always aligned with his desire to get attention, to get noticed. Arthur sought affirmation as a way to negotiate himself into Caleb New's position as the museum's director. Everything he did, every word he spoke, was an attempt to move him in that direction. "We're getting ahead of ourselves, Arthur." I may be small and young, but I can be forceful. I can also be impulsive, as evidenced by my initial certainty that this was the genuine head. But Arthur was gone, popping out as quickly as he'd popped in, leaving P.P. and me looking at each other, holding the proverbial bag, or in this case, the head. "Uh-oh," I said.

P.P. scowled and said, accurately and succinctly, "Idiot." Then he resumed caressing the head. I had to keep reminding myself that the head belonged to him and it wasn't my place to chastise him for not wearing gloves. Somehow, having the head here in the conservation lab, in the midst of microscope, beakers and brushes, lacquers and paints, all the paraphernalia of the science of restoration and conservation, made his stroking seem all the more incorrect.

"Fake would be good," P.P. said.

For a second I didn't understand. "Because you could keep it?"

He nodded, running his finger around and around the whorl of that perfect ear.

"I thought you said it was expensive."

He shrugged.

There was something he wasn't telling me. I pulled the gloves back on and took the head from him. It took some strength, not just because the head was heavy, but because P.P. was firmly attached. I turned it upside down as I wrestled it away and looked at the break, but there wasn't anything unusual about it. It was irregular, rough, one side of the neck extending further than the other. Not cut with a modern saw, or so it seemed. Which was weird, as hadn't the head been cut from the sculpture?

I looked up and out the high windows that lighted the conservation lab, trying to recall what I knew about the theft. The alarm system malfunctioning, the only guard asleep in his office, the head detached at an old break. Ah, yes, that would explain the uneven surface. I looked back at the neck, where one would expect to find some of the adhesive that had attached the head to the body at the old break. I couldn't see any, but I would have Tyler check for it, as it was an important clue to whether the piece really was the original.

Then I looked closely at the stone. It appeared to be the good, fine-grained sandstone typical of Cambodian sculptures. It wasn't concrete or resin mixed with crushed stone and poured into a mold, the way some fakes are created today.

"I'll put it on Tyler's priority list if you don't mind leaving it here for a while," I said. "He really needs to check it under the microscope. Secondly, do you mind if he chips a tiny piece away from the lower section of the neck? So that he can see how deep the skin of patination is and if it's irregular, as one would expect from an old piece. You know, since the discoloration wouldn't be uniform over the surface."

P.P. didn't speak, and I realized that he'd mentally answered my first question and wasn't going to bother to answer my second, impatient, as he always was, with the obvious.

"Sorry, P.P. Let's go to the registrar's office and get you a receipt for the piece."

"Oh, well," he said as we headed for the door.

"What do you know about the people who sold the head? The person who bought it originally?"

He didn't answer.

"P.P., don't get secretive on me now."

"Never should have shown you," he sulked, holding the door open for me.

"Well, that may be. If you want to own a stolen head." He was beginning to irritate me. The greed, the acquisitiveness that I saw as his least attractive characteristic was showing itself in his foul expression. In the corridor, I asked again, "Do you know anything about the former owner?"

"Suspicious death."

"Who? The owner?" I stopped at the registrar's door, but P.P. kept on going, heading for the elevator that would take him out of our basement offices, leaving without a receipt and with my questions unanswered.

I cursed him. But only for a moment. I understood. If you live your life for beautiful objects, they become like lovers. To have one taken from you is not pleasant.

I wondered where I might find Tyler, but decided I couldn't spend my time searching for him. Tyler would be back in the conservation lab soon enough, and I had a hundred things to do. I stuck my head into the registrar's office. "Breeze, we need to get a receipt to P.P. for an eleventh-century Khmer head."

Breeze was responsible for keeping track of all objects in the museum. Any piece brought in, whether it belonged to the museum or not, needed to be noted in the records, and if someone left an artwork for examination or for sale, they needed a receipt.

"Okay. Come in and I'll write it up. I'll let you get it to him."

"I'll be back to pick it up."

"You're really pushing out the boat today," she said.

"What do you mean?"

"I wouldn't bend over in that skirt if I were you."

"You didn't say that two weeks ago when I wore it."

"You must have washed it since then. And dried it."

"You're right. Too short?"

"Way. The last thing you need is to exaggerate those curves. At work, anyway." She rolled her eyes. "It's cute—don't get me wrong—and it does match the purple streak in your hair."

I laughed as I pushed the strand behind my ear. "Thanks."

2

"So tell me about this head that I've found lying on the middle of my work table," Tyler said, the edge in his voice clear even over the phone. "I'll be right there." I hung up, rose from my desk and the pile of oversized papers that covered its surface, pulled my skirt down to a presentable length, and hurried toward the conservation lab. Tyler hated anyone on the staff to deposit art in his lab without consulting him first. Still, he wasn't as finicky as conservators can sometimes be—a trait necessary for their painstaking, exacting work—but his lab could be likened to a dragon's lair, with him the presiding dragon.

TYLER stood with his hands on his hips. Big hands, so big that your eye was drawn to them. He looked like an early Dvaravati sculpture, one of those slender Thai figures with oversized hands. Hard to imagine those hands repairing a fine ceramic piece, inpainting a scarred sculpture, dexterously reconstructing a shattered, delicate Meissen teacup. Harder still to believe he made fine jewelry on the weekends, delicately spun confections, one of which I wore around my neck. He'd made it for me the previous year for my birthday. I felt like a klutz in his presence, as if all thumbs, which I wasn't, except in comparison.

He softened as he looked at the necklace, which I'd unconsciously touched as I walked into the lab. He looked me up and down. "That's some skirt," he said.

"I'm getting that from various sources." I looked pointedly at his jeans.

Tyler wore a lab coat over a flannel shirt and the scruffiest jeans imaginable, the knees sagging and stained. How he felt that he could criticize my wardrobe was a question I wouldn't mind asking, but it didn't seem like the right moment. Arthur Philen had been trying unsuccessfully to alter Tyler's wardrobe, sending out a series of memos that had begun as a general suggestion regarding a dress code and had become narrower and more pointedly directed at Tyler with each new missive. In response, Tyler had taken to wearing his gardening clothes to work.

We both laughed, and as I came to stand next to him, he gave my shoulders a quick squeeze. "I couldn't find you. I asked everyone, but no one knew where you were." A slight exaggeration.

He sighed and braced his meaty hands on the table. "Arthur dragged me upstairs this morning. He'd decided that one of the sculptures in your gallery was leaning, and he wanted me to fix it."

I tried to think which of my sculptures that might have been. I'd walked through the gallery first thing that morning, checking each piece as I did every morning, part of my job as curator. "Was it leaning?"

"Of course not. So tell me about this." Tyler pulled on gloves and picked up the head. It looked miniature in his hands. Neither of us spoke, we just admired, for no matter how he turned it, it was gorgeous. I told him what I knew.

"So you're wanting me to authenticate it?"

"Yes, basically."

"Well, stone is tricky. You know that. There are some obvious things that I can do. I can compare the stone to the Cambodian sculptures that we have and to those in the museum in San Francisco. Will P.P. allow me to chip a little from the lowest part of the neck?" He turned the head over.

"Yes. I asked him."

"Better get it in writing."

"Okay."

"With that chip and that chipped area, I'll be able to see the depth and irregularity of the surface. If it's completely uniform, that would be odd. It would suggest that a chemical has been applied to the surface to make it look discolored, worn, old. But if it does appear that something has been applied, it isn't so easy to see what that application might be."

"In Southeast Asia they use fruits, resins sometimes. Rub it in and voila, you've got an altered surface."

"Yeah. We saw that on that bronze you brought in last year."

"Right." I'd doubted that bronze from the moment I'd seen it, but asked Tyler to look at it anyway. Every fake was a lesson.

"Bronze is radically different from stone." He held the head near to his face, pulling down the magnifying visor he always wore, an extension of his body. "I'll look closely at the cuts, the edges. Try to see the wear, which I'm not seeing at the moment. Or not much." He lifted his head and turned the visor up again.

I said, "I couldn't either, though I was looking with my bare eye. Could be a fake. It's from Southeast Asia, and our starting premise is that anything could be a fake. The modern sculptors are really good." I slipped on gloves.

"Yes, they're good, and they're prolific. Sure is gorgeous." He raised the sculpture in front of him. "I'd like to meet her in a dark alley."

"Right." I didn't want to think about Tyler's sexual longings. I reached for the sculpture. "When do you think that you might be able to get to this?"

"When do you need it?"

"Yesterday, of course."

"I have pieces to get ready for Brian's upcoming exhibition. I have to prepare for the Qing ceramics we're borrowing for your exhibition. I have to write up condition reports. The list goes on." Every object that comes from the outside, on loan for an exhibition, needs a condition report. "I know, and I wouldn't be in a hurry, but Arthur walked in while P.P. and I were looking at it."

Tyler groaned. "A knot?"

"A total knot."

"Okay. I'll try to carve out some time tomorrow. I need to go into the city at the end of the week, and when I'm at the Asian I'll look at their Cambodian sculptures. I'm having lunch with one of their conservators. I'll ask if he knows of any research that's been done on Cambodian stone."

"Thanks so much, Tyler. I really appreciate it." I'd been looking at the carving of her hair. Now I placed her back on the table and gazed at her face, the full lips, the slightly flared nostrils, and the eyes. She was looking straight at me, and I had the eerie feeling that she was trying to tell me something. Did she want to be reunited with her body, or did she want whoever had carved her to carve her a new body? Don't worry, I mentally told her. I'll figure it out.

I sank into her, absorbing her. I ran my gloved finger along her lotus eyelid. She was perfect, and I felt my heart open to her perfection. I felt that frisson of excitement at such beauty and at the mystery before me.

I realized Tyler was watching me and said without looking up, "I won't. Oh, and by the way, if it is the authentic piece, until recently it had been reattached to the body, so you might look for evidence of adhesive on the break."

"I saw that look," he said. "And now you're blushing."

"What are you talking about?" I set down the head and snapped the gloves off my fingers, the sound like a series of slingshots.

"Don't make her any promises, Jenna."

I laughed, pretending I hadn't been caught in the act, "What could I possibly promise?"

Tyler's mouth opened, closed, and he pulled a cardboard box from beneath the table and arranged the head, cocooning it in foam. Then he neatly folded the towel, laid it on the head, and got paper from his desk to write a label. "The receipt. Don't forget the receipt."

I waved as I slid through the door.

My cell phone rang as I headed toward Breeze's office. My mother. I groaned, debated for an instant, and stuck the phone back in my pocket. Not now.

I DON'T need the distraction of the Cambodian head, I thought as I finally settled back at my desk to read through the galleys for the Qing exhibition catalogue. It wasn't much longer than a brochure, but its production had been a headache. The exhibition had a tight installation schedule because of a Western art show of medieval decorative arts that Arthur had shoehorned into our already overloaded exhibition schedule. He often lost sight of the fact that we were a small museum in a small town with a small staff. Brian, the Western art curator, and I had fought to maintain the schedule we'd carefully crafted, but lost the battle to Arthur's aggressive self-promotion and Caleb New's laissez-faire directorial style.

Water under the bridge, I thought. I had to finish my edits today and get them in the overnight mail tomorrow if the catalogue was going to be printed in time for the exhibition opening. As if the exhibition schedule wasn't tight enough, we'd had a kerfuffle about the printing due to an equipment breakdown, which the Hong Kong printer hadn't immediately revealed. When they finally did inform us, we had to scramble to find another printer, so the final galleys had come back to me late. I sighed. The general public thinks a curator's life involves gazing at art, when in reality a museum is akin to a theater company, the next performance always just a week away. To further complicate matters, a museum staff is always slightly out of step. Artists and scholars who run a business—well, need I say more?

I checked the time and was shocked to see that it was already four. I'd hoped to have a leisurely bike ride home, then a popcorn dinner at the movies. A packaged cup of soup from my bottom desk drawer would have to suffice while I spent the evening at my desk. Riffling through the remaining pages I needed to edit, I realized I would be in the office until at least ten, and I cursed myself for riding my bike that morning instead of driving.

Pulling out a page, I saw that the illustration in the upper right-hand corner, which I'd already pointed out to the printer was problematic, was still too red. He'd argued that it looked better that way. I groaned.

3

"Don't talk about it." P.P. grumpily cut me off. I hadn't spoken with him since our discussion in the conservation lab the previous week. We'd just arrived at Fort Mason and the yearly art fair opening, a benefit gala for a San Francisco museum. Dealers from all over the world, collectors, sightseers, and artsy types were rushing through the rain to pour inside the doors.

"What don't you want to talk about?" Brian asked as he shook out his umbrella. I touched his arm, unable to resist the feel of his taupe cashmere jacket. Brian was not only one of the handsomest, best-dressed men I knew, he was also one of my closest friends. Which was a blessing, as we worked together as the only two curators at the Searles. His responsibility, Western art, was as broad as mine. His specialty was nineteenth-century European. Brian, P.P., and I shared an enthusiasm for art beyond your average enthusiasm. We could discuss a single work for hours.

"The head," I said.

"Ah, the head. It looked lovely to me, but you know me, I'm a flat-work person. Give me a print, a painting, none of this three-dimensional stuff. I hate looking at rounded backs of things."

I knew he was joking, but scowled at him anyway. Our tastes were completely opposite, which served us well in our work. I showed him the Asian flat work that came my way, and he consulted me about Western sculpture. We'd both learned a great deal through this arrangement over the past four years, enough that he was now organizing an exhibition of nineteenth-century French sculpture and I was planning to begin work on an exhibition of Balinese painting.

"Don't talk," said P.P.

"Right." Brian pretended to zip his lip. "Maybe we can find a body here that needs a head."

P.P. huffed and marched ahead of us. "You're bad," I said, disappointed that the three of us wouldn't be viewing together. "He's upset about this." I checked my faux-fur coat at the coat check. Brian went wide-eyed when he saw my top, but I ignored his look.

"Just trying to lighten his mood." He peered around me at my back. "Wow. Is your 'year of no men' over, or are you trying to give old men heart attacks so they leave their collections to the museum?" He looked around us. "There are quite a few candidates here, if that's your intention. We know your history with old men."

I accepted the glass of champagne that a waiter offered, and tried to shrug off Brian's comments, but I must have looked pained. My relationship with an older man hadn't ended well. The previous year's foray into relationships hadn't either. After back-to-back hot-and-heavy romances and the crashing end of the second, I had sworn not to be involved with a man for a year. I was discovering a year was a long time.

"Sorry, Jenna. That was uncalled for."

If you can't confide in your gay male friends about the men in your life, whom can you confide in? "Did it work, your lightening his mood?"

"Clearly not." We bumped glasses and watched P.P. dart into one stall and out another. Like a panther, he was on the prowl.

"Am I really too risqué? I just got this shirt and thought it was festive. This is a gala, after all."

"Oh, it's festive, all right."

"So it's too much?"

He shrugged. "You need to live up to expectations, Jenna. You've got the body, why not flaunt it?"

There was nothing I could do about my outfit now. Once again I'd lost in the balancing act between wanting to dress young-attractive-sexy while I still could and being a professional.

"Are you on the prowl?"

He raised his eyebrows in mock horror. "For women?"

"For art, Brian." I knew he wasn't on the prowl for anything else. Brian was in a long-term relationship that I sometimes envied. I was single, and though I frequently slid out of single into couple, I slid back just as quickly.

"No, not really. We just bought that Dürer print, and I doubt I'd be able to raise the money for anything worthwhile now. It may be years before I have the budget to buy a work of art. You looking for anything in particular?"

"Not usually too much Asian artwork at this fair. The material is more up your alley."

"There were a couple of Asian art dealers last year."

"True. I'm counting on their being back this year. Even if I'm not buying, it's always nice to look."

"We've lost him." Brian peered down the first aisle.

"See what you've done." I polished off my first glass of champagne and looked around for a table to set it on. A server whisked it out of my hand as he held out another tray of champagne. "Wait, let me grab another." A crowd was easing the server and his tray away. I started after him, but Brian grabbed my arm and led me toward the art.

"All right, all right."

"You drank that so fast, I'm surprised you didn't pop your cork. Give yourself at least fifteen minutes before you nab your next glass. There will be food up ahead. We always lose P.P. He has to get ahead of us to find the best piece first and buy it." Brian had only taken a couple of sips, so I reached for his glass, but he held on. He appeared to have his antennae set on the first of the stalls in the fair. "Come on, let's get to work." He started off, and I followed. "It's fine with me if P.P. beats us to the punch. He'll probably donate what he gets to the Searles eventually. You can't forget that he has impeccable taste." "True, usually. But he might have purchased a stolen head. Or maybe a fake. Either way, not so impeccable this time." "Yes, we all make mistakes." I looked at him pointedly, but he was examining a small landscape on an otherwise blank wall and didn't notice my dig. Either that or he didn't want to be reminded of the purchasing error he'd made the previous year.

AN hour later, having consumed more sushi rolls and giant prawns than was advisable, I caught up with P.P. and his bulging shopping bag. He was talking with a dealer in front of his stall filled with later Burmese and Thai Buddhas and decorative art. I didn't recognize the dealer.

"Ah, there you are," he said. "I'd lost you." He looked me up and down as if he was buying a horse.

"We lost you—immediately," I said.

"Do you know Grey? Dr. Jenna Murphy, curator, Searles Museum." He turned from Grey to look for Brian. "Brian?"

I shrugged. Hanging on to these two was like herding cats. I'd given up on them both. "Nice to meet you," I said to Grey. "This is your stall?"

"Yes. It's my first time doing this fair," he said with a strong New York accent. He stepped toward me as he spoke, his eyes shifting as if drawing an outline of my silhouette, so that I was well aware of his height, his piercing eyes, his scent, a mixture of perspiration and citrus. I could tell he used his height to intimidate. I didn't step back.

He looked to be in his fifties. He wore a designer jacket and jeans, his hair was pulled into a ponytail that exaggerated the fact it was thinning on top, his earlobe distended by an ancient gold Indonesian earring. Under his deep tan, his complexion was sallow.

He leaned closer. "I plan to come up to your museum at the beginning of the week, once I've packed up. Hopefully I won't have much to pack by then. I live in Bangkok."

"Good luck," I said, turning to look at the sculptures in his stall, moving out of the aisle and in amidst the Buddhas, away from Grey and his hover. "Has business been good tonight?"

"Various people have helped me out." He nodded toward P.P.'s bag.

"See you, Grey," called a youngish man bustling by with his well-dressed wife, the diamond on her ring finger weighing down her hand. An attractive, youngish couple with a look that said tech start-up. At least that's what it said in the San Francisco Bay Area. I'd have killed for her crimson boots.

"Good to see you, Barker, Courtney," Grey said, raising his hand. She slowed and waved. "We'll be back over the weekend."

"Talk with you again about that piece," her husband said, taking her elbow and hurrying her along.

"Who?" P.P. frowned as he watched them weave away amidst the crowd. He was always concerned about the collecting competition.

"Local people. Bought a few things."

"You, too, it seems," I said. I'd ask him later what he'd purchased, though when I looked around the stall, I didn't see anything that seemed particularly to P.P.'s taste. Moving farther into the space and away from the two men, I looked at the small bronzes in a wall case. Two rather coarse Cambodian sculptures sat on the top shelf, while folkish northern Thai or Lao bronzes populated the lower shelves. Two Burmese weights in the form of *karaweik* birds had been squeezed in with the rest. The men's continued conversation hummed wordlessly in my ears until I heard "decapitated."

"Terrible, really terrible. He seemed a very nice man," Grey said. Unable to contain my curiosity, I moved back to Grey and P.P. "Who are you discussing?"

"Tom Sharpen, a local collector," said Grey. "Down in Atherton. I flew here to the States to discuss a piece with him. A terrible loss. He had a good eye."

Clearly for him the loss wasn't the person, but the sale, the promise of more sales. "What was the piece?" It was a rude question to ask, but I hadn't thought before speaking.

P.P. cut me off before I could say anything more. "See you, Grey. Want to finish the fair tonight. Moving, Jenna." He took my elbow and led me away.

"Why did you drag me off?" I said. "He was about to answer."

"Atherton. Where I bought the head. Murder. Be careful about fakes."

That flummoxed me. "What do you mean, be careful about fakes?"

"Don't know. Need to go to garage sale house."

"Garage sale?" I stopped short. "You bought that gorgeous head at a garage sale? That's an important bit of information you didn't bother to tell me. Obviously whoever sold it didn't think it was real. I've had Tyler working on the thing all week. Really, P.P., you are too much."

He shrugged.

"Who held the garage sale?"

"Daughter? I guess."

"Well, that could be useful. What was her name?"

"No."

I gathered this meant that he didn't know. Or he could be saying know, not no. Sometimes translating P.P. was a pain. "But decapitated. That's horrible. His poor family."

"Poor head."

"Yes, his poor head. Did Grey think the decapitation had to do with his collecting?"

P.P. shrugged, and I thought about the dangers of collecting. They didn't usually involve murder, more often money poorly spent, fakery, forgery, excess. "You're right, P.P. We need to go meet the woman who held the yard sale."

"Maybe not related."

"You told me the previous owner died a suspicious death. Decapitation is pretty suspicious." There couldn't have been two murders of collectors of Khmer art in the Bay Area within the past few months I didn't think.

P.P. looked at me apprehensively. He knew I loved to read mysteries.

"I'm not suggesting we go to find her because of the murder. I'm thinking about our research on the head and its provenance. Do you think Grey was the dealer who sold it to him?"

"Yes." But, as usual, he didn't offer more.

I changed the subject. "What did you buy?"

P.P. shrugged and pulled his bag a bit closer to his body.

He wasn't going to tell me a thing about his purchases. Probably still smarting over my concerns regarding the stone head. "C'mon, P.P. Show and tell."

He distracted me with the strands of enormous turquoise beads screening the stall that we were passing. "Real?" he asked.

It was a question I couldn't ignore. I pulled a strand toward me and bit one of the beads. If only I had some matches to test them further. When I turned around, P.P. was gone.

4

"I found him, you know. His body. His head."
Peggy, Tom Sharpen's daughter, ushered us into the room, but hung back in the doorway. Lanky, thin, and tense, she wore an expensive sequined top that had no place at ten in the morning and didn't go with her purple jeans. It was as if she'd decided as she dressed that she needed to look good for us, but then couldn't pull herself together enough to coordinate a wardrobe. "It made no sense. He made no sense."

P.P. and I looked around at the freshly painted walls, the newly finished floor, a little confused as to why we were in the room where Tom Sharpen had been murdered.

Following our eyes, she said, "We had to redo the entire room. The floors. Even though the stains were gone, I still saw them. Like a giant Rorschach, that's what kept going through my mind, so even though we'd cleaned the floor, over and over, I insisted we had to redo it. My brother didn't want to bother, but my father's blood had seeped deeply into that wood, it needed to be cleansed. And the walls. The blood everywhere. Even the ceiling." She looked up. "I still see it and I keep thinking that anyone who might want to live in the house will be able to see it, too."

I knew what she said was true about the blood splatter from a decapitation. I'd gone online and read about decapitation, arteries severed, blood exploding out of the body, up, out. What I'd pictured was blood squirting up from the neck of the Baphuon-style head, not from a living person. Conceivably because it was more alive to me because I'd held it. Funny the mind's tricks.

"He made no sense," she repeated in her trance-like voice. "There he was, over by the desk, but here he was at my feet, his eyes filmy." She took a slight step back as she looked down. Was she afraid that she was stepping on the spot where his head had lain?

P.P. and I stared at the spot.

"I wanted to talk with him. I think I did talk with him. I said, What happened, what happened? The police told me I said it over and over when they arrived. How could it happen? I asked. Then, What happened? How?" She looked away from the spot. "'Happen' sounds like 'happy,' doesn't it? I think I wanted 'happen' to turn into 'happy,' for the moment to become another time. But it didn't. It never will."

Her distress was unsettling and her description so vivid that I imagined the head, the body, the blood. I moved toward her, to comfort her, but she steeled herself. No stranger could comfort her, since no friend had been able to. I felt her unsteadiness, her off-kilter stance, and saw her restless eyes, her self-hugging arms. I said, "It must have been awful. I can't even imagine."

Coming out of her reverie, she looked at me more closely and relaxed a little. "What it is. What it means. It's impossible to explain it to someone who hasn't experienced it."

"I'm sure. The suddenness, the violence, the helplessness. I think all I would want would be revenge."

"Exactly. Someone to find the killer. For them to pay."

We looked at each other.

"Very difficult," P.P. mumbled.

She nodded, then seemed to fall back into her trance. "I just really couldn't understand why he was here and he was there. I asked him, What are you doing? He didn't know what he was doing. I knew that. But it was a question he used to ask me often. A critical question. Like, Why did you spray blood all over the room? Why did you leave your head where someone would trip over it?" She laughed a brittle laugh.

P.P. and I looked at each other. "The furniture," he said, trying to get her thinking of something other than her father's head on the floor.

"Yes," she said, the tangible pulling her back to us again. "They're coming to pick it up today. Or tomorrow. Yes, tomorrow. We sold most of the furniture at the yard sale, but nothing from this room. We dragged a few pieces outside, but they didn't sell. So we're giving what's left to Goodwill. No one will know." She saw our confusion. "No one will know that we had to clean the blood off these. That they were in the room with him."

"And his papers about his collection? They're here, in his study?" I asked.

"They were. My brother went through all his papers." She pointed at the old oak file cabinet. "It's empty. At least he told me it was. Why are you interested in those? Did you buy something at auction?" It seemed to suddenly have dawned on her that we were there for a reason and that the reason might not be to see the scene of his death.

"Here," said P.P.

She looked at him, uncomprehending.

"P.P. bought a life-size head from you at the garage sale."

"Oh, you're the one who bought it. I thought it was the young couple. They came by early, but I guess . . . Oh, that's right. They came back in the afternoon and asked to see it again. But you had already bought it. I couldn't remember then who had bought it. He made me go through the checks, the young man did, to see if I could find the buyer's name."

"Cash," said P.P.

"That's what I told them. The man was rather belligerent. Said he had told me to hold it for him, that he'd be back, but had an appointment first. Or he had to get cash from the ATM. I don't remember." She was thoughtful.

"And the papers, the invoices and notes. Your brother kept them?" I asked.

"Yes, for the auction. He had to. They worry about where things have come from."

"The provenance," I said, looking around the room, then back at that spot on the floor. Her description had been so vivid, so touching, that I could picture it, the blood, the head, this woman standing in the midst of it. My voice caught when I went on. "Yes, they do worry about that."

P.P. stopped trying to move us out of the room and looked at me with concern. I shook my head.

His eyes still on me, he asked, "And the books?" Shelving covered one wall from floor to ceiling. Books filled a good half of the wall, empty niches the other.

"A book dealer over in Berkeley bought the art books. My son is going to pack up the rest for the library."

"Which dealer?"

"I don't recall."

"Is that where he kept his collection?" I asked, nodding at the shelves.

"Yes, some of it. He had the larger sculptures in the living room. Most of them. Some were in the dining room. He even had a space in the kitchen where he put a sculpture. Every time I came over to visit, their placement had changed. As if all those stone and bronze figures could walk around. I warned him he was going to throw his back out if he kept moving those big stones around. Or get a hernia. But he didn't pay much attention. He never did care about others' opinions."

"Stubborn," P.P. said as he finally herded her out the door. She released the doorframe with a glance back at the room. "Stubborn and obsessive. He'd gotten it in his head that he'd bought a fake, and he was doing everything to find out for sure and to see how he could get the person who sold it to him."

"Get the person?" P.P. had managed to lead us to the front door.

"Yes. 'Nail him' was what he said."

"He wanted his money back?" I asked.

"No, the dealer offered him the money back, but he was determined to get this person in trouble. Or ruin his reputation."

"How did the dealer react to that?"

She shrugged. "Who knows? With my father you only heard one side of a conversation. He could be unpleasant."

"I'm sorry . . . " But if she was searching for kind words about her father, they escaped her.

She said, "He was coming here."

"Who?"

"The dealer. From Bangkok. My father was practically gleeful at the prospect. That was when he was talking about nailing him. He seemed to think he could get the man arrested or something. It made him crazy that he'd bought a fake."

I looked at P.P., who didn't look back. We were both thinking about Grey. If P.P. hadn't dragged me off the other night, we'd know now if he'd sold Sharpen the head. "Does your brother live locally?" I asked.

"Yes, he's in the city."

"And he has all the papers related to the art?"

"Yes. But as I told you, I don't think there was an invoice for that head you bought. That's why we were selling it at the yard sale. We figured it wasn't important enough to show to the auction house. And we came across it after we'd given them everything else. He was meticulous in his record keeping, so there was an invoice for everything, as well as his notes. There were even some notes about what different people had to say about the art he owned."

"Different people?"

"Yes, like local collectors. Or some specialists who came here to see his collection. People he met when he went to New York for the big art fair. It's in March, isn't it?"

"Yes," I said. "He bought there?"

"Sometimes. He bought at auction, and he had a few dealers he liked who attended that fair. He said it was crazy, because they all seemed to save their very best pieces for March, and why didn't they want to sell them other times of the year. My brother said they did that because they could get more for them if there were competing offers. Is that right?"

"It's not a bad observation."

She waited expectantly.

"Brother's phone number?" P.P. held out the small notebook that he carried everywhere. She wrote the number in it.

"Could you also put his name?" I asked. "No, never mind that. I remember from the obituary. Tom Sharpen Jr." The obituary was what had led us to her.

"That's right," she said. "I'm sorry. I just haven't been myself."

"No one would be, after your experience." I felt the need to fill the ensuing silence. "Do you think your brother would be available today?"

"He works. He's a lawyer, but he's pretty easygoing. If you catch him in a free moment, I'm sure he'd see you." She looked at her watch. "You might even catch him during his lunch. He doesn't like working then, so he keeps it open."

She shook P.P.'s hand, and he walked down the drive.

"Thank you so much. You've been very helpful. We're truly sorry for your loss." I held out my hand and she grasped it. Our eyes locked. "Good luck."

"If you find anything . . ." she said. She'd seen the look in my eye, just as Tyler had seen it and P.P. had suspected. My determination to solve the mystery of the head, Radha's, though she thought I wanted to solve the mystery of her father's death.

"I'll let you know. I'll let the police know."

"I think Grey was the dealer," I said as we climbed into P.P.'s Porsche. "I wonder if he murdered him."

"Yes."

"Yes, you agree that he might have been the murderer? Or that he was the dealer who sold Sharpen the sculpture?"

"Yes."

Irritated, I looked out the window. We drove through the town streets in silence, then turned north on 280. The tan hills to either side, tufts of green trees on the summits and in the gullies between their low, humping forms. "I didn't much like him."

"The collector?" P.P. sounded startled.

"No, Grey. I didn't know the collector."

He didn't say anything. He'd bought art from Grey, and maybe he felt some kind of loyalty. Or perhaps he felt defensive. Of course, he might be brooding, wondering if the pieces he'd bought at the fair were fakes as the head might be.

"The head. The stone head," he said finally.

I knew what he was talking about. Focus, Jenna, focus on the stone head. Don't get involved in the murder.

"Don't worry," I said. I didn't have time to find a murderer. For that matter, I didn't have time to research his stone head. I looked at my watch and thought about Tom Sharpen's daughter gazing down at her father's head. Would knowing his murderer give her any relief? Solutions often did make one feel better.

I pulled out my phone to call the brother. As I punched in the number, I wondered if the head had rolled, or bounced.

"THANK you so much for seeing us on such short notice. We've just seen your sister at the house."

"She's not doing too well."

"No," P.P. said.

"I can't imagine what it must have been like for her." I looked around the glassed corner office and out toward the Bay Bridge to my right and the glistening water that led the eye to the Golden Gate. I tried to picture the scene without bridges or buildings, but couldn't. They were as much a part of the scene as my eyes, my curvy body, my impatience were a part of me. This was home, had always been home, peopled and constructed.

He shifted the subject to our reason for being there. "You bought one of my father's pieces at auction?"

"Not at auction, at the yard sale."

His generous brows bunched together, a dimple forming in one cheek as he momentarily pursed his lips. He leaned forward then back in his chair in one fluid motion. "We didn't sell any sculpture at the yard sale. Just odds and ends. Most of the work was too valuable. The yard sale was my nephews' idea, though my sister ended up doing most of the work. It kept her busy, and it was helpful, I think, in keeping her mind off his death. At least for a short while.

"But all the sculpture went to auction. Amazingly, the auction house managed to fit it all in at the last minute. I don't know how they produce those auction catalogues so quickly. I think they included my father's estate in the upcoming sale because he had written extensive notes and they didn't need to do too much research. He'd written blurbs on each piece, and they more or less lifted those for the catalogue."

"Your father kept good records?"

"Very good. I think there was only one piece that he hadn't kept an invoice and notes for." It dawned on him. "Is that the piece you bought?"

"Don't know," P.P. said.

"It was a Cambodian head," I said.

"Yes. That's the one. It was shoved to the back of the kitchen cabinet, behind the blender and an old coffee maker. I assumed that it was a modern copy that he'd picked up. He sometimes did that when he was traveling. Bought contemporary sculptures for comparison with the authentic pieces that he owned. He said you had to keep up on the fakes that were being made, so you didn't buy them yourself. He said there were fads."

"Fads?" P.P. asked.

"Yes, fads in carving, fads in types of pieces that people wanted to own. He told a story about being on a street in Ho Chi Minh City where they sell antiques—he always put the word 'antiques' in quotes." He drew quotes in the air. "Each shop on this street had a sixth-century wooden carving. He thought it was hysterical that anyone might buy one of those sculptures. But he said that people bought them once they were in Western galleries, because they didn't know that there was one in every shop on that street. Apparently the forgers had gotten their hands on wood that dated back to that period, so when the wood was carbon-14 tested the date was correct. It was the carving that was wrong.

"So I assumed that head at the back of the cabinet was one of his new ones. I'd already sent the remainder of the collection to auction, and I couldn't find any notes. Plus, he'd been obsessing for months about a fake that some dealer in Bangkok had sold him. He was furious, had had a lengthy exchange with him."

"Do you have that correspondence?"

"No. I didn't find it anywhere. I believe he was speaking with the man by phone, or on Skype. He'd become quite enamored of talking on the Internet. He liked that he could see the person and assess their honesty."

"He wasn't very trusting?"

Sharpen looked thoughtful. "If you'd asked me that five years ago, I would have said he was a trusting person. But the more involved he became in his collecting—and he'd become more involved since he retired—the less trusting he got."

"Because he'd encountered more dishonest people?" I asked.

"I'm not so sure about that. But he'd learned more about the art. And that had made him aware of the forgery trade in Asia. He'd become more skeptical, more critical."

"Not necessarily bad," said P.P.

"No, I don't think it was bad, but it had a negative effect on him. He was more combative. He'd never been one to lie down in an argument, but in the past few years he'd become downright ornery."

"Ah." P.P.'s left leg bounced. Sitting was not his forte. I wondered if he was imagining himself as Tom Sharpen, turning cynical as he learned about the art trade.

"That's too bad. And you think that this head had something to do with it?" I asked.

"I really don't know. Some piece had him bothered. Whether it was that head or some other sculpture, I don't know. It may explain why it was pushed to the back of the cabinet and why there weren't any papers about it. But, as I said, he had been in communication with the person he bought the forgery from—whatever the forgery was—and you would have expected some sort of file on it. Of course, the person who killed him had ransacked his desk and file cabinet, so they may well have taken the receipt or his working file."

P.P. and I looked at each other. "His working file?" I asked.

"Yes, he had a file on each of his sculptures, even the less valuable ones. But there wasn't a file on that one. And the killer went pretty thoroughly through the drawer where he kept his collection information. The drawer was open, files splattered with blood, some half pulled out, others out of order. He was meticulous, so nothing would have been out of order."

"The wood file cabinet?" P.P. asked.

He looked at P.P. "Yes, that's the collection cabinet. That *was* the collection cabinet." His eyes suddenly filled with tears. He looked at his watch and stood. "I have a client coming momentarily, and I need to go over some papers before he arrives. I hope this has been helpful."

"Yes, it has. Do you by any chance have a list of the dealers he dealt with?"

"No. I do have the folder with the invoices. In fact, I have it here. If you don't mind me putting you in a conference room, you're welcome to go through it. I rather doubt you'll find anything about that head, but it's perfectly possible I missed something. I know nothing about Cambodian art."

"That would be very helpful. We'd appreciate it enormously."

He sat back down and pulled out one of his desk drawers, then lifted out a hefty binder. "As I said, he was organized. There are pictures of everything in there, so you can see what he'd purchased."

"Thanks. Would you mind if we got back to you with any more questions that we might have?"

"Not at all. Especially if your research helps in finding my father's killer."

"That would certainly be a positive outcome," I said.

P.P. merely smiled as he shook his hand. Sharpen took the binder and led us to an adjacent room. After he'd left, P.P. looked at me and said, "No murders, Jenna. We're art historians, not detectives."

The length of his sentence told me he was serious, but he didn't need to keep making the point that I shouldn't get involved. The mystery of a stone head was enough for me.

5

"I haven't come to a conclusion," Tyler said as he arranged pieces of a ceramic bowl on his worktable. Some pieces were smaller than my little fingernail, one vanishing between his fingers as he picked it up.

"But any thoughts?" I perched on one of the high stools at the tall table.

"Sure." He moved a small piece from the row where he'd set it and placed it next to one in a different row. Both had bright blue glaze, one of half a dozen colors. It was a complicated 3D jigsaw puzzle.

"What happened?" I asked, motioning to the bowl.

"Mrs. Searles brought it in. Apparently her maid dropped it." I looked more closely. "Is it old?"

"No," he answered grumpily, looking at a photo that he had lying next to him on the table.

"Okay, I won't go there."

"Don't." He looked up from his task. "The conservator at the Asian told me he didn't know of any study of Khmer stone. Surprising."

"Yes, you would think this material was a likely candidate for research. There are so many Khmer fakes being produced."

"I did check out a small sample from P.P.'s stone head under the microscope. The surface patina looked awfully uniform to me. This isn't good, as you know. I'm feeling like I should have taken a larger sample. I called P.P. and asked him to come to the lab the next time he's in the museum, so I can show him how large a sample I want to take. I don't want to take too much off the neck and then discover that the head is authentic, even if I can easily fill and in-paint the area I removed."

"Right. He's due in the building shortly. I'll send him down to you." Tyler went back to arranging the pieces of the bowl. Much conservation work looked tedious to me. I wouldn't want to be the one who actually glued all those pieces together once he got their arrangement figured out. Still, I couldn't resist moving a green-glazed piece next to another of the same color. "What if she didn't bring in all the pieces?"

"That would be a blessing. Then I wouldn't have to complete the restoration. Can't imagine she's going to want to use it once it's repaired."

"No." I leaned forward, looking for more green.

He glanced up and sighed as he realized I wasn't going any-where until he told me more of his thoughts on the Khmer sculpture. "The wear on the head is minimal. A few tiny chips, no breaks. I'm leaning toward thinking it's new. But then I look at it again and the carving is so good, I become uncertain. I'm not a specialist, but the Cambodian fakes that I've seen were obviously fake. This is not."

"I feel that way too. When I first looked at it I thought it was the original. Then when I looked more closely for wear, I got worried."

"If it's wrong, the sculptor is a master."

"Yes, I wouldn't mind having a fake like that one." I pointed at one piece of the bowl and a larger one with a matching angle. As long as it felt like solving a puzzle I enjoyed this.

He moved the small shard of ceramic next to the larger one, and I noticed for the first time that his hands were bare. "No gloves?" I said, surprised.

"I found a bowl like this selling online. It's worth about twenty-five dollars." He picked up the photo and shook it at me.

"And she's paying your fee to have you fix it?" Conservators do not come cheap. I studied the photo. "On eBay?"

"She isn't paying anything," he said with irritation. "Her husband paid for this museum, and his endowment pays our salaries, in case you've forgotten. Yes, of course on eBay."

"Oh." I stood up. He didn't appear to have more to say about the head, and this seemed like a good time to leave.

WHEN I arrived in my office, P.P. was firmly planted in my desk chair, riffling through the papers on my desk. I slouched in the visitor's chair opposite. "Find anything of interest?" I asked ironically.

"No."

"Looking for anything in particular?"

"Catalogue."

"What catalogue?"

"Qing porcelains."

"You're suddenly interested in seventeenth- to nineteenth-century monochrome ceramics?"

"No."

"I sent off the galleys last week. The next version will be the finished product. Or so I hope. Haven't heard a word from them since it went off. A good thing." I picked at a snag in my sweater, though I knew that would only make it worse. "Is there something in particular in the catalogue that you need to read?"

"Date."

I frowned. "The dates of the exhibition?"

P.P. nodded as he began to stack papers.

I handed him the museum newsletter, which was sitting atop a pile he'd just gone through. The cover story gave the dates.

"Ah. Have to get the reservations after the opening."

"What reservations?" I was beginning to want my chair. Usually he would have jumped up after a few moments and begun to pace, giving me a chance to slide back into my spot.

"Cambodia."

"You're going to Cambodia?" This was the first I'd heard of it.

"We're going."

"P.P., I have far too much on my plate to be flying off to Cambodia. Maybe in six months, when the porcelain exhibition has closed. Though I expect by then I'll have something else unexpected on my schedule." Thinking of Philen and his machinations, I said grumpily, "A new project, no doubt."

"I talked with Caleb."

This brought me up from my slouch. "You talked with Caleb before asking me if I wanted to go to Cambodia? If I thought there was any reason why I should go to Cambodia? P.P., you know that Tyler is researching the piece. Hopefully he'll be able to figure out if it's real or fake."

"Arthur's trip." He watched me. "The trip with you."

"What?" I heard my voice rise almost to a screech.

"We'll go first. To Bangkok. Meet the group in Siem Reap, at Angkor." P.P. nodded to himself to affirm his plan.

I was out of my chair, headed toward the door. "Group?" I'd been buried in plans for the Chinese exhibition: first the galleys, then the outreach planning—concerts, visiting potters, movies. What had Philen concocted while I had my head down? "I'm going to talk with Arthur. Is he the one planning this?"

"Caleb. Speak with him."

I hadn't even realized that the director was back in town. "Caleb? He's gotten involved? Why would he condone one of Arthur's wacky ideas?"

P.P. stood up, but rather than recapture my chair, I hurried out of my office ahead of him, down the hall toward Caleb's office.

CALEB New had clearly gone to directors' school. Either that or they found him at Central Casting. He was suave, wore the right—expensive—suits, and fit perfectly into an old boys' network that allowed him access to people able to support an institution like the Searles that depended on private donations. He was always flying here or there, fundraising, his laissez-faire administrative style sometimes creating havoc in the museum. Arthur Philen, who was left in charge when Caleb was gone, furthered the problem with his constant attempts to overthrow him.

"I can't go to Cambodia," I said, charging into Caleb's office. "I have an exhibition opening in a month and a catalogue I need to write for an exhibition that opens in just a year. I should have had it written already."

"How are you, Jenna?" Caleb asked, unruffled as ever.

"Fine, thank you, but really, there isn't any reason to go off to Cambodia just because P.P. has brought in a head that, by the way, may be a fake, and if not a fake, happens to belong to a well-known sculpture." I took a breath.

"Arthur seems to have gotten the ball rolling in my absence."

"Well, can't you stop the ball?"

He handed me the newsletter that just moments before I'd thrust in P.P.'s face. I took it, confused. "What?"

"The back page, I believe."

On the center of the back page was a small announcement about a trip for upper patrons to Cambodia. Led by me, with Arthur Philen also in attendance. "You've got to be kidding. He didn't even ask me about my schedule. This trip is during October, and October is when my Chinese porcelain exhibition will be up."

Caleb nodded. "It did surprise me that you were willing to go then."

"Willing to go? He didn't even consult me. And how did he get it in the newsletter? He had to have gotten it in way past the deadline for text."

A voice behind me said, "It's short."

P.P. was right. The announcement was only two lines. If I was lucky, no one would notice it. That would be the perfect solution to this ridiculous plan.

"He wants to create fanfare about the head." Caleb straightened his cuffs.

"We don't even know if the head is authentic. Tyler is looking at it now to try to figure that out, and at the moment he's thinking it's modern." I was having some difficulty keeping my voice calm.

Caleb raised an eyebrow. "Arthur didn't tell me that."

"That man—" but I saw Caleb's other eyebrow go up. I wasn't sure why he kept Arthur on the staff, but suspected it was because Arthur made him look good.

"Fait accompli," he said, raising his shoulders in an exaggerated shrug.

I could feel P.P.'s hands on the back of my chair. I leaned forward. "Caleb, please, you need to put a stop to this. You know it's just part of Arthur's plan to undermine you. I can imagine the fanfare that he anticipates and his spot in the limelight. He can see the headlines now: 'California Museum Returns Stolen Sculpture.'"

"Yes. Well, it would put us in a good light."

"Not if the headline the next day read, 'Stolen Sculpture a Fake.'"

Caleb missed a beat before saying, "How's the exhibition coming along? The outreach schedule is impressive. You must be very happy." He fussed with some papers on his desk.

The conversation had ended, and I felt as if I hadn't taken part in it. "It's great," I said as I stood to leave.

"Bangkok first," P.P. said.

"Yes, certainly, P.P.," Caleb said. "You and Jenna can go to Bangkok first."

I barely needed to listen to his response. I'd never heard Caleb deny P.P. anything, but I was stunned that he'd agreed with Philen's harebrained scheme of taking a group of people to Cambodia while simultaneously defusing a potentially volatile situation with a possibly stolen head. I needed to come back and discuss this with Caleb when P.P. wasn't around. Or better, I could hope the plan would fade away, though the newsletter I held in my hand suggested otherwise.

Traveling with Philen and P.P., who was demanding in his own way, promised to be a nightmare. I groaned, but P.P. barely glanced at me as he turned to go to the conservation lab. I debated whether I should join him, but I had other work to do. The ceramic exhibition was looming, and the tasks related to it were increasing. I hurried to my office to begin to write down all that I needed to do.

My phone was ringing as I entered. "Jenna Murphy, curatorial."

"Hi, honey," my mother said.

"Hi, Mom. What's up? It's a little crazy here today."

"You sound upset."

"I'm fine. Well, not entirely, but I'll tell you about it when I see you Sunday."

"Have you seen Eric lately?"

I closed my eyes. My brother's problems had woven a web around my family. His drugs, his depression, his dramas. I didn't want to be thinking about him now. I didn't want the worry of him now. I tried to keep from sounding concerned. "No. What's up?"

"He's not answering my calls. Could you give him a ring?"

"Sure, but you know he does this. Winds us up. Worries us to get our attention."

"I don't think it's intentional, honey. It's just the way he is."

I could hear the concern in her voice. "I'll call. You and Dad are coming to the opening of the exhibition, aren't you? You got the invitation?"

"We got it. I have to RSVP. Your Dad isn't coming. He has a previous commitment."

I breathed a sigh of relief and said as unemotionally as I could, "I know he doesn't like these big events."

"It's not that. It's parent-teacher night at the school, and he obviously can't miss that. He has some real problem kids in his classes this year." She paused. "I thought I might bring Sean. Would that be okay?"

"Absolutely. I would have invited him, but was discouraged from inviting too many friends and family." I was always happy to see my brother Sean. "I do have to run, Mom."

"Okay. See you Sunday."

I sat back, my anger at Philen now sidetracked by worry about Eric. I pressed speed dial and waited. After three rings the call went to voicemail, and I knew that he'd seen it was me and turned off his phone.

Nothing I could do about Eric. I'd tried. And nothing I could do about Caleb. Clearly he wasn't going to budge about canceling Philen's trip. I could only hope that not enough people signed up to make the trip viable.

There was one thing I could do, though. I leaned forward and Googled eBay. I could lighten Tyler's workload and buy him that bowl.

6

When I stepped out of my little backyard cottage, the sun wasn't yet visible, but pale pink clouds supported the gray dawn. If I hurried, I could take the rise of White's Hill as the sun burst over the East Bay hills. If I really hurried.

I hadn't planned on riding this morning, but I'd woken early with monkey mind. Choose wall colors for the exhibition gallery; speak with the designer about the didactic panels, which seemed to me to be too small and overdesigned; go with the head preparator to look at fabric for the cases and finish writing labels.

Thank goodness the galleys were off and I didn't have the worry of the catalogue hanging over me. I needed to treat myself, and what better way than an early morning ride out to West Marin. Not too far, just a short ways through Samuel P. Taylor Park, back to my favorite San Anselmo café for a latte, then a shower and work.

The kitchen light was on in my landlady's house, but Rita wasn't in her usual spot by the window. I stopped and double-checked the money in my pocket—I had enough to buy my latte and her mocha, a ritual usually followed on Saturday morning, but I thought she'd be agreeable to sitting and chatting on a Tuesday. That is, if she didn't mind my sweaty self.

I thought of Philen, then pushed the thought of him out of my mind. Best to concentrate on the exhibition tasks rather than the trip to Cambodia, the confusing stone head. And I did until I got to the top of White's Hill.

What is it about sunrise that sets the heart beating faster? The canvas of the horizon—in this case a horizon that included Marin, the San Francisco Bay, and the hills to the east—painted in huge, saturated strokes. Today in pink and an ever-so-subtle orange. Clinically speaking, maybe it was my fast ride through the barely trafficked streets and my acceleration up the hill that had my heart beating so fast. But you'd have a difficult time convincing me of that.

As I stopped for a drink of water, I thought of Radha. I'd printed a photo I'd taken of the sculpture of Radha and Krishna—her head still in place—and hung it across from my desk. If the head in the lab was a copy, it was a darn good one. The photo reminded me of my thoughts when I first saw the sculpture. I'd wondered why it had been identified as Radha and Krishna rather than some other Hindu couple—Parvati and Shiva, to whom the Baphuon temple is dedicated, or Vishnu and Lakshmi.

I realized, after I'd thought about it, that this was as good an identification as any, given the Krishna vignettes carved in the narrative reliefs of the temple. Since the majority of the relief carvings at the Baphuon are scenes from the *Ramayana* and the *Mahabharata*, other identifications are equally possible. But people are enchanted by the stories of Krishna, and there was a precedent for his popularity in the Khmer region, where sculptors had carved larger-than-life-size images of the youthful figure as early as the seventh century.

The story of Krishna, one of the avatars of Vishnu, exalted his boyhood and the amorous adventures of his youth. Women, particularly the *gopis* or young cowherders, swooned before him and took every opportunity to watch him, coyly trying to entrap him, a task finally achieved by Radha. I had to admit that the sculpted Radha looked pleased with herself.

Four men pulled up beside me, two of them saying hello. One drank from the straw attached to his camelback, while the others pulled out their water bottles. A fifth man was still toiling up the hill, his head down. He could have been my brother Eric. He was his size, his build. Except I'd only succeeded in getting adult Eric on a bike once. And getting him on the bike turned out to be different than getting him to ride farther than the coffee shop at the corner of my street. He waited for me there while I rode. When I came back he was chatting up an attractive blonde, with whom he then had a six-month relationship. A long time for him.

"Hi," I said to the men. They were all buff, all about my age, late twenties, early thirties.

"Perfect spot for the sunrise," one said as he nonchalantly repositioned his bike a little closer to mine.

"Yes," I said, turning again toward the east. But the sunrise was giving way to morning, and the pink that had permeated the clouds had faded to a color so subtle that it no longer held interest for me. And though the man pulled me a little, my year without men was not yet up. Soon, but not yet.

I mounted my bike to continue my journey. I'd dawdled long enough, and once again I'd let my mind wander to the stone head rather than concentrating on the exhibition or the lecture that I was scheduled to give the docents at the end of the week.

"Have a good ride." I wasn't leaving because they'd arrived, though I did want to get down the west side of the hill before them. I didn't need the race this morning that the curving west hillside invited. I huffed up the remainder of the incline as I thought of the Baphuon, the Angkorian temple where the sculpture had been found. Now largely collapsed, the gargantuan temple was built by King Udayadityavarman II in the mid-eleventh century.

Why is it that the brain so often doesn't follow one's commands? I succumbed to the mystery of the head, mulling it over all the way out to Samuel P. Taylor Park. On the way back, I thought about Tom Sharpen's head. I'd found a photo of him online. I pieced together the little I knew. His identification of a head as fake, his anger, his threats to a Bangkok dealer, Grey saying he'd flown to San Francisco to talk with him.

I thought about that murder that I wasn't going to try to solve right up until the moment that I ordered my latte and Rita's mocha. I was running late now and wouldn't be able to sit and natter with her, but she would be appreciative when I dropped it off.

THE morning thus far had been peaceful. After my ride, I felt much more centered. But then Breeze hurried into my office, shaking her head as she came, disaster in her mouth. A minor disaster, I imagined, but a disaster nonetheless. It wasn't a big leap to assume it had something to do with Arthur Philen. How he got to be deputy director I would never know.

"Now what has he done?"

"The man is unbelievable. He's announced that P.P. has the head of the famous Radha and Krishna sculpture."

I searched among the papers on my desk for the list I'd written yesterday. "In the trustees meeting this morning?"

"No. I shouldn't say he announced it. He sent out a press release."

"No." I stopped rustling.

"Yes. P.P. is in Caleb's office right now trying to get Philen fired." She leaned against the doorframe, then walked further into my tiny office.

"I don't blame him. We don't even know if the head is authentic. And even if it is, it certainly isn't Philen's place to spread the word about it. If anyone should, it's P.P., the owner."

"I hope he's successful," Breeze said, and sat down. Oh, no, I thought. This is going to take a while.

"Successful?" I said.

She looked at me as if I was mentally deficient.

"You mean getting him fired?"

"Yes. Philen is impossible. He was in my office this morning, ranting about a typo in the collections database. A typo, one typo. There are probably thousands of typos." She raised both hands.

"What did he want you to do about it?"

"Change it."

I shook my head. Philen could change it as easily as Breeze. Any of the curators or registrars could get into the database.

"Uh-oh." Breeze stood and moved to the door, listening. "P.P. has found his way to Philen's office."

I heard Philen say self-righteously, "I thought it my duty—"

"Shut up," P.P. said.

"Later," said Breeze. Like me, she heard P.P. headed my way.

"Fired," he shot as he squeezed past her in the doorway and sat down.

Oh, no, I thought. He had landed in that seat as though it was his safety net. "Unbelievable, that man," I said. More fuel to his fire, but something had to be said, and I agreed with him. Arthur Philen should be fired.

He switched gears. "Tyler."

I waited for more, but it didn't come. "What about Tyler?"

"Come." He jumped up again.

Looking back at my overloaded desk, I trailed him to the conservation lab.

"Trust," he said as he held the door for me. I wasn't certain if he was talking about me, Tyler, or Philen.

Tyler had glued about a quarter of Mrs. Searles's bowl back together. I needed to check the mail; the bowl I'd bought from eBay should have arrived today.

"Seems as if there's one piece missing here." He pointed to the spot, guessing I'd be a willing assistant to his reconstruction. Better to bury my head in that project than in P.P.'s anger.

I took my place at his side, picking through the pieces while P.P. collected himself. He wasn't generally a volatile man, and the degree of his anger now attested how much the situation disturbed him.

"Right or wrong?" he finally asked.

"The head?" Tyler said.

"Of course," I volunteered.

P.P. gave the Indian shake of his head that means yes, but to the uninitiated seems to mean no. Tyler understood it correctly.

"Well."

"Yes," P.P. said. "And?"

Avoiding the line of fire, I kept my focus on the broken bowl that wouldn't be needed once my package arrived.

Tyler stood up. "P.P., I really can't tell you. It's sandstone of a type that comes from Cambodia, or so it seems. I sent off some photos to a friend at the Met who has done a little work on the stone, and he thought it looked correct, but you know that means little. And even if it comes from Cambodia, when was it made? Yesterday or nine hundred years ago?"

He shook his head. "The stone has little wear, which is suspicious. We all know how frequently the nose of a sculpture or some other protruding portion breaks. You have to remember that it sat in that temple, or lay on the ground, for centuries. Something was bound to happen to it. A break when it fell, water pouring over it as it lay."

He was preaching to the initiated. I knew it. He knew it. He knew that we knew it, but he'd shifted into automatic and was explaining as he would to anyone. Maybe he was giving P.P. more time to collect himself. "The sample I took from the neck gives me a surface cross-section that looks awfully uniform. But if I took a sample from elsewhere on the head, it might well be less so."

"You won't commit?" P.P. asked. Tyler was notoriously conservative in his proclamations. He could balance two sides of any issue better than the finest scale.

"No. I think the best you can do is when you and Jenna go to Cambodia, look carefully at the old and see what they seem capable of making with the new. Are you going to Bangkok?"

"We've talked about it," I volunteered, picking up the piece he'd been missing.

"Well, from what you've told me, that's the place to go to look for good Cambodian fakes." He looked at me as he spoke, evidently having had enough of P.P.

P.P. charged out of the lab without a word. I held up the shard.

"Damn," he said. "I was hoping it was gone and I wouldn't have to continue."

"You could always throw these pieces out and buy that bowl you saw online. She'd be incredibly impressed that you got it back together in such pristine condition."

"Don't think that it didn't cross my mind, but when I looked this morning, in a moment of frustration, it had been sold." He focused his gaze on the glue he held in one hand and the shard of bowl in the other. "P.P. seems angry."

"Philen sent out a press release saying P.P. owns the stolen head."

That brought his head up. "Idiot. What was he thinking? No, don't answer that. 'Nothing' is the obvious answer. Wait, isn't Arthur going with you to Cambodia?"

"I fear he is." I prodded another small piece toward him and pointed. "I think this goes here."

Tyler took it. "That sounds like a really fun trip."

"Right. Kind of like traveling with a snake and a mongoose."

I poked half-heartedly at the ceramic shards, but the weight of dealing with Arthur Philen and P.P. in close proximity for two weeks had knocked the wind out of me.

He looked up. "They're both a little much. Each in his own way, of course."

"Of course. Philen, well, he's so absorbed in his quest for power that he wears blinders." I said.

"And P.P. is so engaged in his quest for art that he sees little else."

"That's not entirely true. You have to respect his passion, not to mention his eye. And it's not just that he has an eye for fabulous art. He's very knowledgeable about what he collects. I value his opinion."

Tyler looked at me expectantly. "And?"

"And. He has a sense of humor."

He raised an eyebrow. "Didn't shine through today."

"No, it didn't. It's true that art is at the center of his universe, but it seems to be at the center of ours as well." I swiveled my head around the room. "I'll be back," I said, rising from my stool.

I wished P.P. had never brought that head into the museum. Or that Philen wasn't always lurking. As I passed Caleb's office, he called me in. Philen was standing in front of his desk.

"We'll take the head with us to Cambodia and—"

"No, Arthur," I said. "We are not taking the head with us. We are not going to return the head to the Cambodian government until we know what we have. I'm not certain if it's authentic, and Tyler isn't either." My voice rose as I spoke. I took a seat beside Philen, who remained standing.

"I've already issued a press release that—"

"Prematurely, to say the least." I couldn't restrain myself.

Philen's voice rose to match mine. "When I came into the conservation lab, you and P.P. were discussing a stolen head. Something needed to be done about it."

"And if you'd continued listening to us, you would have heard me say that we needed to authenticate it before we did anything."

"You've had almost a month." He straightened his tie.

"The fact remains, we haven't been able to agree on whether it's fake or real. Now you've put P.P.'s name out there as a collector, possibly of fakes, and by sending out the press release, you've associated us with the head. Which is bad for us. Of course, that might turn out to be good for P.P. if it takes him out of the picture. You'd best hope it does if you want him to stay associated with the museum. He doesn't want everyone knowing he's a collector."

"Well, everyone already knows that," he said prissily.

"Only a small circle of people. Every gift he's given to the museum says "Anonymous" on the credit line. If he wanted to advertise his interest in Asian art, he'd allow articles in art magazines, or put his name on pieces of his that are borrowed for exhibitions. He's not a self-promoter."

Philen ignored me. "I can't believe he came to you, Caleb, and told you to fire me. Just because he has access to you, because he's a trustee."

Caleb evidently had no intention of inserting a single word. "Caleb?" I prompted him.

"Yes. He's extremely angry. Rightly so, as you acted precipitously, Arthur."

It was the most direct attack Caleb had ever made on a member of staff. In my hearing, at any rate. Philen took a step back, as if experiencing it physically.

Caleb softened the blow by saying, "I understand your worry, Arthur. If it belonged to us, I would be very concerned. But it really wasn't your place to send out that press release."

Subtle, I thought. He attacks, then appears to take Philen's side, while simultaneously withdrawing his allegiance to him by saying, "If it belonged to us," a phrase he knew Philen probably wouldn't hear. I said, "How are we going to put out the fire? Someone from the *New York Times* called this morning. There's a message from the *Guardian* as well. The news of the head has already made it to London." I didn't add that my unopened emails from friends at the Met and the British Museum told me the news had reached the museum world.

"Arthur, what do you plan to do?"

My jaw dropped. Caleb was going to leave it to Philen to extricate us from this fiasco?

"Well, I don't know . . ." Philen said. I waited, looking up at him. Caleb swung his chair back down, picked up a paper clip, and bent it open into a straight piece of wire. Finally Philen said, "We'll just have to wait for it to blow over."

"We need to do more than that, Arthur. You've made the museum look bad, and P.P. as well. Add to that the fact you'll be traveling with P.P. in just a few weeks. You'll be together for two weeks, day in and day out. Unless you resolve the situation before you depart, that's going to be rather uncomfortable."

Philen puffed up. "Well, that's what I was saying before Jenna interrupted me. If we take the head back to Cambodia, then it will be out of our hands."

I jumped up and leaned so close to him that I could tell he'd had bacon for breakfast. "That's not a solution," I said, my voice rising, "that's a slither out of the problem." I stepped back. "If we do that, we'll never get any information on whether the head is authentic or not. What people will remember is that we bought a Khmer sculpture that was a fake. The museum will look bad. And I will look bad because I'm the curator in charge of Asian art." As I spoke, I realized that the problem wasn't so much P.P.'s now as it was ours. Damn Philen.

Caleb gave me a look. "Jenna's correct. It isn't a solution." He tapped the straightened paper clip on his desk. "Arthur, I want you to issue another press release saying that the head is presently being authenticated and that you were precipitous in issuing the first release." With a final tap of the paper clip before he threw it down, he said, "I want you to put your name to it."

Philen paled. He'd expected to be in the news, but as the hero returning a stolen object.

"I have a conference call in about five minutes," Caleb said, "and I need to prepare for it. Arthur, let me see the text before you send it out. That will be a new policy, that all press releases cross my desk before distribution."

Philen was out the door before I could blink. "I'm not looking forward to traveling with the two of them. Do you think you can dissuade Philen from going?"

"I doubt it." Caleb already had his nose in a file. Clearly this much conflict was enough for one day. I suspected he'd go out of town on an unscheduled trip to recover.

7

"I don't know where Eric is," my mother said. "You know he's often late."

I looked at the kitchen clock. "It's 7:30. He's not usually this late. We need to eat. I need to eat. I have more work to do tonight."

"It's Sunday night." She wiped the countertop, hopeful that I wouldn't insist if I saw that she was busy.

"It's Sunday night and I was at the museum all day yesterday and again this morning."

"What were you doing?"

"Preparing my talk for the opening, trying to catch up on all the things that have fallen by the wayside as we install the exhibition. The usual." I ran my finger over scars on the kitchen table, skirting the placemats that she'd laid out before I arrived.

"Didn't you ride?" She bundled her hair into a ponytail that she wrapped and then tied into a knot. When my hair was long, I'd done the same.

I am my mother's double. Our height, our auburn hair, our turquoise eyes, wide brow, and small but mobile mouth. Our differences result from gravity, which hasn't yet affected me, and the lines that shoot out from the corners of her eyes and have begun to alter her mouth. Though she exercises at a gym a few times a week and has a friend she walks with the other days, she's become thicker over the years. I thought of her and Polly walking, and wondered what they talked about. Their husbands? Kids? Dissatisfactions? It wasn't that I thought of her as old and her life narrow, just that she was a world apart from me.

"I did ride early this morning, my only fun activity all weekend." I stretched out my legs, trying to relax, to quell my impatience.

"Where did you go?" The question was perfunctory; she was stalling so that Eric would appear and we could sit down together. Sean was out of town. "We rode out the Bolinas Ridge, Pine Mountain, the usual. Really, Mom, I need to eat."

"So do I," said my father, coming into the kitchen, the sound of a basketball game trailing him. He opened the fridge, his belly sinking over his waistband as he bent to pull a beer from the fridge door.

At least it was beer, not whiskey. I wondered what time he'd started drinking.

"We're waiting for Eric," my mother said as she opened the pot on the stove and stirred the chili. Eric loved her chili. I was less enthusiastic.

"Wasn't he supposed to be here an hour ago, two hours ago?" He popped open the beer and watched her as he took a sip.

"Yes, but he's late as usual." She tried to be light about it, though I knew Eric's tardiness drove her as crazy as it did the rest of us. My mother was the classic codependent, a role perfected throughout her years of marriage to my father. She covered for Eric, adjusting her schedule to fit his, making excuses for him, just as she'd always covered for my father.

He took a step toward the TV. "Did your mother tell you he got stopped for another DUI?" There was disgust in his voice.

"No," I said, turning to my mother. "But he doesn't even have a license anymore."

"That's right. They held him in jail. They wouldn't release him until your mother posted bond and he signed a paper saying he'd seek help. Go to rehab."

"Can they do that?"

"Don't know if they can, but they did. May just be an attempt to scare him into sobriety. He said he went to AA last week." He took another sip.

I caught myself counting his sips; it was bad enough counting bottles. "Alcohol isn't his problem. It's the drugs." I turned to my mother, who was probably better informed, "So what's happening with the rehab?"

"He has to go to court first," she said.

"I've washed my hands of him," my father said as he headed back toward the crowd roaring from the TV. Someone had made a great play. "Five more minutes."

"Why didn't you tell me?" I asked my mother.

"I thought I'd let him tell you. We don't know what's happening. When his court date is. How we're going to pay for rehab."

"The court doesn't take any financial responsibility if they tell him that going to rehab is his punishment? So how will he pay?"

"I don't know."

"Let's eat, Mom," I said, taking shallow bowls out of the cupboard and sticking them in the warm oven. "It's pointless to arrange our lives around Eric. And anyway, how would he get here? He shouldn't drive."

"Yes," she said, defeated. "You should have picked him up."

I took a deep breath. We all felt defeated around Eric. His addictions, his self-annihilation so clear, so brutal. Like a train without brakes careening down a track.

My dad, though, my dad. I felt defeated around him too, but for different reasons. Eric's violent swings were hard enough to deal with, but I felt more helpless in the face of my father's quiet self-destruction. He didn't get belligerent, but morose, sinking into weepy depressions. Not talking to my mother, who tried to draw him out by cooking elaborate meals, pampering him. At least he'd never gotten a DUI. He was more sensible in his addiction. Unlike many drunks, he willingly turned his car keys over when he'd had too much.

"Can you put the cornbread on the table?" my mother said, breaking my reverie.

I cut three large pieces and put them on the plate she handed me.

"Four," my mother said, "Four pieces."

But that hopeful action didn't prove to be enough to draw Eric to us.

"DESSERT?" my mother asked.

My father knocked back the last of his beer. "What do you have?"

"Chocolate cake."

It was my favorite, rich and chocolaty, the second piece better than the first. Her making it more than compensated for her cooking chili for Eric. If only she'd told me what was for dessert before I'd taken my second helping of chili.

"So what have you been working on?" my father asked.

My mother and I looked at each other. "The Chinese porcelain exhibit," I said, trying to keep the irritation from my voice. He'd asked the same question the previous week and the week before.

"Oh, right. I heard something on the radio about a stolen head that your museum bought."

"No, we did not buy a stolen head. One of our trustees bought a head, which might or might not be stolen. We're trying to authenticate it." Damn Philen. My father had heard what I'd expected the average person would hear, that the museum was responsible.

"How do you do that, dear?" my mother asked me, trying to deflect the rising confrontation as she watched me watch him

pull another beer from the fridge. A beer to have with his chocolate cake.

"Style, wear to the object, research." I took a deep breath
and turned my attention to my mother. If I didn't watch his
drinking, I might not be irritated. "I visited a book dealer here
in Berkeley this afternoon. He bought the book collection that
belonged to the previous owner. I wanted to see if there were
notations in any of the books."

I took a sip of tea and plunged my fork back into the cake.

"Were there?" She was determined to keep the conversation going.

"No, though there were a number of pages in the books I
looked at, a few of which I bought, marked with Post-its, all of
which appeared to relate to the head. They were in sections of
books about the Baphuon period or in the plates illustrating
Baphuon sculptures." That wasn't a lie. I just didn't mention
that I had found papers stuffed into one of the books. Tom
Sharpen's barely legible and incoherent notes explaining why he
thought the head P.P. had purchased was a fake and what that
meant to him.

"Why did he sell it?" my father asked.

I didn't look up, but I felt his eyes on me. "What?"

"Why did this person sell this head and sell all his books?"

I didn't want the conversation to take this course.

"He died. His family sold everything." I brought another
bite to my mouth. Maybe if my mouth was full he'd stop asking
me questions.

He held the bottle halfway to his mouth. "How did he die?"

The thing about my father was that even when he drank,
he could spot a lie or see one's dissembling a mile away. We'd
been terrified of him as kids. My mother put down her fork and
watched me, aware that my father had zeroed in on something
I'd said.

"He was murdered."

My mother's teacup rattled. "Oh, Jenna. You aren't going to get involved in a murder?" She knew my propensity for getting involved in people's tiffs, neighborhood disagreements—which, in my defense, I attempted to mediate. Though I seemed to have a knack for taking sides.

"No, I have no interest in his murder." That wasn't exactly a lie. I hadn't had any interest in his murder this morning when I woke up, or when I went to the museum to do some work before coming to the East Bay, or even when I'd parked my car at the book dealer's house. It was when I'd stuffed those papers in my purse that there might have been a slight shift. Now I had an interest, though I still didn't have any plans. Not to find the murderer, anyway. Only plans to try to decipher Sharpen's notes. Only plans to try to figure out if the head was a fake or real.

"How?" My father wasn't going to give up. He was undoubtedly ruthless with his students.

"Decapitated. At any rate, I found—"

"Decapitated?" She jumped out of her seat and hurriedly cleared the table. I watched as the last few bites of my cake fell into the compost. I felt about ready to explode, but I would have eaten them.

"Yes, but I'm only interested in the head."

"The head!"

"The stone head. The Baphuon-style head. I was telling you that I looked at his books, and some of them were marked."

"What did they tell you?" my father asked, still watching me carefully, more carefully than the usual drunk can.

"I'm not sure. He seems to have figured out that the head belonged—or was a copy of the head that belonged—to a Khmer sculpture that's in the Siem Reap museum. Well, if you knew anything about that sculpture, you would figure that out. Of course, you'd have to have recent books to come to that conclusion, since the sculpture was only excavated a few years ago."

"And he did."

"Yes. But what that means, I don't know."

"Jenna, promise me that you won't get involved in this murder." My mother was wiping the counter again.

"I told you, Mom. I have no interest in getting involved."

"You say that now, but even you don't know what you'll do. You're so impulsive." Mother's words.

"I have too many other things to do, and I'm going out of town soon."

"To Cambodia," my father said matter-of-factly.

"Do you think I could take home some of that cake? I should get going soon. Work early tomorrow, more to do tonight." I got up, folded the placemats, and put them in the drawer, my father's keen eyes giving me creepies on the back of my neck.

I came out of the house with more than I'd asked for. Half a chocolate cake, a large container of chili, a jar of pear-and-ginger jam, and a down comforter that I didn't need but that my mother didn't need either and foisted on me. The food was in a grocery bag, but the comforter was loose and unwieldy as I struggled to dig my car keys out of my purse.

My feet crunched as I reached to insert the key in the door, but the comforter kept me from seeing my feet, or the car for that matter. I stuffed as much as I could under my arm and saw that I was standing on glass. "Shit," I said. "Not again."

How many times can a person have her car broken into and not feel that she's jinxed? A rear window had been smashed, and glass spread like snow across the backseat and onto the pavement. "Shit, shit, shit," I repeated, setting down the grocery bag on the damp pavement, opening the front door, and tossing the comforter onto the driver's seat. I looked nervously up and down the street, though I didn't really expect to see anyone.

I picked up the bag, shook it to dislodge any glass, and put it in the trunk. I took out a piece of foam board that I could attach to the window with duct tape. It was the third time this year, and I was prepared. My old car invited vandalism, a key run from front to back on the driver's side, break-ins, graffiti written in lipstick on the rear window.

The foam board was awkward, and it was beginning to rain. Luckily the rain hadn't started while I was in the house. Luckily I hadn't had anything in the car. Then I remembered. The books. I threw down the foam board and looked in the backseat. They weren't there, and they weren't in the trunk either. A hundred and fifty dollars' worth of books gone. I cursed the thief, who would have no interest in books on Southeast Asian art. I imagined his disappointment when he saw what he had. It wasn't a consolation.

I considered going to get my father to help me. Four hands would simplify the task of securing the window. But going back to the house would mean my mother would insist that I stay, that I put my car in their garage until I could get the window fixed in the morning. I wedged one side of the foam board down the opening where my window had been and managed to jam it into place, then I taped the upper edge and sides so that it wouldn't blow away when I drove.

I pushed the comforter onto the passenger seat, pulled off my soaking coat and threw it on top of the comforter, climbed into the driver's seat, leaned my head back on the headrest, and closed my eyes, groaning as I thought of the work I still needed to do tonight. Once I'd collected myself, I started the car. A car parked a few cars behind me started too, its lights flashing on for an instant, then going out.

Instinctively I locked the car doors, imagining an arm crashing through the foam board and grabbing me by the throat. Or two arms. Or a machete, its curve falling and in one fell swoop breaking my window and severing my head. Then it dawned on me, my disparate thoughts catching up with each other. This wasn't just a random break-in.

The rain pummeled the window, making it impossible to see. The street was dark, except for my headlights blurring light across the bumper of the car in front of me. I wanted to scream. Instead I reached into my purse, felt the reassuring bulk of Tom Sharpen's notes. This must be what the thief was after. The books meant nothing, the Post-its in the books meant nothing. The notes were what was significant. Of course, the thief didn't know there were notes, or so I hoped.

As I pulled away from the curb, I saw the bedroom light go on in my parents' house. There they were, unaware of the danger. The thief—was he also the murderer?—knew where they lived and undoubtedly knew where I lived. This wasn't about the notes, or the books, or the Post-its in the books. This was about frightening me off. A threat not just to me, but also to my family.

Damn Philen for bringing us to the attention of the killer. The idiot. Car lights came on behind me again, and that same car slowly pulled from the curb.

I braked and started to open the door. Then I thought of Grey and how he had tried to intimidate me with his size at the art fair. His smell and his ridiculous thinning ponytail. Damn that Grey. It had to be him, didn't it? He'd practically admitted it. What was it he'd said? That he'd flown to the States to talk with Sharpen about a piece. That he'd been too late. Or some such. But the point was, he'd come to the Bay Area around the time Tom Sharpen died.

I was sure it was him, a man twice my size. I drove on, turning right, then left, losing the car easily in the maze of streets that wound like snakes around the Berkeley hills.

8

"I'm sorry to bother you again," I said to Peggy as she handed me a coffee mug. I took a sip. It was so weak, I wondered if she'd remembered to put coffee in the filter. We stood in her sunny, butter-yellow kitchen rather than her father's house. Perhaps because of that, she seemed much calmer than when P.P. and I had met her before. "I won't be long."

"Did you speak with my brother?" She pulled a face as she took a sip, then gazed into her mug.

"Yes, he was very helpful." As I spoke, I thought about why I hadn't gone to see him rather than her. His office was closer to Marin, just over the Golden Gate Bridge, I was tired after a sleepless night, and he seemed better able to cope with the murder than she did. Yet I'd rationalized going to her by thinking that I hadn't visited the Cantor Museum at Stanford for quite some time or the Anderson Collection, with its marvelous collection of modern art. I knew these were merely rationalizations. I was drawn to her fragility, to her proximity to the murder, to the possibility that she would reveal a clue.

She looked at me expectantly, and I realized my thoughts had been wandering.

"I went to see the book dealer who bought your father's books. Your brother had remembered his name."

"Oh, were there some books that you wanted to purchase?"

"Yes, always. It's an addiction." I thought of my father. I thought of my brother.

"Did he have what you wanted? That would be nice if you had some of my father's books. He would have liked a young scholar to have them. He was almost as proud of his library as he was of his art collection. He said he had rare ones."

She was right. There had been some rare books, old French publications that were now difficult to find and expensive. "He was right to be proud. Though I fear young scholars can't afford very rare books on their young scholars' salaries."

"Oh, that's too bad. I wish I had met you before I sold the books. We got so little money for them that I would have been happier giving them to someone appreciative."

"Ah, well. Timing. But I did buy a couple of books that I've been wanting, so it was a doubly useful trip." I didn't bother to mention that someone had stolen them. That someone being the same person who had cut off her father's head, no doubt. I didn't tell her. I hadn't told anyone. I'd spent the night getting angrier and angrier, more and more determined. Which, of course, was why I was here.

She frowned. "Doubly useful?"

"Yes, I found some of your father's papers stuck in one of the books." I took another sip, then masked the dishwater taste of the so-called coffee with a bite of one of the cookies that she'd set on the counter in front of me.

She seemed to suddenly realize that we were still standing, and she picked up the cookies and moved toward the kitchen table. "Important papers?"

"Well, I don't know about that, but they do seem to be his notes about that sculpture that worried him so. The head."

"I was so sick of hearing about that hunk of stone."

Taking a seat, I asked, "He liked to talk about it?"

She thought for a moment. "He didn't like to, I think. It was just that it made him so angry. He'd get worked up about it and go on and on to anyone who would listen."

"Ah." I set down the mug with no intention of picking it up again.

"He was convinced that the dealer had intentionally sold him a fake, a copy of some sculpture that he knew. He really was furious."

"I imagine that was difficult."

"Yes. I hated it when he got angry." She picked at a cookie, edging crumbs onto the table.

"I have those notes here with me."

She nodded, a little puzzled.

"I've been trying to decipher them, without success. I thought you might be better able to understand his note-taking."

"I'm not so sure. But I can look."

I pulled the papers out of my purse and spread them before her. "I see here who he bought it from."

She looked. "Yes, that's right. I was trying to remember. Grey. That's right."

That confirmed that. "And of course the invoice has the date of purchase, what he paid, etc."

"Mm-hmm."

"Then it seems he didn't do anything with the head for quite some time, until about a year later—he was very thorough, putting dates for everything."

"Yes, that was him. He was originally trained as an accountant. He was very methodical."

"He dated every note—he researched and confirmed what Grey had told him, that the head was in Baphuon style. That's this paper here. He's written a little blurb describing the head and comparing it to other sculptures."

"Yes, that's what he did, kind of a museum label. That's how he thought of it." She took the paper from my hand.

"Right. Then I get the impression that he purchased a book, or made a trip to Cambodia, or visited a museum, some event that made him go back and look more carefully at the head."

She shrugged. "He went to Southeast Asia at least once a year."

"And that's where I find his notes confusing."

"Why?"

"Because he starts abbreviating things and writing rather obscure comments. That's what I thought you might be able to decipher, since he'd talked with you about the head. Just here, you see?" I pointed to the third and last page of the notes, where he'd written "Radha," then "sR," then "Cambodian," "Radha," and "Krishna!!!" and a few other comments that didn't seem particularly revealing, but that I assumed held the key to what he'd thought.

She took some time looking at the paper, picking it up, studying it. "No, sorry. Doesn't make any sense to me either. What do you think 'sR' might mean?"

"Probably Siem Reap. That's where the museum is that has the original. Assuming his was a copy."

"Well, it would have to be, wouldn't it, if they have the original in the museum."

"Oh, I guess I didn't say that the head of the sculpture in the museum had been stolen." I didn't think I had to explain that the original sculpture included two figures and that only one head was stolen. "We're trying to figure out if this is the stolen head or a copy of the stolen head—a fake, like your father suspected."

She shrugged again. "I have to admit that after the first couple of times he ranted about the head, I tuned out what he was saying. I think I told you that he wasn't easy."

"Yes, you did." I lifted my mug, then put it back down before I made the mistake of drinking.

"You know how fathers are. But maybe yours isn't like that." She watched me expectantly.

I took a breath, thinking about my parents and how I'd left them last night. Had I endangered them? Had Grey, or whoever it had been, gone back after I lost him on the drive down the hillside? Had he gone back and waited? I shook off the foolish thought. Whoever had broken into my car wasn't interested in my parents. At least that's what I wanted to think.

"You look like you've had challenges with your father, too." she said, interpreting my pause.

"My father has a drinking problem. But he doesn't get angry or violent, so I've never had to deal with that. He doesn't rant. Well, not in the same way your father did. He gets—" I searched for the words. "Morose. Emotional. Not pleasant, but not threatening. I suppose my fear as a child was that he would disappear."

"Disappear?"

"Yes, leave us—or kill himself."

"How disturbing. Well, when my father got into his rants, I just wanted to leave, and usually I did." She poked her finger at the page. "So I have no idea what he intended here."

"Would your brother know, do you think?"

She laughed. "My brother was worse than me. He stopped listening to him the first time that he started up about the head. Told him if he was going to waste his money on art, he should expect to get burned. Who did he think he was, to be able to invest in something he knew so little about? Russian roulette, my brother said. Sooner or later you're going to get shot. So my father didn't bring it up with him anymore. Just with me."

"Oh, dear. I guess the more he talked with you about it, the more riled up he became." I understood. I understood her father, possibly too well.

"Yes, I don't think my brother was so happy he'd said that when my father was murdered."

"I expect not."

"At least he wasn't shot. If he'd been shot, my brother would have felt very guilty."

I didn't respond to that. I didn't want her thinking about the head that had lain at her feet. Though she did seem in better shape than when we'd met at her father's house. "Well, thank you for looking at the notes. Do you want to keep them?"

"Not really." She had a faraway look in her eyes. I had the sense that she was seeing that head again.

"I thought that you might want to give them to the police. Just in case the sculpture had anything to do with his murder."

"The sculpture?" Her voice had become shriller. "I don't know what that could have to do with his murder. It was just a fluke, a burglar, and my father happened to interrupt him."

"You're probably right." I tried to imagine a burglar carrying a sword or a machete, something sharp enough to cut off someone's head in a single swipe. Of course, that was an assumption on my part, that it took a single swipe. It wasn't a question that I could ask her. And it was also an assumption that the killer had brought the murder weapon with him. There was so much I didn't know.

"If it did have anything to do with it, which I doubt, I would suggest you let it lie." She sounded like my mother. Looking at me, she gathered the papers up and held them against her chest, as if I might try to wrest them from her. "I'll keep them."

"Of course." To reassure her, I lied, "I'm just trying to figure out whether this sculpture of Radha is the original or a fake, not who murdered your father. How could I possibly do that?"

She didn't look convinced, and it made me realize that I couldn't tell anyone about the car that followed me when I left my parents' house. I could tell about the broken window, the stolen books, but not their connection to the head. If Peggy, who didn't know me, wasn't convinced about my intentions, how would my friends react, knowing my impulses as they did?

As we walked toward the door, she was still clinging to her father's notes. I was glad I'd made a copy before coming to see her. She watched me walk down the rose-lined path and didn't go in when I climbed into my car and waved. I waited a moment before I turned the key in the ignition, thinking about finding the murderer. He'd invaded my space by breaking into my car, and I'd catch the bastard.

9

The last few days before the opening of the porcelain exhibition, I scurried from one task to another. No need to ride my bike to get exercise. And no desire to ride my bike, as the fall rains had arrived with a vengeance. At least here in the gallery, installing the bowls, plates, and ewers, I was able to stand still for a few moments.

"Relax," Rag, the head preparator, said.

"Can't, not even at the best of times." But I tried. I uncrossed my arms and allowed my hands to dangle, my fingers like drooping leaves rather than knotted rope. But I couldn't stop my eyes from swiveling around the room, making sure all was okay.

I spotted some masking tape where wall met ceiling and grabbed a ladder.

"What are you doing?" Rag asked.

"Masking tape."

"We'll get that."

"Got to be doing. You know me." At the top of the ladder I checked my watch. Fifteen minutes to the most odious of all tasks: seating charts for the opening dinner. I bridled at being involved, but Beatrice, the development assistant, claimed not to know enough about the patrons who would be attending. I didn't believe her for a minute. She was the fount of all gossip. I yanked at the tape and it came off in one piece. I climbed down.

The seating plan better not take long. I wanted to be around to make sure that the most fragile of the ceramics were earthquake proofed properly, a necessity in California. I looked down at the elegant pale-blue ewer lying on the table. Clair de lune, they called the glaze, and it was. Cool and distant as the moon, it lay coddled in foam. I stretched out one finger to touch the icy surface, like the slick face of a glacier reflecting the blue of the sea.

I'd known nothing about ceramics when I began this job. I hadn't even known I liked them. Now I was particularly drawn to stoneware, rougher and closer to earth than the refined pieces that filled the cases around me. Still, I could appreciate and enjoy their elegance, the lush, reflective colors, like hard candies, inviting and good enough to eat.

"I'm going to get some more filament," Rag said, holding the earthquake mount for the ewer. The mount was a thin, stiff piece of wire bent to conform to the contour of the ewer and painted pale blue. He would stick it into the floor of the case, then tie the transparent filament around the neck and base of the vessel, attaching it to the mount.

I walked around the room, assessing our installation design, enjoying the silence of the gallery and the proximity of beautiful objects. I belonged here, surrounded by art, not in the ivory tower of a university, where ideas reigned. I loved the ideas, but applied, not abstract.

I stopped and frowned at a row of labels that had been printed on the wrong color paper and mounted on foam board before anyone realized. At first we'd thought the color wouldn't be too much of a problem, as the shade was just slightly off, but the gallery lights turned the labels a glaring yellow. "Why did we ever buy that paper?" I asked Rag, who had returned with the filament. He shrugged. Rag was a big bear of a man, hairy, bearded, muscular, a steady man who moved with an animal grace.

"Guess we hadn't seen it under lights like these." He stepped back to look at my placement of the ewer in the case, then stepped forward and shifted it slightly to the left.

"The difference in color is bizarre. It wasn't nearly that extreme on the table in the workshop."

"Yeah, I guess."

"They need to be redone for the opening."

He looked from the ewer to me and said, "Can't do. I've only got one guy working with me because the education department corralled the others to set up the education gallery. This week of all weeks. You won't believe what they've come up with."

I knew what they'd come up with, but was trying not to think about it. "I'm sure you'll figure it out."

"Not happening, Jenna. One guy, and you want labels remade by tomorrow? We're not supermen."

I knew Rag well enough to know that he probably hated the mismatched labels as much as I did and would do everything in his power to change them before the opening. I walked to the other end of the gallery to get the long view of the ewer, the focal point of the room. "I think the case needs to shift to the left."

Rag scowled, but came over to join me. "You're right. Pick it up."

We walked back together and I lifted the ewer gingerly while he shifted the case. I put it back down and he stepped back to appraise it, then had me pick it up again while he shifted the case another inch.

Beatrice stuck her head in the gallery. "There you are." She waved a stack of papers in my direction. "Seating for the hungry. I've just been going over the menu with the caterer."

"Okay?" I said to Rag.

"I'll be fine without you."

I heard the subtext. "Again?" I said to Beatrice as I walked toward her. "I thought we'd made that decision."

"Yes, well, so did I. But someone's been reading cookbooks, and now they want to feature potstickers with weird fillings. Apparently some fusion restaurant serves them."

"I'm sure you'll figure it all out," I called to Rag as I left, comforting myself as much as I was reassuring him.

"I've got some instructions from Caleb as to where certain people should sit, but I'm feeling a little iffy about one or two," Beatrice said as we made our way through the contemporary painting gallery.

"Such as?"

"He told me to put P.P. at Philen's table."

I stopped. "You've got to be joking. P.P. will walk out of the museum and never come back."

"That's what I thought. He should be at Caleb's table, don't you think?"

"I hate this." I pressed the elevator button and we stood quietly, shaking our heads.

"THAT wasn't so painful," Beatrice said.

"No," I said. "I was afraid it would take us hours. Thanks for doing so much of the chart before enlisting me. And I think we're right in putting P.P. at my table. He'll feel comfortable and I'll survive Caleb's wrath. If Caleb can feel wrath."

"You look tired," she said, glancing at my leggings and oversized sweater.

I ignored the implied criticism. "Getting an exhibition up is overwhelming. Something always goes wrong."

"I hear that you've had more than exhibition woes. This thing with the Cambodian head."

"Yes. That's been a royal pain, and Philen has compounded the problem. Created the problem, I should say."

"He's been scowling around here like the dark lord."

"He put himself in the fix. Caleb told him to extricate himself, and he didn't have any idea how to do it. So Caleb told him to send out that second press release, damning himself." I had to smile.

"Serves him right. No one's happy about it, though."

"Really?" I was surprised.

"We all think he's been looking for another job, and who will hire him now? He's a loose cannon."

"True. Why do you think he's looking for another job? I always thought he was just trying to unseat Caleb."

"I gather he's received a number of communications from a museum back east. Remember when he flew to New York a month or so ago? We think he was interviewing. He was quite cheerful when he returned. But since his last communication from them, he's been especially irritable."

"Sounds as if he didn't get the job."

"Sure does."

Someone was being nosy. I would have to be careful, not that I had any secrets to keep. Well, one secret, but I wasn't looking for another job. "I'm off. Back to the gallery and the woes of the installation." Once the show was up, the press preview and opening were over, the lectures had been given, and those who expected a private tour had been satisfied, maybe I'd be able to relax.

"YOU'RE deep in thought," Breeze said when we ran into each other just outside the gallery entrance.

"Just thinking about all I have to do in the coming week. There's this show, and I won't have a moment to catch my breath before I have to rev up for the trip to Southeast Asia."

"I don't envy you. Well, I do envy you going on that trip, but not with Philen. You should get combat pay for that, at the very least. Or even a couple of weeks off when you come back."

"That would be nice. But what's worse is how angry P.P. is at Philen. Those two will be at each other. Not to mention P.P. and Alam Haque together. They don't get along, though at least they're civil with one another."

"Alam Haque is going? Isn't his interest modern art?"

"That's what I thought. Maybe he has a secret stash of Cambodian bronzes. The bigger question for me—."

"Wait a minute. We both know why he's going." She arched her eyebrows.

"What are you talking about?"

"Don't you remember? The last opening? I told you he was watching you."

"Don't be ridiculous."

"Just wait. Uh-oh."

"What?" I asked.

"Is the year up?"

"Get off it." I tried to change the subject. "I was just starting to say that the bigger question for me is why he and P.P. don't like each other. P.P. rolled his eyes when he saw who had signed up for the trip, and he wouldn't tell me the reason."

"Oh, dear. Jealousy." She did a little jealousy dance, then stopped when Rag came down the hall, a box in his hands. "Conflict from the beginning," she said. "I can imagine people grumbling after being together for two weeks, but to start that way isn't good."

"No, and I either need to mediate or keep them apart. It isn't easy keeping people apart when there are nine at a table for several meals a day."

She said, "Oh, God, do you have to eat together every meal?" The look of horror that crossed her face was replaced by a coy smirk. "Of course, then you'll have much more opportunity to get to know each other. If you know what I mean."

I ignored that. "Lunch and dinner usually. Though I've convinced Philen, with much effort, that people will be happier if they can have a certain number of meals on their own. He's trying to do it on the cheap."

"You're kidding."

"No. That's why we're going in October. It's not high season yet, the end of the rainy season."

"It's still expensive. I thought it was a high-end trip."

"Mmm."

"Excuse me. I need to ask Rag a question," Breeze said, and started after him, humming "Love and Marriage."

"Be sure you comment on how bad the two different-color labels look in the gallery," I called after her.

"I'll let you fight that battle." She pushed open the door to the gallery, and I headed back to my office to hide.

ARTHUR Philen, scourge of the Searles Museum, stood at my door. Pigpen, in the *Peanuts* cartoons, may have been followed by a cloud of dust. A mountain of self-generated trouble followed Arthur.

I opened my mouth to deliver an irritable "What do you want?," but he looked so forlorn, I turned it into a genuinely concerned, "What's up, Arthur?"

"Terrible week," he said, falling into the empty chair opposite my desk. He'd never sat down in my office before. He'd stood in the doorway and barked instructions, hovered over me and issued snide remarks, stuck a foot in as he passed and given me, verbally anyway, a swift kick. But he'd never sat.

I straightened in my seat. Was he going to fire me? Had he heard I'd been deriding him as a fool? I didn't think Caleb would let him get away with firing me, but Caleb was such a chicken, you never knew. In any case, they couldn't fire me right before an exhibition was to open. Probably he was here to try to manipulate me.

He slumped, his posture broadcasting defeat.

I waited, thinking back to my early days at the museum when he'd tried to enlist me as an ally.

"Emily is ill."

"Nothing serious, I hope." I genuinely liked his wife, Emily. Everyone did, and wondered what on earth she was doing with him. We'd placed bets on when she would leave him.

"Not sure yet. They're doing tests, scans, blood, the works."

That wasn't very illuminating. "What are her symptoms?"

The question seemed to bring him to attention. "I really can't tell you. She doesn't want me to say. I shouldn't have said this much." He leaned forward as if to leave, then sank back again. His hands hung limply on the arms of the chair, the nails manicured, the long, thin fingers of an artist. I wondered, not for the first time, if he'd come to art history by way of the studio, but this wasn't the time to ask.

"We all love Emily. I'll keep my fingers crossed for her."

"Yes, yes. And this thing with P.P. . . . ." He didn't go on, which was just as well. I wanted that one to stay vague.

I merely nodded. I wasn't about to be drawn more deeply into his standoff with P.P. I thought of the stone head and it firmed my resolve.

"He's trying to get me fired. Working Caleb, in his ear day after day. I just know it."

"That's not P.P.'s style, Arthur. Being in Caleb's ear would require more words than he'd be willing to expend. You know he hates to talk."

"He's called trustees at other museums."

This shocked me; it didn't sound like P.P. "That I truly doubt, Arthur. But really, why would he do that? And even if he did, people have short memories. They'll soon forget your screw-up."

He didn't seem to hear me. "I'll never be able to get a job anywhere else. I'll spend the rest of my life jumping to Caleb New's every whim. I'll be his dirty hands while he stays the golden boy. It matters, believe me, it matters."

I was suddenly certain Beatrice was right that Arthur was looking for another job. He'd revealed more about himself in the past three minutes than he had in the years I'd known him.

He stood. "We're having a gathering in a couple weeks, the group going to Cambodia. At the home of one of the couples. I want you to give a little presentation."

Before I could speak, he slithered out the door. The conniving, manipulative bastard, enlisting my sympathies about Emily, crying to me about P.P., then the parting shot as he left. I flung my pen down on my desk. This trip was like a series of landmines—the battle between P.P. and Philen, the note in the newsletter, Caleb's support—all interspersed with my real responsibilities, the porcelain exhibition, the everyday work of the museum.

Once we were on the trip, I would have to juggle P.P. and Philen, who were already at each others' throats, P.P. and Alam, who didn't like each other, and God only knew what dramas the others would bring. It was a bloody landmine that wouldn't go away, I thought, then cringed at that word "landmine." Landmines were not something to be taken lightly in Cambodia.

I got up and shut my door, hoping I could breathe quietly on my own for a few minutes before jumping back into the fray.

10

"I've got to get to work," I said to Breeze, trying to shoo her out the door.

"I found this new recipe I want to try out on you." She settled into the chair and looked around my office.

"I need to shift gears. The show's installed, the opening's over. The reviews are in."

"And they were good. Bravo!"

"Thank you, thank you, but really, I need to shift gears," I said.

"Yes, and that's why I'm talking about dinner tomorrow night."

"I need to think about this trip. I have to talk to the group tonight."

I waited for her to take the hint, but she remained glued to the chair.

It wasn't easy to shift. It wasn't easy to leap into a new task, when porcelain had been at the fore for months. Now that the ceramics were encased in glass, I missed touching them, running my hands (in gloves, of course) over their shapely forms. Delicate, thinly thrown ceramics, tactile and elegant.

I said, "There should be some clause in a curator's contract for post-installation trauma. Just a few days off, a spa trip, a long bike ride."

"A dinner," she said brightly. She stood, and we both looked out the window for a moment; the rain was blowing horizontally through the coast oaks. "Not a bike ride."

"Go, go," I said, and as she laughed her way out, I added, "And shut that door."

I typed, "The itinerary." Siem Reap, site of the ancient Angkorian capital, for eight days, then a day in Phnom Penh, the modern capital. Naturally everyone would want to rush to Angkor Wat the moment we arrived in Siem Reap, since it epitomizes the ancient Khmer kingdom of the seventh to thirteenth centuries.

I thought of all the temples we could visit: the towers of the Bayon, with their eerie faces; the charming Neak Pean, set in the middle of a pond; the Bakheng at sunset; the gum trees sprouting out of the vastness of Ta Prohm; and my favorite, the early Bakong.

I'd take them through chronologically, more or less. We'd go see the sunrise at Angkor Wat the first full day, just to whet their appetites. Then we'd drive out of town to the Roluos group and the Bakong. As I typed, I was transporting myself to those temples, seeing the relief carvings before me, the height of the towers, the vastness of faith. Feeling the weariness in my legs, the heat, the exhilaration of the approach as one traversed the causeway to Angkor Wat. And that glorious tropical light, glowing, flickering from the heat, illuminating the past.

This trip wouldn't be so bad. I just needed to stop thinking about the head, the murder, the potential in the group for conflict, and all would be fine. I imagined the helicopter trips, flying over the temples laid out below in their complex, symmetrical plans.

I couldn't wait to go.

P. P. never knocked, he just charged into my office. Today he moped through the door.

"You look glum," I said distractedly.

"Thieves," he said, and sank into my visitor chair.

"What?" I stopped typing.

"Home. Broke in."

"When? Did they take anything?"

"Last night. No."

I waited, but he didn't offer any more. "Were you there?"

"Yes."

I half rose from my seat, panicked, guilty. I should have warned him. "P.P., you need to tell me what happened. Are you okay?"

He nodded. "Took my laptop."

"Oh, no. That's terrible. I would say that counts as something being taken. Is there information on it that would allow them access to your accounts, your social security number? Is that what they were after? Is it business-related?"

In his usual fashion, he volunteered the information he thought worthy of mention. "No art."

"Okay, they didn't take any art. That's something. Did you see them?"

"Yes." Another nod. The man was infuriating. "I shot."

"Shot? You shot the burglar?"

"No. I don't think. I might have shot him. My gun went off."

"Your gun? You have a gun?"

"Protection." He scowled. "I scared him. Might be dead."

"Who might be dead?" My distress made translation difficult.

"Me. I heard him downstairs. Called 911, then went down. Like a mouse."

"In the dark? Tiptoeing?"

"Yes. He didn't hear me." He leaned forward and broke into complete sentences, forgetting for a moment his resolve not to waste words. "He was rustling through my things. My desk. My shelves. He was looking for something." We stared at each other.

"He was looking for the head." I could feel myself going pale.

"My thought exactly." He poked his finger at me. "I pointed the gun as I got to the door. He sensed me, or maybe he saw my silhouette but didn't see the gun. So when he charged toward me—" He stopped, recalling the moment.

"Yes? You shot at him?"

"No. The gun went off. He lunged at me, and I was startled and shot. Then the sirens started."

"The police were coming already?" I was puzzled. "Why would they be coming already? If the gun just went off?"

"I called 911, but he must have set off my alarm system when he entered. We stopped our tussling when the sirens began. Just for a second or two, but it felt like an eternity. His hand on my arm, the gun raised in my hand. It was primal. Both of us frightened by the sirens. Not the gunshot, but the sirens. You would have thought I'd be pleased to hear them, but I wasn't. We're trained to be afraid of the police."

"And?"

"He broke away and ran."

"My God. You were lucky."

He seemed to recognize the stream of words that had just gushed from his mouth and reverted to his telegraphed manner of speaking. "Lost my head."

"Sounds to me as if you kept your head."

"Yes. Might have lost it. He had a machete."

I felt queasy. "No."

"Yes." He thought a moment. "Looked like one in the dark. Police were skeptical. Their expressions, the looks they gave each other said I was imagining things."

I slumped back in my seat. "This isn't good. He's escalating."

P.P. looked puzzled.

"My car break-in."

"What?" He looked at me, his brow furrowed. "Why related?"

"He stole the books."

"You didn't say."

"I didn't want anyone thinking I might want to find the murderer."

Nodding, he said, "Might?"

"Would. Don't you?"

He didn't answer, but he often didn't answer when the answer was obvious.

"Should I tell the police about someone breaking into my car?"

He shook his head. "I did. They didn't understand the connection. Told them it ties to Sharpen."

I waited and when he didn't go on, I said, "So you suspected even though I didn't tell you about the books?"

"They'll look into your car break-in." He grimaced and rubbed his knee. "They lack imagination. 'A Cambodian connection?' one said and laughed." He shook his head. "I don't think they'll do much."

"Are you hurt?"

"No. Would have liked to defend my home." He paused. "Better."

I tried to focus on the event at hand, the attempted robbery. "Your laptop."

"A loss. I have my IT people making certain no sensitive data is released."

"I'd be beside myself. In fact I'm going to back up everything this afternoon."

"Yes." He slouched further down in his seat, then sprang up and began to pace my tiny office, pulling a book off my bookshelf, opening it as he walked back the other way, shutting it as he took the wood-and-iron rice cutter from the opposite shelf and replaced it with the book. It was dizzying watching him.

I said flatly, "The head."

He turned on me, raising the sharp little rice cutter in his hand and said, "Someone was decapitated."

"Yes." He put down the cutter and walked back out of the office, leaving me with my mouth open and with thoughts of Tom Sharpen's head lying at his daughter Peggy's feet. And the stone head, lying on that table in the unlocked conservation lab. And Grey. And P.P. headless, that round head of his rolling away from the round body. It would definitely roll, not bounce.

Sometimes I had the creepiest thoughts.

Then another thought came to me. If people were killing and robbing to get that head, it must be authentic after all. But with Tom Sharpen dead, what trail would it leave? And to whom? I could see the trail back to Grey, but beyond that, where?

11

I was starving. Giving a lecture always made me hungry. Not that I'd given a lecture, just a twenty-minute pep talk about Cambodia. But I had used my brain, and that was enough. Especially since my brain felt largely used up. I raised the glass of white wine to my lips; I don't think I'd put it down since it had first been filled. I might live in California, but that didn't mean I couldn't love French wine. "Lovely wine." I raised my glass to Barker and Courtney Hobbs. He smiled.

"We're so looking forward to this trip," said Courtney from the head of the table. She wasn't much older than me, but she was clearly in a different tax bracket. She wore discreet flash. Diamond earrings as big as the tip of my little finger, a ring to match, a Missoni dress that cost more than my monthly salary, Jimmy Choo shoes. I couldn't see her shoes here at the dinner table, of course, but I'd been very aware of their red soles extending toward me as I stood at one end of the living room giving my talk.

Her husband, Barker, the stem of an arugula leaf sticking from the corner of his mouth, said, "We've been wanting to go to Cambodia for years."

I wondered how Barker and Courtney felt about going on a trip with a group of people much older than them and with whom they had little in common. It was a disparate group. We weren't going to be dancing all night. Martha Payne, who sat opposite me, could easily be in her seventies. Why would the Hobbses choose to go with us, rather than on a private tour with their own guide? At some point I would have to ask.

"I'm sure we'll have a wonderful trip. It's nice to have so much time to explore," said Martha. She pulled back the cuff of her flowing jacket. I'd seen it slide across her salad once, and apparently so had she. Her ample clothes made her head look small, though that may also have been a result of her closely cropped hair and the delicacy of her features, a delicacy that didn't seem in keeping with her rather abrupt, forthright manner. Funny how a person's looks inform our perception of them. I thought of people we meet for the first time over the phone and how we pictured them.

"And a helicopter trip!" said Mrs. Jolly. I'd turned her last name, Jolson, into Jolly because both she and her husband were equally cheery. "I've always wanted to go on a helicopter. The thought of flying over the jungles of Cambodia and arriving at one of those dilapidated temples is so romantic."

"It does, doesn't it, Mrs. Joll . . . , Mrs. Jolson." I flushed as I saw that Courtney and Martha seemed to catch my slip.

I made a mental note to be sure that Mrs. Jolly took the helicopter the day we went to Banteay Chhmar, rather than on our trip to the more intact Sambor Prei Kuk. Nineteenth-century explorers had romanticized the Khmer temples in their drawings and prints of fallen walls overgrown with enormous trees. Contemporary photographers had perpetuated the image. We were still under the spell they had created. "Yes, me too. And the helicopter trips allow us to visit temples farther from Siem Reap than we'd otherwise be able to go. As I said, we can't all fit in the helicopter at one time, since it seats only five, but everyone will get their day in the sky. The limited space is the reason for taking two helicopter trips."

Mr. Jolly was bobbing his head in agreement to everything his wife and I said. I began to worry that they were a pair of those terminally cheerful people. Cheerful is okay, but not all the time. Still, they were full of good questions, both practical and insightful. It would be a pleasure to have people so intellectually engaged on the trip.

Mrs. Jolly said to me, "I met your mother at the porcelain opening. A lovely woman."

"Thank you, I'm rather fond of her," I said, wondering what Mrs. Jolly and my mother might have spoken about.

"She said that you have a number of brothers. Three, is that right? And they all live here in the Bay Area?"

"Yes, I'm afraid I grew up a tomboy. But only two of my brothers live here. The third is on the East Coast."

"But being a tomboy is very good. It explains your apparent independence." She had a soft face, padded with surprisingly smooth flesh for her age.

What did she know about my independence? What had my mother told her?

Alam Haque asked, "Do you think that there will be an opportunity for us to go to Battambang? I understand there's a museum there." I'd managed to get Courtney to seat him at the opposite end of the table from P.P.

"I don't think we'll make it to Battambang. That might have to be your next visit. We'll end the trip in Phnom Penh, so you'll be able to visit the National Museum and the old palace, the Silver Pagoda. It's too bad, I'd also like to see the museum in Battambang." I dug into my salad, hoping to keep those wayward arugula leaves from embarrassing me as they were doing to Barker.

"More wine?" Barker asked.

"No, thanks," I said as I looked at him. "I just realized that I've seen you before." Both he and his wife looked puzzled. "It was at the art fair last month. I was talking to a dealer named Grey. You walked by and spoke to him."

"Oh, yes, of course," Courtney said politely.

"Do you collect Cambodian art? I haven't seen any here at your house."

"A little," said Barker. He looked a bit like George W. Bush, a bland, forgettable kind of man, but now his small eyes and regular features lit up. "We've bought a few things and have been thinking about buying more. But all our Southeast Asian pieces are at our house up in Napa. You'll have to come to see them sometime. It's a modest collection, though. Not even really a collection, just the odd piece."

"What?" asked P.P., peering down the table at Barker.

Barker looked at him, puzzled, creases furrowing his brow under his mop of hair.

"P.P. is asking, 'What do you have?'"

"Oh, a couple of bronze Hindu deities, a couple of stone sculptures. That's all."

"And those pots," Courtney added, pushing the food around her plate without eating it. No wonder she was so thin.

"That's right, I forgot. Some Khmer bronze pots. Courtney's the one who spotted them. They look good with our modern art collection."

"Beautiful abstract forms," she said.

"Have you purchased from Grey?" I said, "I just met him at the fair for the first time. Does he have good material?" I hoped my question sounded innocent. No one there would know that the sound of Grey's name made bile rise to my throat, made anger flare, and the furies take over my heart. Except P.P.

Or maybe I was projecting. Maybe P.P. didn't understand a thing and didn't suspect Grey. I looked at him. He was oblivious to my anger, my determination to make Tom Sharpen's killer pay. Instead he was assessing Barker, whom he now saw as a collector buying in his field of interest, a competitor.

Barker shrugged. "He seems to, though, as I say, I don't know much. We're just learning." He went back to the arugula wars.

I persisted. "What kinds of objects have you purchased from him?"

Philen, ignoring Mrs. Jolly sitting between us, looked at me aghast at my question, and opened his mouth, probably to change the subject, but Courtney spoke up.

"We tried to buy a head from him. Someone else got it."

Barker gave her a look, but she was so intent on making her salad shrink without eating any that she didn't seem to notice. "We bought a small bronze. A Buddhist goddess," he said.

"That's right. I'd forgotten that," said Courtney. "She has a long name I can never remember."

"Prajnaparamita?" I asked.

"Yes, that's it," he said.

"I'd love to see your collection sometime." I wondered why Barker had given her that look, and if the head they tried to buy from Grey was the same head P.P. now owned, the head they had tried to buy from Tom Sharpen's daughter. I looked at P.P., who was still staring squinty-eyed at Barker. I eyed Courtney's plate and all that lovely arugula.

"Of course." Courtney smiled a broad smile, her perfect teeth flashing. "When we get back from the trip. You must be very busy right now with your exhibition."

"Yes, very." I looked around the table, shaking suspicion from my mind.

Courtney turned to P.P. and asked, "Will we be returning your Khmer head in Siem Reap when we arrive? Or does it go to Phnom Penh at the end of the trip?"

I held my breath.

"Not," said P.P.

I leapt in. "Are you the couple who had hoped to buy the head from the Sharpen family?"

Before Barker could deflect my question, Courtney said, "Yes. We were rather upset when we came back and his daughter hadn't held it for us as we'd asked. Especially since we'd tried to purchase it before."

I held my breath, then asked, "From Grey."

"Yes," said Barker. "Now we're feeling relieved that we didn't buy it. I'll be happy to get a chance to look at it again, since you'll be returning it."

"We won't be returning the head." Could this be their reason for joining the trip? I wondered. "I'm afraid the press release was a little premature. We won't know for certain whether it's the original head until we complete our research." Philen looked like he'd shrunk, while P.P. seemed to have expanded. He looked as if he might blow up.

"Philen's press release." P.P.'s hands grasped the edge of the table. His knuckles were white. "Endangered us all." Courtney, unaware of the difficulties, had cheerfully placed P.P. and Philen together.

Silence gripped one and all; the animosity between the two was so clear that a two-year-old would have seen it. None of the party knew what had gotten P.P. so worked up; he had managed to keep the news of his encounter with the burglar out of the paper. Before the moment turned into a shouting match, Martha saved the day. "The deforestation in Southeast Asia is an abomination!" she cried, as if she hadn't seen the flash between Philen and P.P., though I felt pretty certain she had. She certainly had chosen a volatile topic.

"Ah, yes," responded Philen vaguely, relieved to move on to something else, even one far outside his ken.

"We hope to do something about it," Martha said, nodding emphatically and finishing her last bite of arugula with relish.

"Who hopes to do something about it?" asked Alam, deftly cutting those wild arugulas so they didn't splash salad dressing on his perfectly tailored shirt or stick waywardly out of the corners of his mouth.

"The environmentalists." Martha had introduced herself as an avid conservationist.

"I thought you were a member of the Great Old Broads. Aren't they more focused on national wilderness areas?"

"True, I am. Young man, I'm impressed that you've even heard about the Great Old Broads."

"The Great Old Broads?" Barker laughed. "Who are they?"

"A group founded in 1989 in response to Orrin Hatch's statement that wilderness without roads isn't accessible to the aged and infirm. He tried to use us as an excuse to put roads through pristine wilderness areas. The cad."

We all laughed.

"But I'm also a part of other environmental groups, and I'm hoping to meet with people in Phnom Penh. We have an army of people protecting our wilderness in the States, and few in these third world countries where they're most needed. It's time for me to branch out." Her fork still poised above her salad, she said, "No pun intended."

We all groaned, laughing.

"Sounds laudable," Alam said. His dark eyes held hers.

The maid began removing the salad plates, while the cook slipped our entrees in front of us.

Barker said, "I wanted to ask you about the food on the trip."

"We'll have fabulous food, I'm sure." From food, we went on to discussing the practicalities of the trip. The Jollys joined in, while Alam chatted across the table with Martha about petitions and laws and dire conditions in various parts of the world. From the snippets of their conversation I heard, the two seemed to be enjoying each other.

Martha's voice rose above the others. "And what do you do, young man?"

"I'm a doctor."

"In practice?"

"Yes, though I also do research."

"How is it that you can get away for two weeks?" The woman was certainly direct.

Alam's response was drowned out by Philen's ingratiating quizzing of Mr. Jolly. Beatrice had told me that Alam was a cardiovascular surgeon at a local teaching hospital—I had already known that he was a surgeon—and she thought he had invented a piece of equipment that was now widely used in surgeries. If he did have a patent on something like that, it helped explain his ability to collect very expensive contemporary art.

P.P. was scowling at his food, even though it was salmon, which I knew he liked. Then I heard Philen's smarmy voice buttering up Barker. It was enough to make me wince too, and I wasn't sitting next to him.

Philen had made a few overtures to P.P., who hadn't responded, and so now Philen was speaking a bit too loudly to anyone who was willing to talk with him. I overheard him tell Mrs. Jolly not to worry, he was sure that we would be able to . . . But the remainder of the sentence was lost, and I could only hope that he hadn't promised the moon, when all we could deliver was a relatively comfortable ride on an overused tourist minibus.

As the dessert arrived, the Jollys, Barker, and Courtney had found common ground in their alumni status and were comparing notes on fraternity and sorority houses. If I'd joined a sorority at Berkeley, would I now be sitting in my own living room, with a Diebenkorn dominating one wall and a Thiebaud another? Would I want that, rather than my ratty cottage and its secondhand furniture? I didn't think so, but the pleasure of looking at a fine painting while I ate was one that I could get used to. Distracted by the art, I almost forgot to eat the crème brûlée. Almost, but not quite.

12

I decided to take a bike ride in the Napa Valley. I could drop in on Courtney and Barker. Well, not exactly drop in, but let them know that I was in the Valley and would love to see their collection. It would be nice to know their interests, so I could have a better sense of what they wanted to see in Cambodia. And I could find out why Barker hadn't wanted Courtney to talk about the stone head. He'd become extremely quiet after she mentioned it. A visit and a little chat might clarify why.

Or that was what I'd thought as I loaded my bike onto the bike rack of my car at six on Sunday morning. Now that I was here in the Valley, I wondered if a visit was such a good idea. I didn't need any more annoyed people on the Cambodia tour. Courtney probably wouldn't mind if I called. She'd invited me to visit when we returned from the trip. Of course, it had only been four days since I'd seen them, and the trip was still in the future. I thought about the scowl that slid over Barker's face when she talked about Radha's head, and how it had deepened when she talked about me visiting.

It was too early to call now, at any rate. I'd have to do it at the end of the ride. I'd parked near their gate, or what I guessed was their gate, given the nearby wineries they mentioned when speaking about their Napa house, so it would be easy enough to call when I got back to the car or earlier, from Calistoga.

Traffic wouldn't be too bad on this cool fall morning, so I was riding the narrower Silverado trail north. I would pedal back down the west side of the Valley on my return. Since their home wasn't far from St. Helena, the ride to Calistoga wasn't as long as I would have liked, so I'd continue further up Route 29 past Calistoga to give myself a good, solid three-hour ride. Such a luxury.

The low hills barely rose from the Napa Valley floor, across which vines stretched from east to west in rows that seemed to widen the expanse. The occasional vineyard dipped up a hillside: Cabernet, Merlot, some Cabernet Franc. A fellow I'd once dated had explained at length the differences between the grapes that grew on the valley floor and those on the hillside, the geology of the valley, and how the soil contributed to the mineral flavors in the wines. I wished I'd listened more carefully. The sun struggled to peek through the clouds, changing the color of the grape leaves, vivid maroon splashed with yellow, fall-variegated like a crazy quilt.

I pedaled harder, the tension falling from me, doing my best not to think about anything other than the cars that passed; the winery signs and their offerings; the cup of coffee that I would stop to have in Calistoga on my way back down; Courtney and Barker's, and whether they were even there. I did pretty well until I hit the coffee shop.

Sweaty and chilled, I embraced the welcoming warmth and rich aroma of the Coffee Roastery. I ordered a double cap and a scone, then looked around for a table. The long table by the window where I would have liked to sit was occupied by a group of old men. The same group had been there on my last visit a few months earlier, when my biking group rode in the Valley.

Sipping at my overfull drink, I moved toward a table near them that had just freed up, pushing out the chair with my foot, aware of the men watching me as I sat. I wondered if I would end up like them, an old lady sitting in a café in the morning with a group of other oldies who needed a chat. A woman unable to settle on a man, and who in the end was alone.

The men burst out laughing as one, and I looked again. They were a motley crew, linked together by their age but seemingly not by much else. Were they winery owners? Retired lawyers or housepainters? Artists or clerks? Had any of them known each other before aging had slowed them?

"When we were in Africa," one of them said, launching into a story.

"You were driving a Volkswagen van," another volunteered.

"You heard that one already," said the first, laughing.

"A few times."

"We were collecting beads after windstorms."

"Under the pyramids, right?"

Collecting. The word brought up Barker and Courtney. I wondered what their collection would offer up. I tore apart my scone and bit into the outer crunchy edge. A pecan, a raspberry. I tapped crumbs from my fingers and pulled out my phone.

"DELICIOUS, isn't it?" Courtney asked. She leaned her head back, letting her legs float upward in the hot water. "I could boil in this all day."

"Absolutely," I said, looking past her toward the hills. She'd been inviting and effusive when I'd called, saying she was about to take a hot tub, but would wait for me. "Paradise."

"Most certainly," said a voice behind me. Barker set down a tray with champagne glasses, a bottle of champagne in an ice bucket, and a pitcher of orange juice.

"Uh-oh," I said. "I may never leave."

"You may never get out. The sun might be out, but it's bloody freezing. No need for an ice bucket today. I'm heading back into the house."

"Barker, you've put that tray just out of reach. Can you put it over here closer to the hot tub?"

"Absolutely, madam. At your service." He kissed the top of her head as he set down the tray, then hurried away, shivering.

"It didn't seem that cold when I was riding."

"I promise you, we'll be prunes by the time we work up the nerve to get out and all the bones in our bodies will be so warm we won't even notice." She reached over to pour the orange juice.

"Not too much champagne for me. Not a good idea just after a long ride."

"Or while in the hot tub. But it was sweet of him to think of it, so we'd better drink some."

She was right. It was sweet, and not at all in accord with my previous impression of him.

"Twist my arm." I reached for the glass.

WE ate lunch in the dining room. Slate floors and walls, gorgeous wooden table and chairs with jacquard-covered cushions that one sank into. The table was large for the three of us, but the view was so spectacular that I understood why they'd chosen this room rather than the less formal enclosed porch or the kitchen. "Are those your grapes?" I asked, gesturing toward the vineyard that spread before us.

"Yes," Barker said. "But I'm not so foolish as to think I should be making my own wine. A vintner nearby has purchased the grapes from this vineyard for decades, and when we bought the property we agreed to keep that arrangement until he didn't want them anymore. It's worked out very well. Not only does he buy the grapes, but he looks after the vineyard." He raised his glass.

"This is his?" I took a sip. "It's lovely. I like a nice crisp, green Sauvignon Blanc."

"Yes, and he does just as well with reds, so we're quite content." He took a deep breath. "Well, what do you think of our collection? You didn't say much when I showed it to you."

"Barker, don't put her on the spot," said Courtney, who looked relaxed in an elegant loose cashmere sweater and plush leggings.

"You have some lovely objects. Have you had anyone advising you?" I threw a question back at him, hoping he wouldn't insist I tell him what I thought of his pieces.

"Not really, unless you could say that dealers have advised us." He took a bite of his salad after pushing aside the radicchio.

I smiled.

"That's a joke," Courtney said. "Very funny, mister."

"It's a joke of sorts, but I will say, when we first started two years ago—"

"You've put all these pieces together in two years? You've been busy!"

"Yes. We first started when we were in Paris. A short trip, just four days. We went to the Musée Guimet because we'd read how fantastic it is. And we went back every day that we were there. Never made it to another museum."

"That's where you got hooked?"

"Yes. The first day we looked at the Chinese collection on the top floor, then each day we worked our way down, ending up in Southeast Asia."

"I liked that the best," said Courtney. She'd finished with her radicchio and was rearranging the other food on her plate to make it look like less.

"I rather liked the Tibetan thangkas and sculptures. Bronzes. Gilt bronzes. Anyway, by the end of the week we had begun to think that we might like to collect something Asian."

"But we were bickering over which area. He liked the Tibetan art. I thought the Southeast Asian sculpture would look better with our contemporary art."

He gave her an expectant look.

"You have a fine collection of contemporary art as well," I volunteered, thinking of the Diebenkorn and the Thiebaud in their house in San Francisco and the large contemporary paintings by artists I didn't recognize that hung in the living room here.

"Thank you. I know much more about contemporary art, actually. Though I did sit in on a class on Southeast Asian art at Berkeley last year, and I've been attending every lecture on it at the Asian Art Museum."

"She's thinking of taking a course in London next summer." Barker had finished his lunch and poured himself another glass of wine. "But back to Paris."

"Sorry, yes, back to Paris." If only, I thought.

"We were debating what to get, then we walked down this side street in the Latin Quarter and saw that piece in a gallery window." He pointed to a Khmer sculpture in a corner of the dining room.

"We didn't even say anything to each other, just walked in and within an hour had bought it."

"It's from an old French collection. I mean a really old collection, from the 1920s."

"Is the gallery owner the dealer who's been advising you?" I was trying to think who it might be.

"No. He's primarily a Chinese art dealer. I'll just say that there's a dealer in New York and another in London who have been very helpful. I've bought the few other pieces we have from them."

"*We've* bought," Courtney interjected.

"Sorry, honey." He reached over to pour her more wine, though it didn't appear to me that she'd even taken a sip. "She's the one with taste and knowledge."

"He's the one with the pocketbook. And taste."

"But not much knowledge, I'm afraid. So that's our story." He paused. "Since you're here, could you tell us your thoughts on any objects we've purchased that might be problematic?"

"I would have to spend more time with the collection to properly evaluate it. It's a very tricky field, so we all make mistakes."

"Okay, I get the disclaimer. And I get the fact that we've made a mistake. Hopefully not more than one." The irritation that had crept into his voice reminded me of my first impression of him. I hesitated, not wanting to rile him.

"No one wants to be the messenger," I said. "I suggest that you have your sculpture checked by a conservator. Tyler at the museum has a full load, so he can't do it, but there is a freelance conservator in town who is quite knowledgeable about Southeast Asian sculpture. As you know, stone is quite tricky, but there are some clues."

"Are you saying everything is problematic?" He was sitting up straighter in his seat and leaning toward me. Threateningly.

"No, I'm not saying that at all."

"Are there any specific pieces you're talking about, then?"

"Well . . . there is one piece that has some stylistic anomalies."

"Which piece?"

How do I get myself into these situations? If I hadn't decided to ride in the Napa Valley, then wheedled my way into stopping to see the collection, I wouldn't have found myself confronted by an irate collector.

"The female by the fireplace in the living room."

"Damn that Grey," he said. "He assured me that the piece had been in a Thai collection for decades."

"It may have been. Unfortunately, copies have been made for decades. Or the collector could have lied to him. Or I could be wrong. It may be just fine."

"Or he's just a son of a bitch."

"That's possible too. I don't know him well. And as I've said, a cursory glance can't tell me for certain. I would need to do some research on the object." I nodded at Courtney. "Courtney could do some research, too. And you need to have a conservator look at it."

"We're lucky we didn't buy that head," Courtney said, trying to placate him. But Barker rose from his seat. "We have dessert, honey," she said.

"Not hungry anymore," Barker said. "I should have stuck

with the respectable dealers in the West. Buying from some rookie Bangkok dealer was not my best idea." He started toward the living room. "You told me."

Courtney widened her eyes and nodded. "I did tell him," she said quietly. "He's stubborn."

"I'm sorry, it's very difficult when people ask my opinion after they've purchased something. I shouldn't have said anything."

"No, it's better if we know. Thank you."

"Grey, call me back. It's Barker."

Shit, I thought. Now I'd dumped myself in it. I got up and went into the living room. Barker was looking at the figure beside the fireplace, his arms crossed. "I didn't say it was a fake. I said there are some anomalies and it should be checked."

"The guy's clearly crooked. He sold that stolen head, didn't he? As soon as I heard that, I knew I shouldn't have bought anything from him."

"We haven't resolved whether the head is stolen."

"If it's not stolen, then it's a fake, isn't it? Like this one."

"I brought us some coffee," said Courtney, a pot and three mugs on a tray. "Do you take cream or sugar?"

"Damn him," he said again.

"Barker, you need to calm down. Jenna told you that she doesn't know for certain and that more research needs to be done. We can have the conservator come before we go to Bangkok."

Uh-oh, I thought.

"We're going to Bangkok at the end of our trip with you in Cambodia." She poured us each a mug.

I breathed a sigh of relief, thankful that they weren't going at the beginning of the trip, when P.P. and I would be there. I hoped Barker wouldn't fume the entire time we were in Cambodia.

"Oh, shut up," he said, and stormed out of the room.

We watched him leave. "He's got a temper. And he doesn't like to lose. But his bark is worse than his bite."

I thought of Peggy. I thought of Tom Sharpen's head, rolling across the floor. I looked at the beautiful Japanese sword that lay on the mantel, incongruous amidst the Khmer sculpture and contemporary paintings. Did not being able to purchase that Khmer stone head amount to losing, in Barker's mind?

13

"It's just ahead," I said. "The numbering on these Thai streets is a befuddlement."

P.P. and I had walked only a block from where the air-conditioned car had dropped us, but the sweat was already pooling between my breasts, and my white T-shirt was stuck to my back. I was glad I'd worn a skirt, at least. Bangkok is always hot, but Bangkok in the humidity of October gives "wet blanket" an entirely new meaning. When P.P. had pointed down the Soi, the driver gesticulated that he wouldn't drive the narrow street, instead indicating a parking space where we could come back to find him.

P.P. didn't answer, he just looked from right to left, searching for the number of Grey's house.

"Are you still thinking about the burglary?" We'd been talking about the burglary and the car break-in on the way over.

"Robbed, violated, almost killed."

"Yes, terrible." I saw his anger flaring. "We have to keep it cool here."

"I know."

"We can't let on that we suspect him."

"We know."

For a moment I thought he was referring to himself as the royal we, then I realized what he meant. "We think we know it's him. Our evidence is circumstantial."

"Trap him?" P.P. asked.

"How? Say, 'Oh, by the way, did you kill Tom Sharpen when you were in town?'"

He shrugged.

"This blasted number." I looked down at the piece of paper in my hand, as if the number had changed since Grey gave it to me when I'd called.

"By ear," P.P. said, and pointed at the door before us.

"Thank God," I said, whether because we'd found the building or because even from the street we could hear the hum of air conditioners, I didn't know. "Yes, we'll play it by ear."

He moved toward the building, but I hesitated. Were we walking into a trap? Grey had sounded pleased when we said that we were coming. Pleased because he would have us both in the same spot to kill?

THE apartment door was open and from deep within I could hear Grey calling out, though I couldn't make out the words.

"It's dark," P.P. said in a tense voice as the two of us peered into the pitch-dark apartment. Coming from the bright sunlight, it was impenetrable.

Before I could speak, he charged ahead of me into the darkness. "P.P.," I cried, but he didn't listen. I heard him stumble and then I heard a crash. "P.P." I hesitated. No point in both of us charging headfirst into danger.

"P.P.," I said more urgently, as the room had fallen into silence. The cold of the air conditioner and the damp of my sweat formed shivers up my spine. "Shit."

"Damn." I stepped in, trying to understand as I did why the apartment was dark. The front door closed behind me, making it darker still, but forcing my eyes to adjust. "P.P., are you all right?" I had to get him out. We'd walked into a trap. My heart beat wildly and I blinked, willing my eyes to adjust.

"Just a minute. I'll be right there." Grey's voice moved closer.

"Get up," I said, hurrying to P.P. and running into the same obstacle that had knocked him over. I managed to stay upright.

"Just stay where you are," Grey said and I could tell he'd entered the room. With a sword? A gun? A cudgel? He moved closer.

I found P.P. and pulled at his arm. "C'mon," I whispered, but pulling him up was akin to picking up a baby elephant.

Grey pulled open the drapes. "Are you okay?" he asked P.P. solicitously.

"Stumbled." P.P. had risen and was bending over to rub his knee.

"Early afternoon the sun shines directly into this room, so I pull the curtains. I'm so used to navigating the space that I barely noticed when I opened the front door that I hadn't opened them. Sorry about that." He turned, empty-handed.

Still on the alert, I wondered why if he had barely noticed the darkness—had in fact noticed it—why he hadn't done something about it.

"Can I get you some ice?"

"HOW many days do you have?" Grey asked. His ponytail was still in place, and his tan was deeper, his skin color bordering on ochre, a color that matched the chair he now sat in. I wondered if there was something worrying him, or if his sallowness indicated hepatitis, a not uncommon disease in Asia.

"We'll be in Bangkok for just two days."

His apartment was sparsely decorated, very modern and beige, with bright silk cushions as strategically placed as the sculptures and the single hassock that had tripped up P.P. My chair faced a thirteenth-century Lokeshvara, rather damaged, but with the sweet expression that characterizes sculptures from the period of Jayavarman VII. That expression could lull one into complacency. I looked at P.P., who sat opposite a cabinet holding bronzes. He rose almost immediately to pull a small Buddha from the cabinet, leaving the door open for his next foray, apparently forgetting we were here to figure out if Grey was a killer. I was relieved Grey was alone. At least we had the advantage of numbers.

Biting his tongue—P.P. hadn't asked permission—Grey watched P.P. systematically take down one sculpture after another. "I've already arranged for you to see one collector this evening. He may be able to help you meet with others tomorrow. But I meant, how long will you be in Cambodia?"

"Ten days."

"That's a long trip for a tour group." With his eyes still on P.P., he said, "Would you like something to drink?"

"No," said P.P. as I nodded.

"That would be lovely. The length of the trip is probably the reason we only have seven people. Well, nine counting me and the deputy director. The ten days includes the day flying in and the day flying out, so really only eight days of touring."

"One," said P.P., putting back the second Buddha and pulling out a large Burmese weight, possibly the one I had looked at when we'd met Grey at the fair in San Francisco.

"Yes, one reason. The trip was arranged on very short notice. By the deputy director." I changed the subject. "How long have you lived in Bangkok?"

"Seven years. I came for a visit—to source material—and realized that it would be easier—translate, cheaper—to live here than in New York. My quality of life improved by about 100 percent."

"More than this?" P.P. moved from the cabinet and stood in front of a seventeenth-century Thai Buddha Shakyamuni.

"I beg your pardon?"

I translated, "He's curious to know what else you have." P.P. had quickly assessed the objects in this room and found little of interest.

"Not a lot, a few additional bronzes." Grey got up and closed the cabinet door that P.P. had left open. He'd tensed as he watched P.P., probably because he'd showed so little interest in any of the sculptures.

"What does he collect?"

Grey looked at me for an explanation.

"The collector you've arranged for us to meet. What does he collect?"

"Oh, Cambodian sculpture. Isn't that your interest?"

"Yes, definitely. A longtime collector?"

"He's elderly and has collected for decades. I think he's imagining the end coming soon, so he's been selling off some of his collection. That's how I've gotten to know him."

"If we buy, commission for you." P.P. plopped back down in his original seat, though I knew he wouldn't stay seated long.

I got up to look at a sculpture on the other side of the room, annoyed at P.P. for creating an awkward situation. Grey tried to act as if nothing had happened. Of course, that was how he would act; one doesn't act like a murderer if one can help it, I supposed. But he was so comfortable, so casual, so unconcerned. "I'd be interested in seeing your other bronzes," I said. "But I'm also wondering if you would know any of the sculptors working in Bangkok. Good sculptors who are creating Khmer fakes."

He turned away from us and drew a bronze from a lacquered manuscript cabinet, then pointedly closed the cabinet door, keeping his back to us. I wondered if his intention was to hide his expression. When he turned back, he stretched out his hand to give me a small bronze Prajnaparamita. "As a matter of fact, I do. There's one sculptor who's quite well known. He's very good. Carves in old style, but also creates modern works. It's those that I've sold." His eyes didn't waver from my face and I was reminded of my brother Eric, who always looked straight at the person he was lying to, unblinking.

He was slick. He hadn't hesitated to tell us about the sculptor, while being careful to let us know he didn't buy fakes from this fellow. That lying look bothered me, and I asked, trying to sound unthreatening, "Do you know where he sells his fakes?"

"No. I don't want to get involved in that. But his modern work is really quite lovely." He pointed to the small courtyard garden where a large stone sculpture in the style of Henry Moore stood. "This is one."

"Nice," I said.

"I certainly think so. These pieces have been my bread and butter for the past few years. The Italians particularly like them, so I've been exporting to a gallery in Milan." P.P. took the bronze from my hands, pushed his glasses up over his brow, and held it close to his face.

"Do you have photos of his Khmer-style work?"

"No, but I'd be happy to take you there. If I call first, he's less likely to let us come over. It's best to just drop in on him."

This surprised me, and I realized P.P. was staring at Grey, even though he was holding the bronze at nose length as if studying it. "Perfect. We'd appreciate it. Also, could I ask you to look at this list of dealers that we've culled from various recommendations? I've tracked down most of them. We saw one this morning and have appointments with some of the others tomorrow, but there are a couple I haven't been able to find contact information for."

P.P. handed the bronze back to Grey. His eyes flickered at me, letting me know he considered the piece a fake. He seemed to have forgotten why we were here.

Grey placed it back in the cabinet, pulled out another, blocking P.P.'s access as he did, and handed it to P.P., then took the list. He frowned as he looked at it. "I know all but this one. Seems to be a Khmer name." He pointed at another name. "I can give you this one's phone number. She mostly deals in ceramics, though. Do you collect ceramics? I have a very nice Khmer baluster jar, thirteenth century, a lovely, rich chocolate brown."

"We don't have any in the museum, but it can't hurt to look. P.P. doesn't have ceramics, do you, P.P.?"

"No." He stared intently at the face of the little bronze and I knew that he liked it, certainly more than he'd liked any other piece that he'd looked at so far.

"So you don't know the other fellow?" I pointed at the Khmer name.

"Never heard of him, which is surprising. It's a very small community. Let me get the jar." He left the room.

"He's holding back," P.P. said in a stage whisper.

"I'm not sure. Maybe he just doesn't know the person. He's not acting guilty, and he doesn't seem antagonistic toward us in any way." I turned my back toward the door so that Grey wouldn't hear me. "Did you see how he turned away when I asked about fakes?"

He nodded, looking at the door.

"What if he's gone for a weapon?"

P.P. looked at me as if I were crazy, then glanced at the door that Grey had gone through anxiously. "Ask again about the dealer."

I'd pushed enough already, and I didn't have the sense that Grey was lying about not knowing the dealer. He was a bit evasive, though. All dealers have middlemen from whom they get their stock, and perhaps that was what this fellow was.

Grey returned carrying a large, exquisitely glazed baluster jar, not a weapon unless he conked me over the head with it, though with two of us to conk, that was unlikely. The jar was clearly from the thirteenth century, as earlier potters often had difficulty getting the glaze to adhere properly to the surface. "Very nice," I said, looking at P.P. to see if the vessel interested him enough to purchase it for the museum. P.P. took it from Grey's hands, gave it a quick once over, set it down, and went back to examining the bronzes.

"How did your sales go at the fair in San Francisco?" I asked as innocently as I could.

"Quite well. Many small pieces, one larger one. I gained a few clients, which is really the point of doing these fairs." He swiped a cobweb from the side of the jar. "I would have liked to have sold another big piece or two. I decided to leave some things in storage in San Francisco for next year."

"I gather Courtney and Barker Hobbs are your clients." I said, running my finger over a repair on the lip of the jar.

"Yes, do you know them? I didn't realize they had any connections to your museum."

"They live in Marin."

"They'll be here in a few weeks." The light dawned. "They said that they were going to Cambodia. With you?"

"Yes." I took a deep breath. "I understand that one of your clients passed away recently."

P.P.'s eyes widened.

Grey paled. "Sharpen, you mean Sharpen. How did you know that he was a client?"

"He told me when he showed me a Baphuon-period head that he had." I could feel P.P. tense. But I didn't look at him, determined to get the information from Grey even if it meant lying.

The man shrank away from me as if I'd hit him, then pulled himself together quickly and said, "He thought it was a fake."

"Yes," I said.

"Is that why he showed it to you?"

I noticed he didn't ask what I thought about the head. I nodded. "And in San Francisco at the fair, you mentioned you'd come to the States to talk with him about a head."

"Oh, yes. But I never had a chance to speak with him."

"Phone," P.P. said.

"Well, of course—"

"Was it a fake?" I asked.

"The head? No, of course not." Grey's coloring had returned, and he looked indignant.

"But he thought it was," I said. "And was harassing you about it?"

Very primly, Grey said, "He had questions, so I said I'd take it back." He picked up the jar and took it into the other room.

When he returned, carrying a small bronze pot, I said, "And?"

"He wouldn't give it. Said he'd ruin me rather than let people know he'd bought a fake."

"Hard to see how he'd ruin you if he didn't want people to know."

"Oh, he had ideas." He handed the pot to P.P., who held it but didn't look at it.

"I got the impression when I met him that he had a temper," I said, relying on what Peggy and his son had told me about his temperament.

"Yes, he certainly had that. He was quite unpleasant." He took the pot back from P.P. and set it on the table, picked up his man bag, and headed toward the door. In a tight voice he said, "I'll take you to that sculptor now."

Outside, the heat oppressed. Grey walked ahead of us, his spine stiff with anger. Not guilt, I thought, though maybe for him anger and guilt weren't so far apart. I tried to think how Sharpen would have ruined Grey without letting on he had a fake, but I'd tried to figure that out before without any luck.

Had they argued and physically fought? Surely decapitating someone was a premeditated crime. I tried to imagine Grey swinging a sword, but in my imagination his man bag got in the way. Still, he was the person who would gain most from murdering the man—he'd keep his reputation intact.

I stopped. Motive. I'd been assuming the head. I thought of Peggy and her brother. Maybe one of them had killed him. For his money. Because he was abusive.

Grey and P.P. stopped up ahead and turned to look at me.

I began to walk again. Surely the police had investigated them. And I couldn't imagine either one of them swinging a blade to decapitate their father. The only two people I could imagine were Grey and Barker. Were they working together?

14

An ageless woman dressed in T-shirt and jeans met us at the door of the sculptor's home. She paled when she saw us, her dark eyes on P.P. Then, taking a breath and with a nod to Grey, she led us through two small rooms. The first was populated with teenagers lounging in front of a TV, their ages suggesting the woman, if the mother, was in her late thirties or forties. The second room was devoid of people but filled with heavy, carved wood furniture. A formal parlor, I guessed.

We continued down a narrow hallway lined with boxes, a rolled carpet, and a bookshelf filled with small bronze sculptures lying helter-skelter. I didn't have time to look at them closely, but my fingers itched to pick them up, to touch them. They were all in old style—Thai Ayutthaya Buddhas; Khmer images of the spiritual mother of all the Buddhas, Prajnaparamita; a large dancing female *yogini*; and smaller male bronzes of various periods.

We passed through a door that the woman took care to swing shut behind us into a surprisingly large courtyard. A man, probably in his late forties, wiry and dust-covered, worked on a large piece of sandstone, the chink, chink of his chisel greeting us. That sound, the smell of stone dust, the light of the artist's studio flooded me with memories, and my stomach flipped. I had loved that smell once, certain it would nurture me the rest of my life. I stepped back and steadied myself on the nearest sculpture. Only the woman seemed aware of my unsteady moment. She stood, patiently awaiting an acknowledgment, which the man didn't give. Grey sat down in a wicker chair.

I took the opportunity to look at the sculptures in various stages of carving that stood sentinel along the periphery of the courtyard. A roughed-out seated Buddha in ninth-century Dvaravati style; a twelfth-century standing figure, six feet tall, still too rough to be identifiable; a delicate seventh-century pre-Angkorian male, arm raised, probably a Krishna holding up Mount Govardhan to protect villagers from torrential rains. I walked up to examine him.

Krishna's body was incomplete, but the carving of the head was almost finished. The smooth planes of his cheeks, his upturned, smiling lips, and the jaunty angle of the head suggested a young man. The completed eyes perfectly caught the seventh-century style; they were simply drawn and frank in their expression. Wow, I thought.

Although none was finished and all were caked with the powdered stone that flew from his fervent chisel and hammer, each contained the kernel of an image, the beginnings of a sculpture, refined and already identifiable as being in the style of a specific period. The thin, muscled man before us was good. He was very good.

The work closest to completion was the four-foot-tall standing male that he was so intently bringing to life. Here he was giving rein to his imagination, his narrow chisel curving and angling around the perfect shell of an ear. The nude exuded a physical strength not seen in ancient Cambodian or Thai sculptures. The musculature of the torso expressed the sculptor's understanding of the human body—idealized in its perfection, but with no attempt on his part to depict a superhuman individual, a god. This figure was angry—the body taut, a look in the one finished eye that could kill—so angry that I took a step back. This was modern sculpture at its finest. I turned to P.P. and mouthed, "Buy it." Once the words were out of my mouth, I wasn't sure. Would one want to live with this much anger?

But I hadn't needed to say it, because the hunger was already in P.P.'s eyes. "How much?" he asked, and the sculptor stopped, his chisel inches from the stone. He turned and scowled at P.P., then recoiled as if afraid of him. Regaining his composure, he glared at him.

I realized that he was just now registering that there were strangers in his studio. He hadn't heard our footsteps, or the creaking of the chair when Grey sat, or the shuffling of P.P.'s fidgeting feet. "Fifty thousand. U.S." He turned back to the stone and raised the chisel.

"Twenty," said P.P.

"Forty. Last price."

"When will it be completed?"

"Next week."

"I'll be back. Hold it. If happy, I'll buy. Thirty-five."

The sculptor didn't respond, and I knew that P.P. had his deal. I cleared my throat, and again he stopped. He swiveled in his seat and looked at me, taking in my purple shock of hair, my flowing skirt, the T-shirt that clung to me, though it had felt loose when I put it on.

I reached into my bag and pulled out a photo. "Did you make this?" I asked.

Grey raised his head curiously, but didn't get up, seemingly defeated by our conversation at his apartment.

The sculptor's eyes narrowed, his shoulders tensed, then he shrugged and turned back to his sculpture.

"We're just trying to figure out if it's old or new. We're not trying to get anyone into trouble or to get money back, or to create any other problem."

He said a few words in Thai, to the sky, or so it seemed. I had no idea if he had even registered the photo.

The woman touched my elbow and Grey said, "Time to go. Once he's back at it, there's no catching his attention again."

I opened my mouth to object, but she took hold of my elbow and steered me toward the door.

Outside, P.P. said, "Find out more next week."

"You're going to buy it?"

"Told me."

"Yes, I guess I did. Can you live with the anger in that piece?" P.P. nodded.

Grey couldn't contain his curiosity any longer. "What did you show him?"

"Just a photo." But I didn't offer to let him see it, and he didn't pursue the matter. In the world of dealing and collecting, secrets prevail.

"I hope we haven't kept you," I said, seeing him look anxiously at his watch.

"I have another appointment. A collector," he said.

I nodded. What did I have to lose? "The head, Sharpen's head. Stone head. Where did you acquire it? Not from this sculptor?"

Seemingly ignoring me, he said to P.P., "You've gotten a deal on a great piece. I could have sold that for twice as much in Italy." Then he turned to me and said, "I told you. The head isn't a fake. I only buy this guy's abstract sculptures and the rare modern figure he carves. I don't know why you suspect me of intentionally selling a fake."

"I'm sorry, it's just that Sharpen was so convinced."

"Look. The person I bought the head from is so certain it's all right that he wants it back. He's owned it for decades. The provenance is good—it's been out of the country that long. It is not a fake. If I knew where it was, I'd buy it back at full price in a minute." He averted his eyes and mumbled something else.

"I'm sorry, what did you say?"

"I said, if for no other reason than to get him off my back. He's a powerful man and he's angry. Never a good combination. He could ruin me as easily as Sharpen could, more easily, if truth be told."

"I apologize, Grey. I've been rude. You've been very helpful and we appreciate it. I'm pushing because it's important to us to resolve our questions about the head." I tried to mollify him, though the words sounded inadequate. Just in case he was the one who had killed Sharpen. I didn't like the fact he couldn't look at me when he said he didn't know who owned it.

He just shook his head and looked at his watch again. P.P. and I got into the car, but Grey held back. Leaning into the car window, he said, "I'm afraid I can't go with you. I've got this previous engagement. But I've arranged for you to see that collector tonight, and he's expecting you. Here's his name and address." He tore out a page from his small notebook and handed it to P.P.

"Thanks so much for arranging these visits for us, Grey. We appreciate it. And I apologize if I've made you uncomfortable." He really had been helpful.

"No problem." He stepped back, then again leaned into the car. "That head has given me nothing but grief. I've come to expect the worst from anything and anyone associated with it. P.P., will I see you when you come back into town next week?"

"Yes."

Grey waited for P.P. to say more, but P.P. didn't offer. "Well, give me a call when you know your plans. Have fun in Siem Reap," he said to me with a forced smile and walked away.

P.P. said, "Have an appointment. Hotel."

"Back to the hotel, please," I said to the driver. "Who's your appointment with?"

"Could have," P.P. said to the window.

I waited for elucidation, but none came. His cryptic comments usually didn't annoy me, but the heat, and my rumbling stomach, gave rise to irritation. "Could have what?" I snapped.

"Carved it. Murdered Sharpen."

"The sculptor?"

"Sculptor carved. Grey murdered."

"The head. Yes, he's good enough. The Krishna was very fine, wasn't it?" I looked at the car mirror that we were slowly creeping past on the narrow street. "I'm not sure about Grey."

He shrugged, clearly not having an opinion about Grey, then rushed from that topic to the sculptor.

"Talented. Very talented."

"Yes." But I wasn't thinking about the sculptor's prodigious talent. "You know, I don't think Grey has connected that head with the sculpture at the museum in Siem Reap. To him it's just a head."

P.P. tapped a finger on his knee, taking his time considering this, then went back to discussing the sculptor. "He captured style, period."

"He certainly did. The simplicity of the body and the facial details, too. And the other sculptures reflected their intended periods as well, even incomplete." I wondered suddenly if Grey had gone back into the sculptor's house. "Stop the car," I said.

P.P. looked startled.

"I'm going to the museum," I said. "I'll get a taxi at this hotel here. I'll see you later."

I watched as P.P. drove off, feeling only slightly guilty for lying to him.

WE'D only gone a mile or two from the sculptor's house, but the taxi I'd jumped into got stuck at one of Bangkok's endlessly long lights. Finally the driver turned down the Soi, unafraid of the narrow streets that had hindered the hotel car driver, and stopped near the sculptor's house. I told him to wait, and he nodded.

The sculptor's wife opened the door again, shaking her head. I barged past her, through the rooms, and down the hall, lingering for a moment at the bronzes. She rushed along behind me, calling out in Thai, but I ignored her.

The courtyard was deserted, stone dust eerily floating in the bright light. I moved quickly to the open door on the other side of the courtyard. It had been closed when we were there before. She let out a little yelp and hurried after me.

Stone dust covered the shelves of the storage room so thickly that it took me a moment to realize that the shelves held stone arms, legs, and heads. Despite the dust, the meticulousness of the man was evident, for the heads were arranged by style and chronology. Breeze would have loved it—a registrar's dream. I moved toward the later heads, toward the Baphuon period. But there wasn't another head like the one that P.P. had bought, that Tom Sharpen may have been killed for.

There was, however, a space on the shelf, a space with no dust, a space that half an hour before had probably held a head. I picked up the head next to it. The pointed headdress, the jewelry, the shape of the eyes all pointed to Angkor Wat style, twelfth century. "He can do anything," I said aloud to myself. Or to the head.

"Seems like he can," said Grey behind me.

I jumped. "Oh, my God, you scared me."

The sculptor's wife continued her tirade. Grey said something to her in Thai, and she shut up.

I didn't like that he'd given no indication that he could speak Thai when we'd been here earlier. "What are you doing here?" I said.

"I might ask you the same thing."

"Your husband," I said to the woman. "Where is your husband?"

"She doesn't know," he said.

I didn't believe him.

A young girl appeared at the door to the courtyard that we had come through. Probably one of the lounging children; I hadn't gotten a good look at them. She listened to her mother, then turned to me. "My father has gone out. He will not be back. Not today."

"Thank you," I said, and turned to leave, but Grey blocked my exit. His eyes, which at the fair had looked at me as a possible conquest, seemed to now be watching me as prey.

"Why did you come back?" he asked.

"I wondered if *you'd* come back. I also wondered if he had another head like the one that P.P. bought." I flushed as I realized what I'd said. Now he knew that P.P. owned the stolen head.

There was no change in his expression, and I realized that I'd been right in thinking he knew it already. Which meant our suspicions might be right: he could have been the one who robbed P.P., broke into my car, and killed Tom Sharpen.

"I need that head," he said calmly as he moved a step closer. "The original owner is insistent. And, as I said earlier, he is a powerful man one doesn't want to cross."

He was leaning toward me, too close already, but I took a step forward and said, "Do you need that head enough to kill for it?"

"I told you, I didn't kill him." He backed up.

More children had left the TV and gathered around their mother. Feeling somewhat protected by their presence, I strode past Grey, past them, picked up speed as I went down the hall, and jumped into the cab that waited just outside the door.

"Oriental Hotel," I said to the driver. "Quick."

15

I had settled in a comfortable chair on the patio of the Oriental and ordered a coffee when P.P. arrived and canceled my order. Sitting by the Chao Praya River was not to be. P.P. hurried me along, hurry having become our modus operandi. His hurry usually meant he wanted to buy a work of art, while mine was a headlong rush into some trouble or other. Now we hurried together to the collector's house.

I would have liked to stay on the terrace, watching the light changing as the sun set, the boats passing. It was a different sort of life. I recalled the summer my parents had hired a boat on the eastern Mediterranean. A boat too small for the six of us and the captain, but cheap enough for them to afford. It was part of our education, financed largely by a small inheritance from the death of my maternal grandmother. My parents said they didn't want to raise a batch of provincial brats, unaware of the rest of the world. They'd met traveling in Europe after college, and traveling ran deep in both of them.

My brothers remember fishing during that Mediterranean trip. I remember the ruins we visited on the Turkish coast and the light in the evening as we sat on deck awaiting dinner—bread and feta, tomatoes and olives, cucumber. The sun sinking, the quiet broken by voices amplified by all that blue water, the slight rocking motion, the harsh light of day giving way to the softening dusk.

No sooner had I relaxed into the memory than P.P. announced our arrival. He hurried me out of the car as he sprang to knock on the collector's door.

The tough little man who answered hesitated, as if deciding whether to let us pass. Clearly against his better judgment, he ushered us in, stepping to one side and taking my measure, my height, my weight, the proportions of my body. Once done with me, he did the same to P.P.

The three of us stood there, P.P. and I waiting for him to tell his boss we were here, he waiting for something I couldn't discern. Like the sculptor, he was small and wiry, but they were not alike in any other way. The sculptor had a detached, dreamy mien, while this man's tight musculature and the way he stood poised on his bare, crooked toes was that of a hunter, a lithe cat in search of its prey, though his wizened feet made me wonder if he could really move all that quickly. It was difficult to take my eyes off those feet.

Finally, after what seemed like minutes but was probably only thirty seconds, he said in excellent English, "One moment."

"Weird," I said after he'd left, but P.P. had walked away from me to look at the sixteenth-century bronze Thai Buddha that stood on a pedestal at an angle to the wall. The diagonal placement exaggerated the forward motion of his slightly extended foot, while the piece of pale green silk that hung behind him enhanced the warmth of his stunning green patina. Skillful installation, I thought. Not that it took much to make a Thai walking Buddha look good. A well-executed one is among the world's finest sculptures. This one was a monumental work, even though it was only a foot and a half tall.

"Lovely," P.P. muttered.

"Welcome, welcome," said our host as he bustled into the hall. He grasped my hand quickly and released it just as fast, then turned to P.P. and laughed. "I am Mr. Cha."

I saw his reason for laughing, though P.P. didn't seem to grasp it. The two men were cast from the same mold, short and rounded, all circles and globes. The details differed—P.P. had little hair and Mr. Cha a full head, and while P.P.'s features were rather delicately placed in the center of his face, Mr. Cha had a broad nose and a generous mouth. Even the way that their clothing hung on them differed: P.P.'s jacket was custom tailored, perfectly cut, while Mr. Cha favored a looser, more casual look. Still, from behind or in silhouette one might easily mistake them.

"My brother," Mr. Cha said.

P.P. frowned, then, catching on, laughed.

"Come in, come in. Our dinner is prepared. I hope Grey told you that we would eat."

"No, he didn't. We don't want to impose. We had planned to dine at the hotel." Dang, I thought, no terrace, no dinner at the Oriental.

"No imposition. I'm very happy to have you. Come, Mr. P., this is not the only beautiful sculpture in my house. I will give you a moment's peek into my living room, then place you at the dinner table so that you can see the sculptures in my dining room and courtyard. You will have two feasts. One for the eye and one for the mouth." He leaned toward me and said confidingly, "I do believe that I have the best cook in Bangkok."

"Well, then. I look forward to our meal."

"This is the living room. We will have our dessert here." He swept his arm to indicate the room, the sculptures, the Thai banner paintings that hung on the wall, the profusion of orchids and minimum of furniture.

"Oh, dear. It's difficult to leave this room," I said as he hurried us through.

"You will be happy where we dine. I assure you," Mr. Cha said.

A lovely room, the teak walls offered a fine backdrop for the gallery of sculptures that lined one wall. "Your house is built of old houses, like the Jim Thompson house, isn't it?" Jim Thompson was an American ex-pat who had built his fabulous house in the 1950s. It was now open to the public, and I never missed an opportunity to visit it, to see the wonderful art collection he'd accumulated before disappearing under mysterious circumstances.

"Yes. But rather than retaining the complete houses, I have purchased walls from decaying buildings, which I then have had built into a modern design. I have employed a prominent Singaporean architect, who was pleased to be able to work with old materials while maintaining his very modern style." Before seating us, he led me to a window that looked out on a courtyard dotted with sculptures placed fetchingly among the verdant planting.

"You can understand his design most clearly in this courtyard. If you look off to the left, you see those rooms are linked by open walkways. The room shapes are unusual—geometric glassed rooms, a trapezoid there, a pyramid. The pyramid is difficult to see from this spot, but you will see it from the living room. A mini-Louvre, so to speak. He is a very ingenious man, this architect. He understands the climate and has created a comfortable and cool home for me that also serves as an excellent home for my collection."

Clanking dishes interrupted his description.

"But my cook will become irritated at me, and we do not want that. Like a child she clanks the dishes, a little warning. One time she threw additional chilis into the curry to punish me for rambling on to my guests. I have been obedient ever since." He raised his hands in mock terror.

P.P. paid little attention to our chatty host or to the view of the garden. His glasses pushed to the top of his head, he stood eye-to-eye with a Baphuon-period god, leaning in to study its features. The thin, barely clad stone deity gazed serenely back at him.

"Lovely, isn't it? The most elegant of all Cambodian sculpture, the Baphuon-period work," said Mr. Cha.

P.P. said, "Yes."

"I will put you here, Mr. P., just across from this sculpture, so that you can give him your attention during dinner. Do you collect Cambodian sculpture?"

"Indian," said P.P., watching the servant who had opened the door now enter with a lacquer bowl filled to overflowing with rice.

Seeing that P.P. didn't want to give his collecting interests away, I added, "P.P. has a fine collection of Indian miniatures. But the Searles Museum, where I'm a curator and P.P. is on the board, has a few Cambodian sculptures."

"Ah, very nice. And what is this Searles Museum?"

"It's a small private museum in California. George Searles, who passed away a few years ago, made his fortune in industry and tech and from an early age was an avid collector. When he was diagnosed with cancer, he began to think about what would happen to his collection when he passed away."

"He had no family?"

"He had family, but his children weren't interested in art, or not interested enough to want his huge collection. His wife encouraged him to donate the collection to a museum. But no museum would meet his terms."

Mr. Cha looked puzzled. "Terms?"

"He wanted a large percentage of the collection on display at all times, and museums are cautious about agreeing to that."

"I see."

"So he decided to build a museum. He lived in San Francisco, but he chose Marin County, north of the city, as a suitable place for the museum. More land available, no museum to speak of, and the rest is history. Not a very long history, though. The museum has been open only three years."

"How long?" P.P. asked Mr. Cha, who frowned.

"How long have you been collecting?" I asked.

"A very long time, but when I tell you how long, you will know that I am an elderly man who is looking young. Close to forty years."

He already looked elderly to me, but when you're in your twenties, anyone over fifty looks elderly. "You must have begun when you were still in your cradle." My compliment triggered a cascade of memories.

"Ah, yes," he began. As he rambled on, I looked from one sculpture to another, seeking an old break, greater wear on one side of a stone where water had run over it, discoloration that looked centuries old, or a modern hand. P.P.'s stone head had put me on my guard.

"More, miss?" the old servant asked gruffly, holding out a curry for me to serve myself. My skin crawled as the pungent aroma of the chili crept into the pores of my body.

"Oh, no, thank you, I've eaten more than I need." I looked up at his face and was riveted. He had the blankest eyes I had ever seen, deep wells of nothing. I felt for a moment that I was falling into them. His life must have been difficult, I thought.

"No. Butterflies," P.P. was saying.

"Butterflies! My first collection was knives. The blades take so many forms. I believe you in the West prefer to look at the hilts, and, of course I have come to appreciate the hilts, but in the beginning I was drawn to the blades. The glimmer of metal, the sharp curve."

He looked like a man having an orgasm. I listened in astonishment as these two round men traded lives. Astonished not because they were trading lives—that's natural enough when people first meet—but because Mr. Cha understood P.P.'s brevity. I had become used to being his translator.

P.P. tilted his head toward a spectacular large bronze that stood on a pedestal by the window.

"Ah, yes, that piece. I think it is best not to tell you that story." He leaned confidentially toward P.P. "Not while there is a museum curator in the room."

I ignored the comment. He was baiting me, and I wasn't about to be hooked.

"Do you worry about those sculptures out in your courtyard?" I asked. A conservator's question.

"No. There is a cloth ceiling that we draw over them during the rainy season. What do you call this?"

"An awning," I said.

"Yes, an awning. I have removed it for your enjoyment this evening. We will put it back up tomorrow." He changed the subject. "Are you organizing an exhibition?"

"No, thankfully. At least not while I'm here. I just installed a show last month. Later Chinese porcelains—Qing period—the monochrome wares. We were given a collection, and two of our trustees have good collections with pieces that we were able to borrow."

"I like Qing period porcelains. I have a few of them myself, but they are in my home in Siem Reap."

"You have a home in Cambodia?"

"Yes, of course. Who could collect Cambodian sculpture and not live some of the time amidst that candy shop of temples?" He tapped the corner of one eye. "It trains the eye. It must be the same for you, Mr. P. You must visit the temples of India when you return to your homeland."

"Yes," said P.P., rising. He couldn't sit still any longer just a few feet away from half a dozen sculptures.

"Yes, yes, this is correct. Let's adjourn to the other room and coffee and some dessert. Though I fear this is my cook's one failing. To her, dessert is fruit, no elaborate pastries or those crunchy cookies you have in America."

"Thank goodness. I couldn't fit a cookie in sideways." They both looked at me as if I were mad.

As our host hurried us out of the room, P.P. looked back longingly. For a moment, I wondered if Mr. Cha didn't want us to look too closely. Suspicion was fast becoming my middle name.

SETTLED with my coffee and a small plate of fruit, unable to move after consuming such a large dinner, I watched as P.P. and Mr. Cha discussed one small bronze after another. Jet lag had hit me, and though I'd made it through every stone sculpture in the room, detailed observation was now beyond me.

"When did you arrive?" Mr. Cha was standing in front me, and I wondered if I'd dozed.

"Last night. Actually, early this morning."

"Oh, my, you must be very tired."

"Yes, I think we'll have to get going soon."

P.P. glared at me, but only for a moment. He was lagging too. His leg didn't bounce as it normally did when he was sitting.

"I hope you had a relaxing day today."

"I'm afraid not. We ran from one dealer to another."

"Did you buy anything?"

"No, we were just trying to get the lay of the land, see what was available."

"Sculptor," said P.P., watchfully.

"You visited a sculpture studio?" He seemed surprised.

"Yes, Grey took us to see a sculptor. He was very good. Frighteningly so."

P.P. nodded in agreement, stood up to replace a bronze in the cabinet, and picked up another.

"Do you recall his name?"

"I'm sorry, I don't. Do you, P.P.? I have it written down, but it was a very long Thai name, and in my present state I just can't recall."

"T."

"It began with a T," Mr. Cha said. He narrowed his eyes. Then, realizing that we were looking at him, he said, "Ah, yes, I know whom you mean."

"Good," said P.P., pointing at a bronze.

"Yes, this one is very good. Not the best, but very good."

Thinking we might not be leaving for a while, I took a few sips of coffee. Strong, very strong. I surfaced from my daze to see Mr. Cha again standing over me.

"I think Miss Jenna is asleep in her chair. You must take her home. We will look more some other time. You really must come see my home in Siem Reap. I have a few sculptures there. My Khmer cook will prepare a meal for your group, and they can see how the locals live. I will be there next week on business, so the timing is perfect."

"That is most kind," I said. "I'm certain they will appreciate it."

"Knives." P.P. was standing before a wall case that filled one corner of the room. "The blades are gorgeous."

That complete sentence was certain proof he was as tired as I.

"Those are just a few. I promise you, my friend, when you come back I will show you more. You have told me you go to India frequently, and it is easy enough to stop here in Bangkok. We will have an entire day of knives, of blades of all sorts."

I joined them at the case, but in my current state one knife blurred into another, and they frightened rather than engaged me. I faltered and took P.P.'s arm. He didn't resist.

16

A message had awaited us back at the hotel the previous night, saying that Grey had arranged another visit to a collector early the following morning. So, still exhausted, the sun bright and blazing down on us, we found ourselves once again in a hotel car, breathing the dense Bangkok pollution. It was kind of him, but it was hard to feel grateful right then.

I'd wakened during the night and only gone back to sleep at five. And now I would miss having breakfast on the Oriental Hotel's terrace. I'd experienced it only once before, but it was a favorite Bangkok memory. Sitting by the Chao Praya River, where speedboats and barges, water taxis and ferries evoked Bangkok's past. The Venice of the Orient, with its hundreds, thousands, of canals and few bridges. Certainly it would have been quieter a hundred years ago, with the boats under sail or paddled, not the outrageously loud engines of today, but it would have been the same sort of activities, the same variety of vessels.

I scowled out the window.

"Hungry," P.P. muttered, more to himself than to me.

"It would be nice if we could get back for a late breakfast on the terrace." But I knew that once we had reached the other side of the city, where two of the dealers we needed to visit lived, we wouldn't come back. The traffic would be too daunting. "We could take a later plane tomorrow morning."

P.P. shook his head.

I knew that would take a great deal of effort: getting new airline tickets, rearranging cars to take us to the airport in Bangkok and pick us up at the airport in Siem Reap. I would just have to come back to Bangkok. P.P. would definitely be back, when he returned to pay the sculptor. That would let him escape the group, and Philen, at least for a day. I wondered if that was the reason he had bought the sculpture. I couldn't think of any excuse that would let me escape as well.

"THANK you for coming to my home. I have not prepared a meal for you, but I knew that you were leaving your hotel early, so I do have some small food and tea."

"You're very kind," I said. P.P. had made a beeline for the sculpture standing just inside the collector's living room, not even seeming to notice the man.

"Please come this way. I understand from Mr. Grey that you went to see Mr. Cha last evening. I should warn you that I do not have a collection that even begins to compare to his. Still, I do have a few quite fine pieces, I believe."

The contrast between this man's house and Mr. Cha's was extreme. His living room was small and messy. No tasteful decorations, just comfortable chairs and tables piled with books and notebooks and the occasional object. Two large manuscript cabinets, lacquered with scenes from the *Ramayana*, filled the one wall. None of the objects before us were of the quality we had seen last night, yet I felt more comfortable here, more excited to see what he had. Clearly he wasn't wealthy; he was a scholarly man engaged with the material he collected.

"This," said P.P., holding up a small folkish bronze of a monkey seated before the Buddha.

"Ah, you have chosen my first piece." His eyes lit up as he told us the tale of its purchase in the northeast of Thailand. It remained a favorite, both for sentimental reasons and because of its genuine charm. P.P. and I both bent our heads to look, engaged by this warm man.

WE had seen most of the pieces in the living room when he led us to a small case in the corner of his dining room. The top shelf held a head that could have been the sister to P.P.'s.

Before P.P. could speak, I said, "This one is lovely. Could you tell us about it?"

"Yes, I bought it recently. It is my new prize. As you see, it is Baphuon style. Very lovely." He proceeded to give us a lesson on Baphuon sculpture.

I could almost feel P.P.'s hands itching to hold the head. Finally, he said, "Hold?"

"Yes, of course it is old," the man responded.

"No. May I hold it?" P.P. spoke as if to a child.

"Oh, sorry, I misunderstood you. I would prefer that you did not hold it. I do not want to get oils on the surface, and I do not have gloves."

"Could you open the glass door so that we might see it more clearly?"

"Oh, of course. I'm glad that you like it. I am very pleased with it."

"Where?"

The collector looked at me.

I cleared my throat in embarrassment. "He's asking where you bought it." I glared at P.P.

"Ah." He smiled, but didn't answer.

P.P. stuck his head into the cabinet to get a better view, then stepped back to let me do the same. The carving of the eyes was almost identical to P.P.'s work, though the delineation of the braided hair seemed more sharply realized. "Very nice," I said.

"Time to go." P.P. pointed to his watch.

I tried to make up for his abruptness. "We have such a brief time here in Bangkok, I fear that we've overbooked ourselves," I said, looking longingly at my half-eaten pastry. "It was so kind of you to let us come on such short notice. You have a lovely collection."

P.P. was already at the front door.

"You will come back the next time you are in Bangkok."

"That would be very nice," I said.

He accompanied me to the door, and we exchanged cards as we watched P.P. hurry down the path.

"FAKE." P.P. said as I shut the car door.

"That head was awfully similar, wasn't it? It was smaller than yours."

"Cornrows."

"Yes, the braids were different, but the eyes were almost identical. We'll know more once we get to the museum in Siem Reap tomorrow."

He rolled his window down, letting in a blast of hot air and car exhaust.

"Please put that up," I said irritably. I'm impatient myself, but P.P.'s fidgeting made me look relaxed in comparison.

He closed the window again.

"P.P., you can't let this head dominate our trip. It's ridiculous. What did you pay for it?"

"Not the money."

"What is it, then?"

"Pride. Conned."

"No one tried to con you. You bought it at a yard sale. Really, your response is out of proportion."

"Philen," he said. "That damn Philen."

"It's true, Arthur made it worse by bringing the existence of the head to everyone's attention."

"Your car. My house."

"Yes, but really. We have a long trip and the opportunity to look at some wonderful temples and sculpture. We've already seen some terrific objects." I was talking to him, but I was really trying to convince myself.

He didn't say anything. I didn't like sulky P.P. "If the head is why Mr. Sharpen was lying decapitated in his study, then I would advise you to take another tack. You don't want to end up like that, with your blood on the ceiling."

"No. I could have. Would have without the gun." His leg stopped jumping, and he rubbed his finger back and forth across his knee.

"We'll find out what we find out. You've tried to discourage me from getting engaged in detecting the mystery of the head, and now here you are doing exactly that." I dug in the bottom of my purse for my lip balm, thinking for the millionth time that I needed to put it in the side pocket. "From what we've learned so far, the head is probably a fake. That's all we need to know."

"That was before. We both want the murderer."

I knew he was right, but I had moments when I saw the folly of it.

"Admit it."

I sighed. "It's true. I want to get that Grey."

"If him."

"Yes, if it's him. I think it's him."

P.P. didn't look convinced. I probably didn't either. We were taking turns believing it was Grey. Wavering, debating. It just showed that we didn't know a thing.

We continued on through the horrendous traffic, stopping far too often at the endless stoplights. Exhaust plumed from the three-wheeled tuk-tuks and encircled us like a blanket.

As we climbed out of the car at the first dealer's shop, P.P. said, "We must."

We must what? I thought. While I tried to recall what he had said last, P.P. hurried ahead of me. Oh, dear, I thought. We'd been talking about finding the murderer. He was right. We must.

17

"All right, all right. Let me hang up a couple of shirts to get the wrinkles out." I unzipped my suitcase, then reached into the closet for hangers. I didn't really care about the wrinkles, but I wanted a few minutes to make the mental transition from Bangkok to Siem Reap.

P.P. bounced in the middle of my rattan-furnished room. Management had accessorized with local products—bamboo cups and soap dish in the bathroom, locally woven wastebaskets and bedspreads. The muted greens and golds, with an occasional accent of maroon, were the colors found in traditional Cambodian weavings, and P.P., in a green-and-gold-patterned Hawaiian shirt, fit right in.

"Museum," P.P. said again.

"We have all afternoon, P.P. The rest of the group doesn't arrive here until tonight. We've been in our rooms fifteen minutes." Putting a shirt on a hanger, I went to the window to look out at the view of the grounds. I had a balcony.

He huffed and walked out, saying, "Room."

"What's your room number?" I called after him. If he answered, I didn't hear. I breathed a sigh of relief. I hadn't ever had P.P. in such large doses. Usually it was a lunch or dinner, a visit to a museum. Once we were in New York at the same time for Asia Week. We previewed the auctions together, but most of the time he was off on his own to visit the dozens of dealers who take over the city and to visit friends he rarely saw.

My time with him had begun three days ago, across the aisle from him on the plane. That I wasn't complaining about, as he had provided me with a first-class ticket. We both slept for eight hours. The easiest trans-Pacific flight I ever took. One could get spoiled in the lap of luxury.

Then P.P. in Bangkok. We'd run from one dealer to the next, eaten one fabulous meal, taken in a few museums, and visited two collectors and a sculptor. All that activity had resulted in a good night's sleep the second night. I now had a head start on the group, who would undoubtedly find themselves jetlagged for the next few days.

I hung another shirt, put my toiletries in the bathroom, and left my pants thrown across the bed and my underwear on top of the dresser. With the appropriate level of chaos in place, I picked up my key and headed out the door to find out what room P.P. occupied. I knew he was in the old building of the Grand Hotel, as was most of the group, while I was in the new addition. The only other time I'd led a group and experienced being Mama Mandarin, waddling along with her ducklings close behind, I'd learned the importance of having my own space.

The two men behind the reception desk were moving their heads back and forth, as if watching a tennis match. P.P. had that effect on people, which was one reason why I enjoyed being with him. His impatience masked my own. I'd learned as a child, from my mother's constant admonitions, to sit still when I needed to. My inner me still balked at the command, while my exterior could, when push came to shove, appear calm. P.P.'s mother had clearly never been able to slow him down. Now here he was, pacing from one side of the lobby to the other.

"Let's go," I said. "What's keeping you?" I was out the front door and halfway down the steps before he caught up with me.

"Car," he said.

"No, we can walk. It's not far, and we've been sitting on the airplane. If I'm going to survive ten days of buffets and banquets, I need my exercise."

He looked meaningfully up at the sky.

"It's not far," I repeated, and set off.

"Tuk-tuk," he called from behind me, as if the open vehicle might entice me. In fact, the exhaust terrified me.

"Go ahead, I'll meet you there." He did, and I was relieved, a sensation I attempted to keep at bay. I was already feeling the pressure of having one person following me; what would I do for eight days when I had eight? I'd begun counting Philen as one of the ducklings, as I assumed he would be on my trail along with the rest of the group. Just the thought of the man's name made me want to groan.

Car exhaust enveloped me. When I'd charged out of the hotel, I hadn't considered the tour buses presently returning to town so that tourists could eat lunch and take a siesta after a morning of temple viewing. They would set out again later in the afternoon once the temperature had cooled down. Now they returned in droves. I coughed and covered my face with my hand.

P.P. didn't give me a glance as he tuk-tukked by.

Hotels lined the road; they'd multiplied since my previous visit just a few years earlier. The number of vehicles on this, the only road leading to the temples, had greatly increased, too. I could see the recently built museum up ahead. It was a great improvement over the warehouse where many of the finest works of Khmer sculpture had been housed for decades.

P.P. stood at the entrance, hands on hips, tickets in hand. I smiled at him. "Excited?" I joked. He didn't respond, the issue of the head not a joking matter, just turned on his heel and rolled forward.

As I followed him toward the entrance to the first gallery, I realized he'd lost his sense of humor the day he brought the head to the museum. I knew it wasn't because of what he'd paid for the head. A mere hundred and fifty dollars, he'd finally admitted. His ego and his collector's greed were fighting for predominance.

"Wow," I said as we entered the first room of the museum, with its display of Buddhist art, rows of Buddhas set upon increasingly elevated receding shelves. One was more beautiful than the next. Most were seated in the *bhumisparsha mudra*, the earth-touching gesture that the Buddha Shakyamuni made when he called the earth to witness his resolve. I slowed. "Fantastic, isn't it?"

But he didn't answer, calling over his shoulder, "Hindu." Then, sensing rather than seeing my hesitation as he moved determinedly forward, he said, "Come back later."

I started to follow, but stopped in front of a particularly refined Angkor Wat style Buddha Muchilinda, the Buddha seated beneath a serpent.

When I caught up to him, he was standing in front of Radha and Krishna. My heart stopped. Radha had her head. Had they recovered the original? "New," said P.P.

He was right. The head fit perfectly—style, attachment, and angle of attachment. But the color of the stone differed.

"Fake," he said.

"Well, as you said, newly carved. They haven't made any effort to disguise the fact it's new. Look, they've intentionally used different-colored stone just as a Western museum would do to let the viewer know it's a replacement."

"Mine is fake."

I looked from the head to the intertwined bodies of the lovers. Her leg nudged his. His hand rested on the swell of her hip. Her long skirt, with its incised pleats, contrasted with the smooth cloth of his sarong and her braided hairdo, rows of braids gathered in a chignon, differed from the fat curls that cascaded down his head and over his shoulders.

"I think your head might be closer to this new one, don't you?"

He didn't answer my question, but nodded to himself. "Get him."

"Who are you going to get?" The question came out more shrilly than I intended. I lowered my voice. "Don't you remember that the reason Sharpen lost his head, literally, was because he became obsessed with the stone head?"

He didn't seem to be listening. It was almost as if the head had cast a spell over him. The same spell it had cast over Sharpen. "Same carver?"

"No, the head is new; the sculpture is old."

Impatiently, he said, "Same as mine."

I hadn't willfully misunderstood him. I looked again at the sculpture, focusing on the head as I walked to get a side view. Radha's lovely ear. Were ears really as lovely as this? The whorl of the lobe, like a fine shell. I looked at Krishna's ear; it was very similar. "Well, the sculptor has copied the original." I pulled out my camera.

"Don't know for sure."

I looked at him. "Don't know what for sure?"

"Why he lost his head." He nodded once, twice, turned, and walked out of the gallery. I opened my mouth to say something, but there was nothing that I could say. He was angry, hurt. I'd only seen him fuming like this once before, and I hadn't had any luck pacifying him that time. I doubted I'd have any luck now.

Letting him go on his way, I glanced around the room and found another Baphuon sculpture to study. It was a fine piece, and mentally I compared it to the Radha and Krishna behind me. But then I looked again at Radha and Krishna, and the other sculpture seemed nothing in comparison. Radha and Krishna held the room. The person who had designed the gallery knew that, and had made them the focal point. The sculptures hugging the wall faded, and this single sculpture of man and woman filled my eyes. He was a good head taller than her, and as I looked at her nestling against his side, I imagined the hardness of his body and the coolness of his flesh, for somehow she exuded warmth and he an aloof distance. Though he accepted her leaning into him, I knew from my own experience with men that he had done nothing to lessen any distance between them.

He stood erect. No, not exactly erect, for his left foot extended slightly forward and his hip tilted slightly toward her, so that they stood united in a reverse S-curve. The musculature of his chest, the voluptuous folds of flesh below her naked breasts, the three lines in her neck, and the slight dimpling of his chin—the sculptor had given them humanity, fitting for her, but, for this avatar of Vishnu, unusual. Especially since the sculptor's skill, his insight, had made the god accessible, had brought him down to earth, had allowed me to join with him.

I'd moved forward without realizing it, and reached out my hand to touch her.

"No touch!" yelled the guard.

Jolted awake, I realized I'd fallen under their spell.

I wandered through the remainder of the museum in a daze, and as I walked home I thought about P.P.'s head. The good news was that P.P. would not have to return the head, since it was a fake. Still, there was the question of why someone had broken into my car, why someone had burgled his house, why someone had murdered Tom Sharpen. Maybe we had been wrong. Maybe they weren't after the head. But if they were, then either they thought it was real or, for some reason, didn't want us looking too closely at a truly fine fake.

18

As our minibus crept along the busy road, I was aware of Alam sitting behind me. Not that he was leaning over me breathing down my neck, or even leaning forward to speak with me. When I turned around to survey the group, he seemed not to notice, but continued gazing out the window. I wished Beatrice hadn't suggested he was coming on this trip because of me. He hadn't done or said anything to express interest in me, but his body language, the steady gaze of those brown eyes, made his interest clear enough. No doubt about it, I found him attractive. If he hadn't been someone I saw on a regular basis, I might have been interested. Once such a relationship ended, for one had to assume an end, it would be awkward.

Siem Reap had grown since my first visit. It now extended into the countryside, a bit closer to the Roluos group of temples where we were headed. But it was still a provincial town, not the grand city it had been in the twelfth century, and within a few minutes we were rolling through rice fields.

Vuthuy, our local guide, stood at the front of the minibus, microphone in hand. "Hariharalaya, where we are going today to see the Roluos temples and the terraced Bakong, was the mid-ninth-century capital of the Khmer kingdom. Hari-Hara is a composite of the Hindu gods Vishnu and Shiva, and so this capital was dedicated to these two great gods."

Vuthuy and I had tussled briefly over which temples to see first, but he had conceded when I explained that I wanted to start with the earliest to give the group a sense of the development of the architecture. My concession had been to go at sunrise to the twelfth-century Angkor Wat, which we'd visit at length another day. We'd had a taste of the temple, walking around it to the eastern gallery to see the famous relief of the Churning of the Ocean of Milk, best seen when the sun was low in the sky and the gallery roof hadn't yet shadowed the shallow carving.

After returning to the hotel for breakfast, we set out again. I just needed to keep them awake for the rest of the morning. In the afternoon, which we'd deliberately left free of temples, everyone would fall into bed for a nap. There had been a few complaints, but I suspected that after this excursion, all would be ready to concentrate on readjusting their time clocks.

I should have been listening more closely to Vuthuy's soothing amplified voice, so that I didn't repeat what he had said when they asked questions, but I was pondering the Alam dilemma.

Courtney squealed, "Stop, stop! Look at that darling horse and cart. And, oh, lotuses."

Before I could speak, the driver pulled to the side of the road and she dashed to the door. She was right. It was a photo op. With Mr. Jolly's help, she managed to get the driver of the rustic wooden vehicle, piled high with lengths of bamboo three times as long as the cart, to position himself before the small roadside pond, green with algae and pink with water hyacinth. I'd have to point out lotuses to her elsewhere. There might be some in the moat of the Bakong.

Seeing that the photograph had been so artfully arranged, a few more of the group got off the bus. Vuthuy looked at his watch, then at me.

"It'll be okay. We can have a long morning since they can rest this afternoon," I said.

We would first visit Preah Ko, a charming group of temples dedicated to the king's ancestors, then the early temple mountain, the Bakong, one of my favorites. The third group of temples, at Lolei, was in worse shape than the others, and if push came to shove we could forget our visit there.

A group of children had materialized. Mrs. Jolly assumed the job of arranging them around the cart. She had a good sense of the tableau. Vuthuy assisted, as much to help as to encourage the group to get back on the bus.

I didn't want to set a bad example by joining them. If we stopped at every photo op, it would take us forever to get to the temples. Plus, Alam had stayed. He was like a magnet, pulling me toward him.

He said, "Terrible poverty."

"Yes, the average Cambodian makes about one or two thousand a year. Farther away from the cities, it's far less. It's inconceivable for us." I looked at the children's feet. None wore shoes, though their clothing was in pretty good shape. "These kids don't have it as bad as children farther out in the countryside. Tourism is feeding them."

"Yes, not necessarily an easy diet."

Vuthuy was herding the others onto the bus. Martha was first. She leaned over me and said, "You're right. They are both very Jolly. I can't call them anything else."

"Oh," I said, startled. "I . . ."

She patted my arm, as if to say, not to worry. It's fine. Before I could say anything in response, she'd sat down. P.P. boarded next and found a seat, but when Philen sat across the aisle from him, he moved. I inwardly groaned.

AFTER seeing Preah Ko, the temple named for the Sacred Bull sculpture that stood at its entrance, we were driving toward the Bakong. Typical Southeast Asian houses on stilts lined the road. Under one, a woman worked her loom, the bright colors of the plaid cloth she was weaving visible from the road, while children played in the shade of a neighboring house. One owner had penned his pigs beneath his dwelling. Not so nice to sleep above them, I thought.

The road dead-ended, and the five terraced levels of the Bakong, with its single temple spire, rose before us. Oohs and ahs filled the bus. The driver made a left-hand turn to take us around the moat toward the entrance, then paused. It was a photo op not to be missed, this enormous stone structure isolated in the midst of lush growth and surrounded by the murky green water of the moat.

Water, I thought, the key to those ancient kings' power. The moat would have irrigated the area around the temple, but it was the tanks, the giant reservoirs, that allowed an extensive population to exist here, a population that could then be put to work building temples. Of course, there were never enough people, and wars were fought to gain slaves to help construct these public works.

I tried to imagine the Bakong partially built, people swarming over the structure, primitive methods of raising the huge stone blocks, brought from fifty kilometers away, from the ground to the top of the building. What I pictured was something like one of those old movies of the Egyptian pyramids being built, not least because of the pyramidal structure of the Bakong.

Driving on, we came to the bridge with its *naga* (snake) balustrade, the entrance to the complex; the pyramid was set amidst smaller temples, all arrayed symmetrically around it. As we climbed off the bus, vendors thrust postcards and hats, cokes and coconuts, toward us. They were not allowed beyond the first step onto the sacred ground, for as soon as we had placed our feet on the stone bridge, they stopped and turned to wait for the next arrival. We stood on the causeway, silenced by the immensity of it all. The single temple rising from its steep terraces, the subsidiary buildings around the periphery, all spoke of its builder, Indravarman I, a king with a vision. Surprisingly, we were the only ones here. But I knew this solitude wouldn't last long. Another tour bus would surely arrive, even though this temple was not on the short list, the brief itinerary.

"It's a dollhouse compared to Angkor Wat," said Philen dismissively. "Everyone over here. Gather to hear what Jenna has to say." Vuthuy sank, deflated by Philen's unthinking suggestion that he hadn't told us anything. Seeing that Mr. Jolly, busy with one of his cameras—he had a photographer's vest full of them—was ignoring him, Philen bustled up to him and took his elbow. "Jenna is going to tell us about the temple," he said, not understanding that Mr. Jolly wanted the pristine picture, the scene devoid of people.

"I'll be there in a moment," said Mr. Jolly, sloughing off Philen's hand.

Letting go as if he'd grabbed a hot ember, Philen looked around for other wayward members of the group. He moved toward P.P., who had walked to the moat, but as he approached, P.P. looked up and glared, stopping him in his tracks.

Then, to my surprise, P.P. walked up to him, nose to nose, and said, "Stay away from me."

I looked around to see if anyone else had heard and was relieved to see that only Mrs. Jolly was aware of the confrontation. She looked at me and I shook my head. I hoped that she wouldn't broadcast the extent of P.P.'s hostility.

"What's that building over there?" asked Barker.

"A modern monastery," I said.

"Right on the grounds of the ancient temple?"

"Yes. The temple was originally Hindu, now Buddhist. Sacred space often continues to be sacred to peoples of different faiths. Think of Jerusalem."

They all nodded.

"This was a sad place in the 1970s, during the time of Pol Pot. I imagine the monastery helps make amends for all that happened here."

Vuthuy pointed to the temple tower at the top of the pyramid. "It was filled with skulls at the end of the Pol Pot time. This was a killing field."

"At a temple?" asked Courtney, moving a little closer to Barker. He poked her. "They were communists."

"What does that have to do with it?"

"Communists don't believe in religion," he said, exasperated.

"Vuthuy has given you a very thorough explanation of the temple," I said. "As we walk through the grounds, I'll be happy to answer any questions, as will Vuthuy."

Martha stood next to the young man. "Yes, we're so lucky to have you. You don't always get such a knowledgeable local guide."

"Hear, hear," said Mrs. Jolly, clapping.

I looked at Philen, who gave no sign of knowing what had just transpired.

As each one headed off in his or her chosen direction, I looked toward the tower and tried to imagine the horror throughout the country during the genocide and in the years since, as graves were discovered, oral histories taken. Four short years and two million people dead, a quarter of the population of Cambodia. But I couldn't wrap my brain around it. It felt remote from me, remote from this place, so lovely, so calm, so devoid of people.

As we wandered among the smaller buildings that surrounded the central pyramidal structure, Vuthuy and I answered questions, volunteered information, mentioned the wonderful group statue of Indravarman and his two wives that we would see at the museum, but that had originally been placed here. Then we gathered to climb the central tiered structure. Halfway up, I showed them the small section of relief carving that had survived the elements. I wondered if they could imagine, like me, the entire surface of the temple carved with reliefs.

"It looks like Angkor Wat," Martha said, pointing up at the tower.

"It doesn't look anything like Angkor Wat," Philen spit out, still smarting from P.P.'s anger.

Martha looked at him, startled.

"The tower was constructed in the twelfth century, probably replacing a tower that had fallen down," I said. "So it's contemporary with Angkor Wat. Is everybody ready to make the final ascent?"

Philen looked abashed.

"The subsidiary buildings were built at the time of the dedication of the temple," I said, pointing them out from the summit. "You can see that those towers are quite different from the one at the top of this tiered temple. They held ancestral images. The king gave himself a lineage in building them."

I thought of family, of my family. Would I dedicate a building to my father? To my mother, yes, but to my father? Family life was no less complex in the time of Indravarman I. After all, he had married those two queens to consolidate his power. Did he ignore his parents' flaws and quirks? Substance abuse might not have been such a problem then.

Mr. Jolly broke my reverie. "Why a pyramid?" Evidently he had been focused on his photography when Vuthuy was explaining the pyramidal form.

"The temple is a recreation of Mount Meru, the axis mundi, the cosmic mountain, the center of the universe. It's a glorified place, a wonder. To recreate it on earth is to recreate the heavens on earth. It's sublime." I started down the steps.

The temple, in its sturdiness and simplicity, seemed to encompass the most basic character of the cosmic mountain. But it meant more to me. Through the combination of the horrors it saw during the Pol Pot period and its esoteric symbolism, it represented not only history gone awry but the ancient Khmer kingdom. A kingdom that had thrived for hundreds of years, then vanished into the jungle until revived in modern times as an artifact, a reminder of what man can achieve and what, at his worst, he is capable of inflicting on his fellow man.

"Heads," said P.P.

"Yes, skulls."

"Decapitated."

I looked from him up to the tower, a lovely spire, a tower like a lotus bud. Filled with skulls. "You don't think—" I didn't finish my question. Surely there couldn't be a connection.

19

Courtney chose some stir-fried vegetables, then passed along the fish curry and the shrimp dish without taking any. I realized I hadn't asked if anyone had any dietary restrictions.

"You don't like seafood?"

"I'm allergic."

"To all seafood?" I started to tell her that the bite of vegetables she had just taken had probably been cooked with fish sauce, but I'd only heard of people being allergic to shellfish, not to all seafood. I suspected, though, that "allergy" just meant she didn't like seafood. "Do you like Southeast Asian food?"

"I love Thai and Vietnamese—we have it all the time—but I don't know much about Cambodian. The food is one of the things that drew us to the area at first."

That settled it. Fish sauce is a key ingredient of those foods. These dishes weren't going to harm her. "I'll be sure there are always meat dishes that you can eat."

"I'm a vegetarian."

"Ah, well, then I'll be certain there are multiple vegetarian dishes for you. If you like greens, you'll learn to love the water spinach. It's the one certainty on every menu. But we'll see if we can get some more interesting vegetarian dishes. Does anyone else have any dietary restrictions?"

"Lactose intolerant," said Mrs. Jolly. "But that shouldn't be a problem here."

"No, it shouldn't. I have a friend who discovered he was lactose intolerant while living in Cambodia. Suddenly the gastrointestinal problems he'd had for years vanished, and he figured out it was because he wasn't eating dairy." Everyone around the table seemed to be diving into their food, even Courtney. Good, no complainers.

I said to Alam, who was sitting next to me, "I was traveling with a group in graduate school, and the group leader asked if anyone had any dietary restrictions. By the time he had gone around the room, we had someone allergic to, or not eating, every form of protein—one couldn't eat chicken, one couldn't eat fish, and so on. We had a vegetarian, we had a vegan . . . You get the picture. I thought the group leader was going to shoot himself."

Alam laughed. "Californians especially. You won't find a group of people with such complex food requirements anywhere else in the world."

We concentrated on our food for a few moments, then Alam said, "The temple this morning was truly magnificent, the Bakong. I think I liked it better than Angkor Wat."

"I can see that. Its strength lies in the simplicity of its form. Angkor Wat is magnificent as a building, and one has to love the details. It presents a mystery as you move from the causeway, ever closer, until the towers disappear because you're below them, then they reappear as you get to the center of the temple complex. With the Bakong, what you see is what you get."

"Do you love Angkor Wat, with all its details?"

"It's a bit refined for my taste. I like to be slammed in the face by the power of a building or a sculpture. Though I have to say that the Churning relief that we looked at in the morning light could convert me."

"Yes, it's certainly a tour de force."

"It reminded me of certain medieval reliefs," Philen interjected. Alam and I waited for him to expand his thought, but he'd turned to answer a question Martha asked. He patted her hand as he spoke, a patronizing gesture that she watched as if hypnotized.

P.P. frowned at him from the far end of the table, shook his head, and went back to eating. I didn't know if it was merely Philen's presence that bothered him—though he was sitting as far from him as he could—or if it was his Eurocentric view of the world.

"Tomorrow we have our first helicopter trip," I said. "I don't remember which trip you'll be taking." That was a lie; I knew very well which trip Alam was taking.

"The second one. I'm looking forward to it. I've read a little about the temples we'll be visiting."

As the dessert arrived, Martha stood and announced that she was going for a walk. She was gone before any of us could say a word.

"Smart," said P.P., rising too, though it must have been difficult to ignore the crème caramel that had been placed before him. "Walk." He followed Martha out of the room.

"Sorry, I can't resist crème caramel," I said. "You'll all need to put up with me for the remainder of the meal."

"Me, too," said Courtney. "I might even eat P.P.'s. By the way, where did he get that awful name?"

I laughed. "Those are his initials, not what you're thinking. When he came to the States to attend Harvard—"

"He went to Harvard?" Barker seemed surprised.

"Oxford and Harvard, yes. When he arrived at Harvard to get his MBA—he already had a law degree from Oxford—one of his fellow students called him P.P. to mock him. Making certain he knew that it was mockery. Apparently he joked about his physique, his name, cast aspersions on his intellect. The fellow was a racist, it sounds like. Though when P.P.'s startup catapulted into the stratosphere, he asked P.P. for a job."

"Did he give him one?" Mr. Jolly asked.

"I gather that he did."

"Doing what?"

"I believe he put him in charge of janitorial services."

The table laughed, except for Philen, who had a strained expression. Perhaps he was imagining himself in charge of janitorial services under P.P.'s influence.

"He speaks in such shorthand. I thought maybe he had difficulty with English," Barker said.

"No, he just thinks people talk too much. He's decided to use as few words as possible. To cut down on noise pollution."

"Well, I have to say that I find that commendable. People do dither on," said Mrs. Jolly.

I eyed Philen's untouched crème caramel, but he raised his spoon and began to eat.

"Here, dear, you can have mine," Mrs. Jolly said. "I'll get a little fruit."

"Are you sure? Thank you." I pulled her dessert next to the one I already had eaten.

When I'd finished, I said, "If none of you mind, I'll excuse myself." I had designs on the swimming pool, but didn't mention my intentions for fear someone would join me.

"I'm heading up, too," Alam said.

We made our way to the lobby and turned right to go to the new wing. Alam was the only other person in the new wing, a fact I found disturbing, especially since he'd requested moving there from his assigned room near the others. Neither of us spoke, the day's activities catching up with us. I decided I could get into the tub instead of finding my way to the pool. But neither happened.

A doorman rushed up behind us. "Madame, madame, one of your friends has hurt herself on the street. A lady."

It had to be Martha. "Where is she?" Alam asked.

"The Indian man is helping her. She has hurt her foot."

"Oh, no." A foot injury the first day of a tour was not good. We rushed out to help P.P. assist Martha up the steps.

"What happened?" I asked.

"A pothole," said Martha. "Who anticipates a pothole in the sidewalk?"

"Oh, dear," I said.

"Did you twist it?" Alam asked.

"I don't think so. Fortunately. It would serve me right. I was wearing the sandals I wore to dinner rather than my sneakers. Very foolish."

"How could you know?" I should have warned her, though I had been too intent on my crème caramel.

"I was charging along, oblivious to the dark and the treacherous sidewalks."

Inside I could see that blood was dripping from her foot. I turned to the doorman. "Can you get your first aid kit?'

"Do you know what you cut it on?" asked Alam, helping her sit and examining the wound.

She held up a rusty piece of metal. "I knew you'd ask that. And to answer your next question, I had a tetanus shot before coming on the trip."

"We will call a doctor," said the manager.

"Let's let him look at it first." I gestured toward Alam. "He's a doctor."

Alam squatted on the floor to take a look. "It needs stitches," he said. "I doubt the emergency kit will have everything I need, but let's see. Get me some boiling water and soft towels."

When the kit arrived, it didn't include a needle and thread, so the front desk called the on-call doctor.

"I want you to stitch it," Martha said to Alam.

"I'm sure the doctor will be qualified to put in a few stitches, but I'll stay with you while he works."

I held her hand, though she was a trouper and kept trying to get us to leave her alone, not to worry.

The hotel manager pulled me to one side. "Can we move her to her room? She will be more comfortable there. I have brought a wheelchair."

A number of people had gathered around, and the hotel probably preferred that this drama continue in private quarters. "Alam, can we move Martha to her room for this?"

"Sounds like a good idea," he said. One of the room boys brought the wheelchair, and Alam helped her into it.

As she was wheeled away, Martha called back to me, "I'm supposed to be on the helicopter tomorrow."

"Don't worry. We'll get someone to switch with you." I looked around for P.P., the most likely candidate, but he was gone. I'd give him a call in his room.

20

"They were lovely," Martha said as she adjusted her foot on the stool the bartender had placed before her. She was relaxed and elegant in white, while we were grubby and dusty after our day flying to remote temples and charging through jungles. Well, the last was hyperbole. A hundred years ago, we would have had to cut away the growth from the temples. A hundred years ago, it took one month to cross the tiny country of Cambodia. Now, even at the most remote temple, we were besieged by children selling us scarves, small stone replicas of temple towers and Buddhas, and bamboo toys.

"One or another of the staff kept me company most of the day, and I learned all about their lives. Did you know that a large percentage of the population is under thirty?"

I didn't answer. I didn't want to remind her that their elders had been killed by Pol Pot and his gang in the 1970s.

Courtney said, "I wonder where Barker is. I should go and get him."

"I spent some time here in the bar. Drinking iced tea, of course. But it's so pleasant. You feel as if you're living in an earlier time." Martha nodded contentedly. "I'm sure he'll be down."

"You're right. And boy, am I thirsty." Courtney sat down.

A waiter set water glasses on the low table and asked what we would like to drink. The lobby bar, with its potted plants and rattan furniture, recalled colonial rule, though now the windows looked over an enormous swimming pool rather than an exotic garden.

We ordered beer. All the way home we'd been fantasizing about beer, wondering what the best local version might be.

"I feel like I've crossed the jungle on an elephant," said Courtney, fanning herself with her hat.

"That rackety helicopter was horrid," said Philen. "And it was so dusty. I hope I never have to go on one again."

We all looked at him. I hope so too, I thought.

"Was it marvelous?" Martha asked.

"Absolutely," said P.P. "Early temples."

"Jenna said the temples were on an early trade route," said Courtney. "Wouldn't it have been fun to follow the river that leads from those temples all the way to the South China Sea?"

"The Vietnamese might not have been too happy," Philen said. "Swooping over the border in a helicopter. There must be some collective memory there of the American choppers during the war. They probably would have shot us down."

Under his breath, P.P. muttered, "Oh, shut up."

I agreed with him, but wished he would tamp down his anger. I opened my mouth, but Courtney spoke first.

"Seeing the ancient trade routes, even from the comfort of the sky, would certainly be interesting, wouldn't it?"

"Yes," I said. I was beginning to realize that the entire group had chosen to ignore Philen.

"There you are! You're back!" cried Mrs. Jolly, taking a seat beside Martha and asking her solicitously, "Did you have a good rest?"

"Yes, very nice." Martha turned to me as she patted Mrs. Jolly's hand. "And we had such a lovely visit earlier."

Mrs. Jolly turned to her husband. "We've had a delightful and relaxing day chatting together and talking with the staff."

"I have my cosmopolitan," Martha said, raising her glass, "my foot elevated on a royal stool, and the conversation of the adventurers. This is marvelous, but we want to hear about your day."

"It was wonderful," said Mr. Jolly. "Wait till you see my photos. I got some doozies."

"Yes, do tell us all about it," Mrs. Jolly said.

"It was very tiring," said Philen. "And loud, horribly loud."

I looked at him. Complaint can be contagious, and I didn't want the group to catch it.

Before I could frame words to slow him down, he was saved by another arrival.

"Well, hello, hello," said Mr. Cha, hurrying across the lobby. "I've found you here. It looks as if you have just arrived from a sojourn to the temples." One of the waiters sped toward him, but he shooed the man away.

I introduced Mr. Cha to the group and asked him if he could join us.

"No, thank you so much. I came to see if I might invite you all to my home tomorrow night. For dinner. I have an excellent Cambodian cook." He looked at the beer arriving. "And cocktails, of course."

"Lovely," said Mrs. Jolly, as a few other heads nodded. The group appeared ready for any adventure, including dinner with a complete stranger.

We settled the details, and he gave me the address, telling me that it was a narrow street and we should probably come in cars rather than a bus.

As he was about to leave, I said, "We do have one vegetarian with us."

"No problem, no problem. I will be certain to tell the cook." He was gone before we could raise the beer glasses to our lips.

"How do you know him, Jenna?" asked Mr. Jolly, waving at a waiter and pointing at the peanuts. He was one of those tall, thin men who eat constantly.

"One of the Bangkok dealers introduced P.P. and me to him when we were there so that we could see his collection. He also has a home here in Siem Reap, with another collection."

"It will be very nice to see how the locals live," said Mrs. Jolly.

"I imagine his lifestyle is a bit beyond what the locals can achieve." My comment set Martha off on a recitation of what the staff had told her about their lives, their homes, their children.

I leaned into the cushions and clung to my icy beer. I didn't need dinner tonight, just a few more bowls of nuts, a good mystery, and a very long and hot bath. Not necessarily in that order.

"You're back," said Alam, approaching. "How was your journey?"

It wasn't a profound question, but the words sent goosebumps up my arms. Or maybe it was the voice, its depth, the soft, low tones. Since he'd grown up in the U.S., I couldn't blame it on a charming South Asian accent.

Courtney answered him, and he pulled a chair next to her. He smiled a greeting at me, then turned his full attention to Courtney, who was regaling him with visions of the temple and showing him the photos she'd taken on her smart phone. She was the most excited I'd seen her.

He certainly does give his full attention when he listens to a person, I thought. I'd seen it the first night we'd had dinner back in the States in the way he engaged with Martha. He was clearly a doctor who didn't have a problem with bedside manner.

That thought led to other thoughts that had more to do with beds than manners, and I had to shake myself to unstick wanton thoughts from my brain. Not a good idea, I thought, over and over. Then I looked at his hands. Fortunately, Philen saved me from further forays into folly. Standing, he announced, "We shall have dinner at seven."

I looked at my watch. It was six-fifteen. "Maybe—"

"I will see you all then," he cut me off.

"I don't think we can get ourselves together by then, Arthur," said Mr. Jolly. "My wife and I would like to relax here a bit longer here, then I want to get out of my dusty clothes."

"Me, too," said Martha. "Not that I have dusty clothes, but sitting here is so, well, so colonial, if I'm allowed that politically incorrect fantasy. And such lovely conversation. I'm sure everyone would like to have a lengthy soak. I think tonight would be a perfect night for everyone to eat at their leisure."

"Of course," Philen said sourly, and turned on his heel.

What an awkward man, I thought. What an unhappy man.

As he disappeared around the corner, Mrs. Jolly began to speak, but Mr. Jolly said, "Now, dear." She shut her mouth, her words about Philen unsaid.

I was beginning to like this group. Philen's plan to amass backers to help him shinny up the museum's administrative ladder was clearly not working. I looked around me. Rebels one and all.

21

Mr. Cha's house appeared modest from the outside. A stucco affair quite unlike his wooden home in Bangkok, it was very modern, a wall of glass surrounding the foyer. The door opened before we could knock.

"Welcome, welcome." He ushered in the Jollys and Martha, who were in the fore. "I am so happy that you could come. I have the hors d'oeuvres on the patio. The air has cooled and it is lovely."

"This is exquisite," said Mrs. Jolly, surveying the living room, a much larger space than the exterior suggested.

The living room furniture was mid-century modern: a Saarinen chair by a wood-burning stove; what looked to be a Breuer credenza on the other side of the room; and in front of it, two Finn Juhl bwana chairs, each with its own ottoman and covered in the original leather upholstery. "Where on earth did you find this furniture in Southeast Asia?" I blurted.

"Not in Southeast Asia. I brought it from Europe. I think it fits very well in this house." As he spoke, he was hurrying the group through to the patio.

"The house is Bauhaus influenced, isn't it?" I lagged behind. Alam did as well.

"Yes," he said, seeming pleased that I was interested. "I have my antique home in Bangkok, but thought it would be nice to have something different here. I commissioned an architect to design a home that was very light." He swept his arms across the windows. "A home where this furniture would have a place. It's attractive, I think, and quite comfortable. I also thought that a house of this design would be a good setting for my textiles."

On the wall in front of us hung three Khmer textiles, ikats woven in intricate geometric designs. The other walls also displayed textiles, not all of them Cambodian. "Don't you worry that they'll fade in all this light?"

"No, the windows are all, what is it called, polarized? Even the glass tiles in the hallway. And you see that I have shades, which I pull down during the day."

On the patio, Mrs. Jolly and Martha were studying the landscaping, one particular plant having caught their interest. Courtney joined them. Mr. Jolly and Barker had made a beeline for the hors d'oeuvres.

"I thought we would sit outside for our cocktails, then move into the dining room. It's better to be inside to eat in the evening. The bugs, you know. Have you had a good day of sightseeing?"

"Yes, very." I said, "Though I fear that everyone is already tired."

"It's the third day of jet lag, the worst day," said Alam. "It's so kind of you to have us for dinner. Your home is very lovely. Do you mind if I take a moment to look at your textiles?"

"Please, of course, of course. I'll join the others and leave you to look on your own. If you have a question, please ask me. Though I'm certain Miss Jenna can tell you all you might want to know." He took in the two of us at a glance, pairing us.

Embarrassed, I looked up at the framed sarong above the wood-burning stove. I couldn't imagine ever using the stove in this climate, but it fit the spirit of mid-century modern. Alam examined another sarong, one of three or four that had been thrown over the back of the couch.

"Ikat," he said, fingering the silk. The pattern in an ikat is achieved by dying the pattern into either the warp or weft threads before weaving them. In this instance the weft threads had been dyed. Alignment on the loom is tricky and time-consuming.

Surprised, I asked, "You know about Southeast Asian textiles?"

"A little. They're so much in the aesthetic of modern art. If you collect one, you have to collect the other."

"It's true." Several Lao textiles dominated one wall, their bold patterning very much like abstract paintings. "Mr. Cha might know a dealer here or in Phnom Penh that we could visit, so you can take home a little souvenir of the trip."

"I'd like that." He put down the sarong and picked up another. "Look at this. The tiny squares all over. Brilliant, isn't it? Do you like textiles?"

"Yes, I even have a modest collection. Very modest, just a few pieces. Southeast Asia and a couple South China examples. They've gotten expensive."

Mrs. Jolly's voice rose over the others' as she spoke with Mr. Cha. "The museum was lovely, absolutely lovely. My husband didn't get past the first room, the room with all the Buddhas. We're going to have to go back one afternoon, so that he can see the rest."

Courtney said, "And they have a nice shop."

"Yes, dear, they do." And almost in the same breath, she added, "I want to see that sculpture that P.P. owns the head of again. It has a head, the woman, but Jenna said the original was stolen. Do you know about that?"

I groaned inwardly. I couldn't hear Mr. Cha's response, but I saw him turn his attention to Mr. Jolly, who said, "Yes, that's right. Stolen right off the sculpture. Jenna and P.P. were trying to figure out if the head he owns is old or new. I gather that it's often very difficult to resolve this issue."

P.P. was either ignoring the conversation or didn't hear, because, like us, he'd stayed in the house and was now studying a sculpture in the dining room.

I walked over to the Lao textile above the credenza. It deserved a closer look.

Alam walked up beside me. "I have one like this. Not as nice, a little damage. That type of Lao textile and some of the Burmese textiles are my favorites. The colors, the boldness of the one, the subtlety of the other."

"Join," called P.P., sticking his head into the living room to glare at us before walking out to the patio.

"He's right, we should. Maybe we'll have a chance to look at more in the dining room while we eat," Alam said.

I was struck by Alam's calm in response to P.P.'s hostility. "I don't understand why you and P.P. don't get along." I said, but as I spoke I felt funny asking him about it rather than P.P., whom I knew better.

"Ah. He didn't tell you?"

"No."

"You may have heard that I made some of my money from a small invention?"

"Yes, I have. Something to do with open-heart surgery."

He laughed. "Hardly. No, a toy. When I was a teenager, I created a puzzle that sold very well."

"A puzzle?"

"Yes, a small metal puzzle that you untangle. Not so different from a lot of others like it, but I had very good marketing, thanks to my father who had a friend who had a friend. It sold very well the first Christmas it came out. It became a fad for a brief time. It's never sold as well since, but a steady stream of puzzles goes out the factory door, yearly. The perfect stocking stuffer, or so I'm told."

"And what does this have to do with P.P.?"

"I invested the money I made from the puzzle in a tech start-up." He looked at me expectantly.

I got it. "P.P.'s company?"

"Yes. I'm one of the primary stockholders. P.P. doesn't like his stockholders, especially those on the board who don't always agree with him. He's tried to buy me out a number of times."

"Well, that explains a lot." I looked out at the others, and though I would have preferred continuing our conversation, it was time for us to join them. "We'd better go out."

"I suppose so," he said, without taking his eyes off me.

Mr. Cha and P.P. were plunged deep in conversation, their heads bent forward, their voices lowered. Mr. Cha looked up and smiled when he saw us. "You've come outside just in time to go back in for dinner," he said as he stood and ushered the group inside.

I hung back and managed to catch P.P.'s attention before he entered. "What were you two nattering about?"

"Collections. Head."

"You were talking with him about the head?"

He didn't answer. Obviously that's what he meant. I rephrased my question. "How did the topic come up?"

He pointed inside at Mrs. Jolly.

"Damn Philen," I said, and looked at Philen. He was chattering ingratiatingly at Mr. Cha, who was arranging seating and only half listening. Philen seemed to want to get something out of everyone; I wondered what he thought he would get out of Mr. Cha. "What did he want to know?"

"If I returned it."

"And when you told him that you hadn't?"

"I told him it's a fake."

I waited. Occasionally that tactic worked with P.P.

"Said there are some good fakes. Said I might be wrong and maybe it was the original head."

"We certainly saw some good fakes at the sculptor's the other day," I said. "Let's go inside."

Mr. Cha had saved me the seat at his right, while Martha was already seated at his left, Philen next to her, and Alam next to me. As soon as we were seated, the servants, two young women and the old man we had seen in Bangkok, began to serve. The first course was the traditional fish soup cooked with tomatoes and pineapple, but the broth was unlike any I had ever tasted. The cook had gone beyond using the traditional lemongrass and sweet and sour, but I couldn't identify the additional ingredients.

"This is delicious," I said.

"Thank you. I do not know what she does to this soup, but it is far better than any other version I have had." He took a sip of his wine. "I understand that you went to the museum today."

"Yes. It's impressive. A real education."

"Of course, some of the greatest Khmer sculptures are in Phnom Penh in our National Museum, or Paris for that matter. But the installation and the works here are quite remarkable."

It didn't seem worth beating around the bush. "Including some newly discovered works."

"You mean the Radha and Krishna." Mr. Cha stroked his spoon across his soup.

"Yes. It's a tragedy that the head was stolen, though the modern replacement is quite fine. I wouldn't mind meeting the sculptor."

"Indeed."

"There couldn't be too many sculptors of his caliber in Southeast Asia."

"No, probably not." For a collector of this material, he didn't seem to be too interested.

Martha asked, "What line of work are you in, Mr. Cha?"

"I have many different businesses."

"Including here in Cambodia? I understand you are from Thailand."

"That is correct. I spend most of my time in Thailand, and most of my businesses are there."

"Manufacturing?" she persisted.

I could see where she was headed.

"Some, though my manufacturing is in Thailand. It is not so easy to control that kind of work here in Cambodia. Would anyone care for more soup before we begin our main course? Was your vegetarian soup to your liking, Mrs. Courtney?"

"Delicious. I'd love to get the recipe."

"I'm afraid my cook does not speak English, and she does not seem to have written down her recipes, but I will see what I can do."

"Thanks."

Martha opened her mouth, but Philen jumped in first and drew Mr. Cha into a conversation, annoying Martha.

Mr. Jolly asked me, "What will we be doing tomorrow?"

I told him a little about Banteay Srei, the temple we would visit, which lay an hour outside of Siem Reap. "It's a little gem— small and jewel-like." Everyone seemed content, chatting about what they had seen, what they had read about, what we were going to see, and how delicious the food was.

P.P.'s phone beeped and he pulled it out of his pocket. Martha and Mr. Jolly glared at him. Philen started to say something, but stopped when he saw my raised eyebrows, then went ahead and said, "Really, P.P.," as if he were scolding a child. P.P. slid the phone back in his pocket, got up, and walked to Philen. Speaking very carefully and clearly, he said, "Don't talk to me." Then he calmly walked back to his seat, picked up his napkin, and sat down.

Mr. Cha was looking at him, astonished. Martha spoke to Mr. Cha to distract him, and he turned to her.

Without missing a beat, P. P. said to me, "Grey. Here. To-morrow night." He said it as if we were the only two people in the room. Mr. Cha and the Hobbses would have understood what he was talking about, but the rest wouldn't have known if Grey was a person or a color.

This was a bit of a surprise. Grey hadn't said that he would be coming to Siem Reap. He had probably rounded up a work of art that he wanted to try to sell to P.P. or trade with him. He clearly wanted that head.

Mr. Cha spoke to his servant in what sounded like Khmer. I was surprised it wasn't Thai. The old man nodded and left the room.

Martha, putting on her most innocent old lady face, started grilling Mr. Cha again. "I understand there's a great deal of logging that goes on here in Cambodia. Given the landscape in this area, it's difficult to imagine what they're logging."

"There are hardwood trees in more remote areas. Southeast of here, for instance, there are the Cardamom Mountains, on the Thai border."

"Is that where your company logs?" She took a stab.

"Yes. The transportation is difficult, but the profits make it worthwhile."

"What sort of trees are found there?" she asked.

I could see her hackles rising. Not that I disagreed with her. The rate of deforestation in Southeast Asia is horrifying.

"Rosewood. Very rare."

Uh-oh, I thought.

He was revealing a great deal. I now saw clearly the advantages of being an old broad. She could ask questions that others couldn't without raising suspicions about her motives. He probably thought she was just being polite. Philen was looking to me to divert the conversation, but I couldn't see how, nor did I particularly want to. I pretended not to register his looks and focused on the *hamok* that had just arrived. It's my favorite Cambodian dish—wonderfully spiced fish wrapped in banana leaf.

"The Cardamom Mountains are home to eighty rare species. I understand that most of the logging that is undertaken in that region is illegal."

I had to give her credit. She stood by her beliefs.

"I assure you, madame, I do not log illegally. I have permits." I tried to recall when I had seen this look on his face before. He turned to Mrs. Jolly. "Is your food to your liking?"

The old servant, who had come in with a serving dish, nodded at his boss, who said something to him. The servant nodded again, then thrust the dish toward Martha, but she wasn't to be diverted. "I would hope so. I'm looking forward to visiting that area at the end of our trip."

He smiled. "Very good," he said and shifted his attention to me, turning his shoulder to Martha.

THE hotel had sent two small cars for our return. Luckily, we didn't have a long ride. "Lovely food," I said, squeezing in and trying to inch my shoulder from Alam's arm. I thought of the Cake song: "I need you here with me, not way over in a bucket seat."

No one said anything, before Alam finally agreed.

The driver pulled out into the street and headed toward the hotel.

"Evil," said Martha.

"Yes," said Mrs. Jolly from the backseat. "The epitome of evil, really. Rather oozed off him, wouldn't you say?"

I started to speak, but realized I could only make it worse. I bit my tongue, literally.

"Normally I would say that 'evil' is too strong a term, but not in this case," Mr. Jolly offered in his usual calm tone.

I couldn't stop myself. "You don't think that's a bit strong? He was very kind to have us for dinner, and I really don't see what he gained by having us. You might not agree with his business practices, but it was generous of him to invite us."

"Our host?" said Martha. "He's predictable. A businessman, a profiteer. He's evil by nature. Which isn't to say that all businessmen are that way," she added for Mr. Jolly's benefit.

"I certainly hope not," said Mrs. Jolly complacently. "But it isn't him we're talking about, dear."

"I beg your pardon." I was confused.

"The old servant. When he reached his arm over me to take my plate, it gave me goosebumps. Not the good goosebumps you feel when you're happy, but the kind that make you want to rub your skin, wash yourself. He exuded it, like, like . . ." said Mrs. Jolly.

"Like sweat," said Alam.

I'd been so focused on Mr. Cha that I'd barely been aware of the old man. I pictured him, his eyes like empty sockets, and a shiver went down my spine. I remembered that blank look he'd given me the night we dined with Mr. Cha in Bangkok and the goosebumps I'd attributed to the chiles in the curry. "I imagine he's had a difficult life. You can see it in his eyes, though it doesn't necessarily mean he's evil." I paused. "He *is* creepy."

"That's kind of you, dear. Giving him the benefit of the doubt," Mrs. Jolly said placidly. "Creepy. Yes, creepy."

22

I hadn't remembered to ask the concierge if they had bicycles available, so instead of riding I snuck into the pool early and swam laps until my arms hurt. As I was drying off, the man who cleaned the pool arrived and gave me a long-suffering look that suggested I wasn't the first guest to disobey the rules. I knew the pool opened at eight, but I didn't care. I hadn't interfered with his work. Tomorrow I'd be riding a bike.

I thought about Grey, who hadn't turned up the day before, much to P.P.'s annoyance. Nor had he texted or called.

I took a quick shower and threw on some loose pants and a T-shirt. I wanted to beat the group to breakfast, to have a few moments to gather my thoughts before our morning visit to Angkor Wat. We'd walk around the galleries to view the reliefs and climb up the towers and discuss the architecture.

HOTEL buffets wreak havoc with one's weight, even for someone with my metabolism. A pound or two on my small frame looked like five or ten on a larger person. I tried to put on blinders as I headed for the fruit and granola, but couldn't help glimpsing the eggs, meats, salad, congee, beautiful cheeses and breads. A table of temptations.

I could come back for seconds, a little piece of cheese, a slice of dark bread. I did swim this morning, after all.

"Coffee or tea, miss?" the waiter asked as he pulled out my chair.

"Coffee, please. You don't have espresso, do you?"

"Yes, miss. Would you like a single or double?"

"Oh, a double, please." I'd be nice and revved up for our tour.

"Would you care for a newspaper, miss?"

"Please." I took a bite of jackfruit, loving the perfumy fragrance and the dry texture on my tongue.

He set down the folded Bangkok English-language newspaper and headed off to get my espresso. I glanced at the front page, where Grey's photograph filled the upper left-hand corner above a headline that read, "Foreigner Decapitated." I picked it up, then dropped it, feeling like I'd been punched.

The waiter said something as he set down the espresso, but his words didn't register. I'd fallen into a hole filled with decapitated heads. My hands shaking, I picked it up again and focused on the brief story. Well, what does one need to know beyond a fact such as decapitation? The word alone conjures a sharp blade, geysering blood, a head crashing to the floor. I shook myself. What could I do?

Nothing, I told myself. The police were investigating. Of course they were investigating.

"Good morning. May I join you?"

I looked up at Alam, my tears blurring him.

"Are you okay?" He touched my wrist.

"Yes. No." I pointed at the photograph. "I knew him."

He read the story. "Is this the Grey who texted P.P. the night before last?"

"Yes."

"So that's why he didn't show up yesterday. I overheard P.P. asking the receptionist if he'd had a visitor."

"Right." I pushed my bowl of cereal away and gulped my espresso. It burned the roof of my mouth. Had Grey died because he'd been talking with P.P. and me? Were we to blame? Was I to blame? Had he done something rash when he'd realized P.P. had the head? "I thought he was a murderer. Or at least, was responsible for a murder."

"I don't understand."

"The man decapitated in Atherton. I thought he killed him." Thunder sounded, and I turned to look out, half expecting the huge, ominous clouds to roll into the room. "Oh, god," I said. "I thought he was the murderer."

"What can I do?"

"Nothing." How could I have been so wrong? Poor Grey.

"Rain," he said unnecessarily.

"Yes, but it probably won't last long. It often just bursts. We can always leave a little later."

"Can you explain? About the murders?"

"No, no, it's not important. Never mind." I didn't need to pull anyone else in. Had P.P. and I pulled Grey in? How had he been involved? I put my head on my hand, though bending my head meant Grey's photo was in my face. I closed my eyes. When I raised my head, Alam was watching me.

Alam looked at the cereal I'd pushed away. "I'll get you a roll. That might be easier to get down. We'll be doing a good bit of walking and climbing in the heat, and you'll need something in your stomach."

While he was at the buffet, I reread the article, as if it might have a different ending this time. Two men decapitated on opposite sides of the world. Two men connected by a single work of art. A work that P.P. now owned.

Panicked, I looked around the room for P.P., though I knew perfectly well that he always ate breakfast in his room. My thoughts twirled and stumbled over each other. I cursed Alam for trying to make the morning ordinary. A roll, a bowl of cereal, what did I care? Grey was supposed to have come the previous day, flying from Bangkok to see P.P. Why? To convince him to sell back the head? To sell him something? It had even occurred to me that he was coming to Siem Reap to kill P.P. to get the head. Guilt surged to the fore.

And then I felt disappointment. Disappointment at his death. I had suspected him of killing Sharpen, imagined getting my hands on his passport to see if he was in the U.S. the day Sharpen was murdered. Now I didn't have a suspect. Of course, if I could figure out why Grey was killed . . .

Could it have been because of our appointment with one of the collectors? Or maybe because he'd taken us to the sculptor? I didn't think the sculptor looked like a murderer. Mr. Cha had reacted strangely when we said that Grey had taken us to see the sculptor, though I hadn't known why. Was Mr. Cha involved? P.P. had announced at dinner, in front of everybody, that Grey was coming. At the time, I'd thought the only people who knew that Grey was a dealer were Barker and Courtney and Mr. Cha.

Barker. I thought of his temper. Where had he been yesterday? He'd had food poisoning, Courtney said. He hadn't come to dinner, and Martha had commented that she hadn't seen him all day. The flights to and from Bangkok were morning and evening flights. He could have flown over in the morning and returned this morning, or last night. Which would mean that he was back at the hotel by now.

As if I'd summoned him, Barker walked into the dining room with Courtney. He didn't look rumpled, like someone off a flight. He looked perfectly healthy. After being too sick to join us at the temples. Too sick to join us for dinner. Not even around, as far as we knew.

They greeted me and sat at a nearby table. I wondered what he'd get to eat. You could be wobbly for days with food poisoning.

"Coffee for both of us," Courtney said to the waiter.

"Espresso for me," he corrected.

"The paper, madame."

"Thank you."

"I'll take a section of that," Barker said.

"Are you feeling better?" I asked.

"Much." He didn't look at me as he spoke.

"There's only one section," Courtney said. "I'll read you the headlines. Strikes in Bangkok. Oh, goodness, that dealer lost his head. I mean, someone cut it off. How awful."

Barker paled, but before he could say anything, Mr. Jolly appeared and asked, "What are you talking about?"

"That dealer Grey, he's been murdered," said Courtney. She sounded shaken.

Barker was busying himself with his napkin. He looked rather queasy. Of course, I'd probably look queasy too if I'd been ill with food poisoning all day, not to mention hearing about someone you knew being murdered.

I watched the sky darkening, the clouds bunching closer and closer. The smell of rain preceded the actual event. I closed my eyes and breathed it in, then turned my attention again to Barker.

Alam, returning to the table with his food, was watching Barker as well. Maybe it was because he saw me watching. We're drawn to look where others look, after all. Or maybe it was because Barker was acting oddly. Uncomfortably. He adjusted his seat. He picked at a packet of sugar until it opened and spilled onto the table. He looked around for the waiter, for his coffee, and finally reached for the paper. "Let me see."

Courtney had begun to cry. Barker scowled over the article and said, "First that guy in Atherton and now Grey." He was pale, definitely pale.

If he had killed them both, would he be connecting the two now? Was he dissembling? My previous vague suspicions about him hardened.

He continued, "I don't know about Sharpen, but sooner or later someone was going to wring this guy's neck."

"Stop it," she said, her voice shaky and brittle. "We knew him. He shouldn't have died. No matter what he'd done. You can't joke about it."

"Yeah, well, he should have thought of that before he began selling fakes." He threw down the paper, then glanced our way. He seemed startled to see us watching. "Let's get some food," he said to Courtney.

I jumped up.

"Where are you going?" Alam asked.

"To see if P.P. is all right."

"I'll come with you." He told the waiter we'd be back and followed me out of the dining room.

At the top of the stairs I almost ran into P.P., who was just coming around the corner. "Oh, thank goodness. I was afraid." Then I burst into tears.

"Come on. You need to get something into you to steady yourself," Alam said.

"What?" Even confronted with my hysteria, P.P. had little to say. He looked pointedly at Alam's arm around my shoulder.

"Your friend Grey was murdered yesterday," Alam said, leading me back down the stairs.

"Decapitated," I said, trying to control my tears. Alam's arm was very reassuring.

P.P. voiced my earlier thought. "Not the killer."

"No, clearly he wasn't." I choked out. "I wish we knew why he was coming."

"We do," P.P. said.

Alam and I stopped midway down the stairs and looked up at him.

"Danger," P.P. said.

"Fill in the blanks, P.P. We both know you can." Alam's irritation was obvious. It seemed that murder ruffled his otherwise placid exterior.

"His text said there was danger."

I wiped my eyes. "You didn't tell me that."

He shrugged.

Alam asked, "Danger for whom?"

P.P. took a deep breath. "He said whoever owned that head was in great danger."

"P.P.," I exclaimed.

Alam tightened his arm around my shoulder.

23

"What are you going to do with that machete? Take up agriculture on your country estate?" Mosquitoes and moths swarmed around the bulbs lighting the corridor to our rooms. We were walking slowly, not from the lethargy brought on by our enormous dinner, but to prolong our time together. Alam had been close at hand and attentive all day. I appreciated his concern and didn't want the day to end.

He'd bought the machete from a young boy as we climbed onto the minibus outside Angkor Wat that morning. "Very funny, though not far from the mark. When I was a child and we visited my grandparents' farm in India, I fell in with an old man who worked for them. He seemed old when I was a child, but he was probably about forty. He let me get underfoot, taught me his tasks. Certain that I'd grow up to own the farm and be his boss, no doubt."

"So he taught you to use a machete out in the fields?"

"Not really, no. I helped him more with the work he did around the house or in preparation for going out to the fields. Seemed as if every time I was about to head out with him, my grandmother made me do a chore closer to home. I never did learn how to handle a machete properly."

"They didn't want you seen in the fields?"

"Most likely. Anyway, one of the many things he taught me—"

"Because he was, of course, the wisest of old servants." I patted one pocket after another in search of my key. "Not-so-old servants."

"Something like that, wise guy." He gave me a long-suffering look. "As I was saying. One of the many things he taught me was an appreciation for tools, but more to my taste, how to sharpen them. I could sharpen a tool for hours. Well, at least half an hour. So it soon fell to me to sharpen all his tools."

"You enjoy that sort of repetitive task?"

"Yes, I do. One time I sharpened his favorite machete so long that it broke the next time he used it. So over the years we've joked that someday I'll buy him a new one. This is beautiful. Look at the handle. Feel it. The balance is perfect. There's nothing like a tool where the balance is perfect." He ran his hand along the handle, then let it hang limply, hoisted it, then let his arm and the blade drop again.

"Thanks, no. I believe you. Do you have any qualms?"

"Qualms about what?"

"The machete, that it might have been used to kill somebody. Or many somebodies, during the genocide."

He stopped in his tracks. "I hadn't thought of that." He held it up to the light to get a closer look at the blade. "No, this is a new machete."

"Good. Well, here we are." I put the key card into my door. The green light blinked on, and I pushed the door open slightly.

"Lovely day. Aside from murder, that is," said Alam. He hesitated. "Would you like to come in for a nightcap?"

"We're standing in front of my room," I said. "That would be my line."

"Yes, well. You didn't seem to be saying it, and since my room is only about fifteen feet away, it seemed to be up to me."

I hesitated. I did and I didn't.

A door opened down the hall, and one of the hotel boys walked out, dirty towels hanging over his arm. The spell, if there was one, was broken.

"Not tonight, thanks. I'm tired."

"Yes, well."

There was a pregnant pause while I wondered if he was going to give me a kiss goodnight. Or if I was going to give him a kiss goodnight. Or if it would be one of those romantic comedies where the actors fling themselves at each other and tear all their clothes off before they make it halfway to the bed.

"Have a good night, Alam. I'll see you in the morning."

"Good night," he said.

I pushed open the door, flipped on the light, and whispered, "Alam."

Four feet inside my room, a very large snake was curled on the carpet. Of course, anything over a foot would be a very large snake to me. Apparently it felt quite at home in my room; to him, I was the intruder. "Alam," I called again, before I realized that it wasn't goosebumps on the back of my neck but his breath.

"Viper," he said. "Not sure what kind. We need to choreograph this."

I took reassurance from his perfectly calm tone. "I think you aren't supposed to move."

"True, no sudden movements. He's looking sleepy, not ready to strike."

As if to prove Alam wrong, the snake stirred and with a slight movement of its head acknowledged our presence.

Behind us a voice said, "Is there a problem, sir?"

"Viper," Alam said.

"Not possible, sir."

I felt the boy peer around my arm. "Even if I wanted to move," I said, "you two have blocked any possibility of escape."

"I don't want to move." Alam gently laid his hand on my hip.

I wanted to lean back into him, but this probably wasn't the time.

The boy, the least visible to the snake, said, "I will go to get a weapon, sir."

"Here," said Alam, slowly passing the machete over his shoulder.

"I read somewhere that most snakebites occur when someone tries to kill the snake. Wouldn't we be better off just allowing him an escape route?" Now I did lean back a little, so that my shoulder was grazing his chest. He moved forward a little as well, not grazing, but pressing.

The snake twitched its tail, as if talk of its demise did not make it happy.

Alam's hand had crept around my waist, and as I was wondering if this was the best moment for him to be making a move on me, he suddenly lifted me and pulled me into the hall. As if he and the boy had practiced the dance of the snake dozens of times, the boy, machete in hand, leapt forward, and I heard the sound of blade meeting flesh.

Alam had wrapped his other arm around me and was, as we said in my childhood, squeezing the kishkes out of me.

"Got him!" shouted the boy, raising the machete in triumph.

The man across the hall stuck his head out his door and said, "Could you keep it down out here? I'd expect a little more quiet in a place . . . Jesus, what is that?"

The boy went into the room and picked up the phone. I heard him babbling excitedly.

Alam spun me around. "Are you okay?"

"Except for my kishkes."

"Your what?" He was now pressing me to him frontways.

"My guts."

He released his grip, though not entirely. "I thought I'd lost you."

An odd phrase for someone who didn't have me. I think I actually blushed. "Well, um."

He was poised to kiss me when the boy came excitedly out of the room. "This is a poisonous snake, you know. Deadly. You swell up, and if you don't die, probably you have the leg cut off. This is a bad snake."

"No more," I said, struggling to get into my purse. Alam seemed disinclined to let me go, but loosened his hold when he realized what I was doing.

"I have this." He pulled out his wallet and handed the boy a hundred-dollar bill. The boy began to protest, but Alam raised his hand. "Put it away quickly before your friends see it." Then he handed him a twenty. "You can show them this."

"Thank you, sir." Three other hotel employees, followed by the assistant manager, rushed down the hall, and both the hundred and the twenty disappeared before they arrived. Up and down the corridor, doors opened as irate tourists prepared to give us noise-makers hell, but news of the snake quelled their complaints.

Our neighbor across the hall said to the room boy, "I want you to come in and check my room. Now."

"This is the first time ever that we have had a snake in the room," the assistant manager said excitedly. Realizing that all heads were turned his way, he repeated this to one and all. But the other guests, some ready for bed, others clearly just awakened, all wanted their rooms checked too. The corridor filled. Neighbors introduced themselves. "Where are you from?" and "Do you know so-and-so?" and "What temple did you see today?" could be heard from both directions.

Once we had assured everyone that we were fine, the staff headed into my room to clean up. I couldn't help staring, mesmerized, at the mutilated snake.

"We will give you a different room, madame," said the assistant manager.

"No, that's fine. I'm settled here. But you might check the room thoroughly for more snakes, if you don't mind. Little baby snakes, especially, just in case." I held my hands inches apart. Somehow the thought of a sneaky snake just that size worried me as much as a big one.

"Of course." He peered into the room, as fearful of what might still be there as I was. "I have no idea how it got in. We are very careful about such things. We have snake traps around the grounds."

"Jenna, come to my room while they clean up."

"I will clean your weapon, sir, and bring it back to you tomorrow," said the snake killer.

"Thank you." Alam pulled me toward his room. Everyone was watching us, or so I thought. One woman raised her eyebrows and gave a quick nod to her husband.

I didn't resist. "I think I'll have that nightcap now."

24

"The water in the Tonle Sap, the largest lake in Southeast Asia, is fed from the Mekong, a river that rises in the Himalayas, then flows south through many of the countries— Vietnam, Lao, Thailand, Cambodia." Vuthuy strained to be heard over the sound of the revving engine as the boat pulled from the dock for our sunset cruise on the lake. "The flow of the tributary that feeds the Tonle Sap from the Mekong changes course twice a year and raises and lowers the waters nine meters."

"My goodness," said Martha.

"Incredible," said Mr. Jolly, his camera pressed against his nose.

Arranging an attentive expression on my face as I sank into my thoughts, I tuned out Vuthuy, thankful to have a few moments to think. We'd visited temples that morning, had our siesta, then headed for our late afternoon cruise on the lake, stopping at a village and a monastery on the way. It felt peaceful sitting on the boat, even if the engine made a racket. As usual, Philen was already complaining—about the noise, the smell of fish, the fine spray showering us.

As we cleared the estuary and entered the lake, I realized that Vuthuy was quiet and that Alam had joined me. We'd traveled past the docks where the hospital boat, the library boat, the dozens of houseboats, and the boats ferrying tourists sat. We were now among the overflow of small residential boats. During the dry season all of the houseboats would be moored further out in the lake. I wanted to ask Vuthuy how it was decided who could dock along the shore of the estuary, but Mr. Jolly had cornered him.

Alam sat quietly at my side, looking out over the bow. I feared conversation. My mind was racing as I sought an escape. Since this was a small boat, just about the only place I could get away from Alam was into my mind. I wanted last night not to have happened, for it to be a dream, for him not to have any expectations.

Even though I resisted, his presence was a comfort, not unlike the press of his chest as I'd leaned against him when the viper was curled on the floor before us.

"Oh, my," Courtney exclaimed. "I can't stand it."

The locals made some of their income from drying small fish for fish sauce, and the reek of drying fish had pungently accompanied us from the moment we got off the minibus. Barker laughed at her. "Just hold your nose. We're out on the lake now, and the smell will dissipate."

"Look at that! What a picture." Mrs. Jolly had moved next to me, and I pulled myself back to reality, thankful she was the one talking and not Alam. Thankful that her presence provided protection.

"Isn't it, though?" I said. Every boat was a different color, cheerful backdrops to all the activity. Small children catapulted themselves into the water, trying to sink others who floated on inner tubes. Two boys on a skiff made out of rotting pieces of wood were paddling with palm fronds. The skiff was under water until one or the other of them tilted off for a swim, when it bounced up. A girl and boy tossed a ball between boats, while a younger child in the water retrieved it and threw it back to them. On one boat a woman bent over, slapping a T-shirt against the gunwale, while another bathed her baby.

In this floating town, life didn't differ much from village activities ashore. It was just wetter here. Everyone waved at us as we passed, just as people wave from boats on the San Francisco Bay. What is it, I wondered, this waterlogged friendliness? Is it because of the distance between vessels? Because of the calm brought about by the rustling of waves, the soothing back-and-forth of the boats, the shared experience of no longer walking on land?

We wove our way among the small craft, the water at its highest, the boats all within easy reach of the larger community vessels we'd first passed.

"How are you doing?" Alam asked quietly.

"Fine. It's lovely out here. Look at that." I pointed out a particularly colorful boat to Mrs. Jolly. A woman dressed in an orange sarong and purple top stood at the rudder, hands on hips, surveying our progress.

He wasn't to be diverted. "And the snake."

"We know how he is. Very dead."

"Someone's dinner, no doubt."

"Do they eat snake?" I asked, startled. The glint in his eyes told me he was teasing me. "Really, I'm fine."

"Are you tired?"

Now he wasn't talking about the snake, but our night together. Feeling trapped, I braced myself for what he would say. "I'm fine."

"That's good. It's begun." He looked toward the west. "This is going to be a lulu of a sunset."

"I'm sorry it happened."

He knew I wasn't talking about the snake. "I'm not."

"It was just once. I was, I was—"

"Vulnerable?"

Mrs. Jolly walked away, and I wondered if she'd been listening to our whispered conversation. Probably. "Yes. It's not appropriate. I'm sorry." I got up and followed her. As I reached her side,

I pointed out another boat, as if she and I were continuing a conversation.

"In November," Vuthuy's voice announced, "the Tonle Sap River, feeding the lake, will reverse its waters, and we will have our yearly celebration. The waters will have flooded the land around the lake then, allowing us to plant wet rice in the flooded area."

"How do you celebrate?" asked Barker.

"Boat races." Then Vuthuy's voice was drowned out by a nearby boat revving its engine.

Was Alam only talking about the sunset when he said, "It's begun"? I hoped he wasn't talking about us too. He'd taken advantage of a moment last night. Well, I'd taken advantage of it, too. Did I regret it? Yes. No. It depended. I can't go further, I mentally repeated to myself as the huge orange globe sank before my eyes and the clouds on the horizon kaleidoscoped color.

All the while, I felt his eyes on me.

"BUT how did it get into your room?" Courtney asked, her voice rising hysterically.

We had managed to keep the tale of the snake quiet all day, but as we sat in the bar before dinner, the assistant manager asked me if I was all right, and somehow the word "snake" slithered into his question.

"I can't stay in a hotel where there are snakes." She turned to Barker. "I hate them."

Barker tried to calm her, not very successfully.

"You don't need to worry, dear. I'm sure it's a one-off," Mrs. Jolly said, smiling serenely.

"We're moving. Find us a room," Courtney ordered her husband.

"Someone put it there," P.P. said.

We all looked at him. I kicked his foot. "What are you talking about?" I said. But I knew exactly what he meant. Throughout the day I'd repeatedly pushed that same thought to the back of my mind.

"Grey's decapitation. A consequence of talking with us? The burglary. The snake." Seeing the puzzlement on the surrounding faces, he translated himself. "It could have killed her."

"What's this?" Mr. Jolly said, deftly taking charge. Philen tensed, his usual reaction when another man asserted his authority. "Tell us what you're talking about."

I shook my head. "Could someone have put that snake into my room?" I asked the assistant manager.

"Why would someone do that, madame?" He looked mortified at having stirred things up by mentioning the snake.

"Miss," I said automatically. "I'm not asking why, I'm asking whether someone could have done it."

"No, madame. Miss. They would have needed a key, and the only key is with you and our staff, who are very trustworthy."

"You see?" I told the group. "It isn't possible, and there's no reason for it. Unless Arthur wanted to finish me off so that he could lecture."

Courtney laughed.

He flushed. "Of course not."

"Well, that settles it. Another beer, please." I held up my glass to the waiter.

I thought of the housekeeper who had been walking out of another room, towels over his arm. The same housekeeper who had macheted the snake and been given a hundred and twenty dollars for it. There were others who had keys to our rooms too—the cleaning staff, probably the manager, maybe the assistant manager.

"I want to move." Courtney was drawing attention to herself once again.

I thought of ways to kill someone, if somehow I wanted to commit murder. Knife, gun, poison, strangulation, drowning.

It was a long list, and decapitation and snakebite were not possibilities that would have crossed my mind.

"We're not moving," Barker said firmly. "Get a grip on yourself. No one would try to kill Jenna. P.P. was making a bad joke."

I glared at P.P. before he could respond to that. Except my brothers, I wanted to say. My brothers had tried to kill me in various ways throughout our childhood. But it wasn't the time to be flippant.

Frown lines creased Alam's forehead as he processed P.P.'s "joke."

"I'm starving. I wish the bar had something other than nuts," I said.

"Yes," said Mrs. Jolly. "Me, too."

Martha rose deliberately. She'd been awfully quiet all day. I suspected her foot hurt more than she let on. I'd have to ask Alam to look at her wound. I glanced at him again, and the frown lines were still there. I hoped he wasn't planning on taking care of me.

25

We were flying shoulder to shoulder with clouds as flat as pancakes. More like fog than clouds, really, since Siem Reap is close enough to the Tonle Sap to get fog off the lake. Above us, confections of whipped-cream clouds built palaces across the sky.

"I never want to land." I said to no one in particular. Being in a helicopter is nothing like being in a plane. Flying in a plane is like taking a double-wide trailer aloft. But in a helicopter one feels small, like a bird—granted, a big bird—and you get a sense of what it would be like to spread your wings and fly.

"I love it," Mrs. Jolly's voice squealed through the headset.

I turned in my seat. "You okay, Martha?"

She gave me a weak nod.

"Do you want the motion sickness medicine now? We'll be taking off two more times today. It's that sinking stomach at liftoff that's hard to take."

She nodded and stretched out her hand.

I pulled my backpack onto my lap. We'd already passed far beyond Siem Reap, where the majority of the Khmer temples had been built, and now looked down on a patchwork of fields, many of rice, but other crops distinguishable by their varied greens, though not clear enough to identify. "They'll be harvesting soon," I said. "Those fields of acid green are the rice. Lovely, isn't it?"

"Spectacular," came Alam's voice. He was seated directly behind me, and I imagined I could feel the heat of him.

"Do you have any idea what the other crops are?" I asked the Australian pilot beside me. I found the medicine in an outside pocket of my backpack and handed Martha a pill.

"Afraid I can't tell from up here. They all look alike, except for the tapioca and the rice. But those fields are pretty much what we'll be seeing from here until we get to the Dangrek Mountains on the border with Thailand. We'll spot them from a good distance."

"Are the mountains high?" asked Mr. Jolly.

"No, generally about five hundred meters, a few up to seven hundred meters. They're hills, really. But they stand out because they're all that breaks up the line of the plain. They're interesting, as you'll see. Primarily sandstone, but they're organized in a series of plateaus that stick out like fingers. Preah Vihear sits on top of one of those fingers. Very dramatic."

We flew in silence for most of the next forty minutes, until the temple came in view. It certainly was dramatic. I was glad the pilot had put me in the front seat, though I felt a bit guilty that none of the others had this best of all views.

He circled the temple, keeping a good distance, he said, so the vibrations of the helicopter wouldn't disturb the structural integrity of the buildings. Though I'd seen numerous photographs of Preah Vihear, the view still took my breath away. Angkor Wat had too, when we flew around it after taking off, but in a different way. That temple struck one numb with its scale, its elegance. This one made me wonder at the madness of men, the extent of loyalty to a king, the devotion to the god Shiva. Each of those stones had to be dragged to the top of the plateau along the causeway that bled down the hill in a straight line.

I considered the planning that was involved—climbing hill after hill, arguing over where to put the temple, disagreeing over orientation after they'd chosen this finger of land, debating details of the temple carvings. This flight around the temple tied me to its past. To those people. I didn't know them, but I knew them, I knew how their hearts beat for their god, for their king. I knew that they aspired to something grander than most of us can imagine. I thought about all that, but "Wow" was all I said.

Sticking to the established fly zone, we landed quite a distance from the entrance, close to the small stalls selling the tourist goods that had sprouted even here, miles from any visible populated area.

"No eye contact," muttered Mrs. Jolly as we climbed out of the helicopter. The salespeople always seemed to single her out. They knew a sucker when they saw one. To deter them, Alam took her arm, and we set off toward the temple.

I felt a lightness in my step, the adrenaline of the flight buoying me. Beside me, Alam said, "If this was all we did on this trip, it would be worth it."

I smiled in agreement. Did he feel it? I wondered. Did he feel as I'd felt as we circled the temple? That pull of the past, that connection with the anonymous people who had imagined this place?

When we got to the entrance, I told them about the temple, begun in the tenth century and expanded in the eleventh and twelfth centuries. "It's dedicated to Shiva, the great Hindu god, who resides atop Mount Kailash, so this is an appropriate spot for his temple. The causeway runs north-south instead of the usual east-west."

"To fit on the plateau," said Barker.

"Yes, exactly. The direction of the axis was dictated by the configuration of Pey Tadi, the plateau upon which it sits. You can see that it's bisected by five *gopuras*, gateways, on the approach. Look for the carving of the Churning of the Ocean of

Milk, the myth that you've already seen in the eastern gallery of Angkor Wat."

Their eyes began to wander past me, searching for the carving I had just mentioned. They were anxious to get into the compound and to stretch their legs after our flight. "I'll be walking around, so feel free to ask me anything as you explore," I said, releasing them. Martha and Mrs. Jolly had already gone ahead, Barker solicitously taking Martha's arm and laughing at something one of the women said. Alam lagged behind as if he wanted to walk with me. I took my time finding my water bottle, and he took the hint and walked off by himself.

WE wandered separately, coming back together at intervals as a group, or a partial group, then parting again. As I sat on a low wall, Martha joined me. "I'm trying to imagine it populated," she said. "But it's hard to fill in just what it was like in the twelfth or thirteenth century. I feel so sorry for the people who built it."

"The common man. Yes, it must have been horribly difficult. At the same time, I respect the vision and dedication that it took." I nodded at her foot. "How are you feeling?"

"It's sore, but improving." This was more revealing than her usual bravado.

When she had rested enough, we began to walk back to the helicopter, "Better from the air," Martha said.

"It's certainly spectacular—exhilarating. But, you know, I like the quiet of the place—not just because it has fewer tourists, but its isolation adds to its mystique."

"Yes," she laughed. "My impression may be as much a part of my discomfort as anything. What next?"

"Banteay Chhmar. A Jayavarman VII temple, with very interesting Buddhist iconography. I think you'll like it."

"I know who that is. J7. He was that late twelfth-century king."

I laughed, pleased that the information that Vuthuy and I had been imparting was sinking in. "Yes, you've got it. Late twelfth century, early thirteenth."

"I'll be with you in a minute," she said, and headed for the tourist restroom.

Without Alam to protect her on her return to the helicopter, Mrs. Jolly had been more or less dragged toward one of the T-shirt stalls. I followed her, thinking I might buy a Preah Vihear T-shirt for my brother Sean, the black shirt with an image of Preah Vihear in white. "How much?" I asked.

"Three dollars," said the young woman.

I pulled out three dollars and handed it to her.

Startled, Mrs. Jolly said, "You aren't going to bargain? You said we should always bargain."

"Honey, we flew in on a helicopter," I said in my best gangster voice.

Her expression of dismay transformed into laughter. "Well, I guess we did. And it must take some initiative for these people to come all the way up here and set up their stalls each day just to make a pittance. I think I'll buy three T-shirts for my grandsons. At full price. My grandsons will think this old girl was quite adventurous to get on a helicopter."

UNLIKE Preah Vihear, Banteay Chhmar wasn't in very good shape. Where seeds had rooted and grown into gigantic trees, the roots had destabilized the structure, causing the stone walls to crumble. Furthermore, J7, who had commissioned the temple, had been in a building frenzy, erecting more temples in his thirty-seven-year reign than any previous Khmer ruler. The result was sloppy workmanship, both in the architecture—sloppy joins contributed to walls falling down—and in the sculpture.

This showed clearly in the ubiquitous *apsara*, the celestial females who adorn the exterior of Khmer temples. The artists during J7's reign had taken little care in carving them. In earlier centuries, sculptors had meticulously placed stone breaks at non-critical spots—above the shoulders, at the knees—as they carved the lovely women into the walls of the temple. But during J7's reign a face might be carved into two different stones, creating a jarring visual for the viewer and suggesting that completion of the temple was the priority.

"Dang," I said as we walked toward the entrance.

"What?" asked Barker, who was close on my heels. He'd been very friendly since Grey's decapitation. I guessed he'd seen my suspicions dash across my face.

His friendliness wasn't working.

I pointed at the sign and barriers the Global Heritage Fund had set up to keep tourists from climbing over the fallen stones while they restored the site. On my last visit I had enjoyed scaling the destroyed walls and skirting the gigantic silk-cotton trees in search of carved details. Not this time. We would have to walk around the barriers, kept from seeing much of anything because of this badly needed restoration.

"I know I should be happy about this," I said.

"About what?" asked Alam. We were standing before the scaffolding that had been placed in front of the famous reliefs of Lokeshvara, bodhisattva of compassion. Unlike most of the earlier temples of the ancient Khmer empire, this temple, like its builder, was Buddhist.

The multi-armed forms of Lokeshvara, unique to Banteay Chhmar, rose boldly the height of the wall. I felt an affinity to them, this bodhisattva so beloved of Buddhists. I'd written a paper about these particular carvings as an undergraduate. I hadn't seen them in person when I wrote the paper, but because of that work I now felt linked to them, intellectually, emotionally. Because I knew them, I supposed, and because it was that paper that had hooked me on Southeast Asian art.

"I'm happy that they're restoring the temple, but sorry that you don't get the full impact of these wonderful carvings," I said as we strained to see around the scaffolding poles.

"Yes, it is too bad," said Martha. Alam stood beside her, vigilant about her foot. The last thing we wanted was for her to get an infection. But she was intrepid, and I'd seen some exasperation on his usually calm face.

"No photos here, unless you want pics of a bunch of metal poles," said Barker.

"There are plenty of photos on the Web," I said.

"I imagine there are," he said. "Are there many temples with these fellows?"

"No, this is the only one. Oops, I take that back. Neak Pean also has Lokeshvara images. This particular form of the bodhisattva is drawn from a specific text, the *Karandavyuha*. You see the noose that he carries." I pointed at one of the figures with its multitude of arms and attributes. "He saves people by lassoing them. The king identified with Lokeshvara. He must have fancied himself a compassionate man, building hospitals throughout the kingdom." I paused. "That's not fair. He could well have been a compassionate man."

We peered around the scaffolding at the carvings. "He transported multiple images of Lokeshvara to look over the far reaches of his kingdom, further attesting J7's preference for the bodhisattva. Those figures were also multi-armed versions of the bodhisattva. In Southeast Asia Lokeshvara was more often depicted with only four arms."

Behind me, a voice with an American accent said, "We found one here. One of Jayavarman VII's freestanding Lokeshvaras." We all turned. I was surprised to see a young Cambodian man. "I can show you if you like," he said. "You're a small group and it's our lunch break."

We agreed, and he led us to a small covered area that protected remnants of sculptures and carved architectural details.

"We came upon this freestanding sculpture of Lokeshvara. a multitude of arms like the reliefs you were just looking at, plus rows of tiny Buddhas carved on his chest. This is a cosmic version of the bodhisattva. As you can see, he's in fine condition. Most of the sculptures that we've found buried here at the site have been quite heavily damaged. There are few complete works."

The Lokeshvara had pride of place, standing on a pedestal in the center of the shed, flowers at his feet. He was right. The figure was pristine, and I couldn't take my eyes off it.

"Fantastic," said Martha.

"Yes," he agreed, watching me carefully. "Our great find during the restoration of the temple. Each day we hope some other sculpture as fine as this one will turn up."

"How far will you go with the restoration?" I asked, moving closer, searching the sculpture for wear, damage, age.

"Well, we clearly can't reconstruct the entire site. It's too badly damaged. But we do want to make it safe for anyone wandering around. And, most importantly, conserve the Lokeshvara reliefs that you were looking at. They're the highlight of the place, and, as Dr. Murphy has told you, are very rare."

Startled that he knew my name, I looked more closely at his face.

"What will you do with this sculpture?" Alam asked.

"We're debating that now. Some want to build a small building here to house it. Others want to take it back to Siem Reap to the museum, while others want it in the Phnom Penh museum. As you can imagine, there's been a great deal of discussion." He smiled at me. "Do you remember me? My name is Leap."

"Oh, my gosh," I said. "You were in a Southeast Asian art history class when I was the teaching assistant."

"That's right. You're the reason I'm here today. I was just taking the class to fill a requirement. I was a geology major until then, but that class completely changed the course of my life."

"Gives me the shivers," said Mrs. Jolly. "Are you Cambodian?"

"Yes, though my family moved to the U.S. when I was very young. I have the advantage of speaking Khmer, so it was pretty easy getting a job here in Cambodia when I finished conservation school. I'm a rookie conservator who's lucked out. Found my life's work, really. And married a local Khmer girl, so I imagine I'll be spending a good many years here. In fact, I hope I can introduce you to her." He turned to me. "If you're still in Siem Reap this coming weekend, I'd be happy to have you all to a modest Cambodian house for a home-cooked meal. I'm scheduled to have a week off and will be coming down on Friday."

"Yes, please," said Martha and Mrs. Jolly in unison.

Another member of the conservation team approached him. "I'm sorry, but I'm going to have to drag Leap away," he said. "He's invaluable to us. For one thing, he's our lifeline to the local workforce, and one of them has gone missing."

"I'm grateful we got to see this," I said. "Would you mind if I looked a little more closely at the Lokeshvara?"

"Not at all," the man said. "If you're the reason Leap is here today, I'm glad to assist."

"I'll come find you before we leave," I said to Leap. "It seems you'll be having some guests for dinner. But I should warn you that there are four more people in our group."

"The more the merrier," he said over his shoulder. "I've told my wife about you. She'll be very pleased to have you in our home."

We all crowded around the sculpture, though the others soon became bored with my close inspection and wandered away. Alam stuck it out longer than the rest, but at some point I realized that he was gone too. I'd seen a few of the Lokeshvara sculptures that J7 had plopped around his kingdom, marking his land like a peeing dog. I began by looking at the style and iconography of the stone, which was correct down to the tiny Buddhas that covered the figure's chest. Then I looked at the carving of the narrow edges of details, to see if they had any sign of wear. Finally I turned my attention to the details of the head.

The shallow bowl of the earlobe. The gentle swirl, the soft, natural curve. So fine. So perfect. So distinctive. I could imagine the sculptor's hand at work, the gestures of his wiry body, the tilt and punch of the chisel, and his full attention on that ear. I looked at it until I was ready to make a decision, then I went looking for Leap to ask him more about the discovery of the sculpture. He was busy and only had a moment for me, but I knew I would be seeing him in a few days and could ask the most important question then.

26

"Of course I'm certain."

"Why?" P.P. held his single-malt scotch gingerly. He had a duty-free bottle in his room, and we had sequestered ourselves away from the group to imbibe and to discuss my visit to Banteay Chhmar. His room was twice as large as mine, the advantage of being in the old section of the hotel. The ceilings were high, the bed capacious, and the floor—I wanted to get down on my knees and caress the teak flooring with its luscious patina.

"Why am I certain the Lokeshvara sculpture at Banteay Chhmar is modern?" Oh, dear, I'd begun translating P.P. to myself. "No wear, though it was buried. No breakage, ditto. And there's something modern about it, though I can't verbalize what that is."

He didn't seem to be listening, his mind racing on to the next question. "How?"

"How did the sculptor plant that large stone at Banteay Chhmar and manage to fool everyone into thinking that it was old? Transporting it to that relatively remote spot, burying it where it might be found? Burying it where he assumed it would be found? God only knows." I gulped, my eyes burning from the heat of the scotch. I could get used to Glenfiddich.

"Bury?" He leaned forward in his chair. It was one of those colonial-style chairs that had extendable arms that you could put your feet up on. I wondered if he'd trade seats with me. I'd seen them in films, but never tried one.

He was looking at me expectantly, his expression making his round face even rounder. "Of course. Not only was it buried about a foot underground, but stones had been piled on top of it. Not little rocks, but big stones from a crumbling wall, heavy enough that it would take a couple of people to move them." I stretched my arms a foot and a half, then moved them around to create a cube.

"If they brought it there, they could move stones." He bounced from his chair, took a few steps, walked back, and sat.

I hadn't been quick enough.

"Well, sure. Whoever planted the sculpture could surely move a couple of stones. But that's not the point. Burying the piece, yes, but piling stones on top? That's what's flummoxed me. How could they be sure that the people doing the restoration to the temple would even find the sculpture?" I looked out the window toward the pool. Courtney was coming out of the spa, probably having had a facial, a massage, her nails done. I looked at the state of my nails and tried not to think about the state of my skin.

"Insider." He swirled his icy glass, the color of the scotch shifting from dark to light.

I looked at him. "You mean someone working there? That's a possibility. I didn't think to ask exactly who found the stone. I asked about where it had been found."

"Where?"

"Near the entrance to the site."

"Not far."

"No, once they got it there by truck, they didn't have too far to transport it. I think they would have had a guard at the site. Of course, it wouldn't take much to pay off a guard, but the villagers nearby would have heard a truck roll in the middle of the night. Or so you would think."

"Nearby?"

"The village isn't adjacent to the temple, but close enough. And there isn't so much traffic out there that you wouldn't hear a truck."

"Daytime? Archaeologists?"

"You're suggesting they brought that sculpture in during the day, and the archaeologists working on the site are in cahoots with the sculptor?"

He nodded.

"I seriously doubt that. What would they gain?"

"Glory."

It was true. Archaeologists liked the find, the discovery. We've all seen *Raiders of the Lost Ark*—the movie was over the top, but it wasn't the first to depict archaeologists' greed for the discovery. Not for their own pockets, necessarily, but for the glory. I thought about the people I'd met at the site. None immediately fit the bill, and I dropped that line of thought.

"I think the more important question is why," I said. "Why would they do it? It had to have been more than one person. It couldn't have been easy, and what could possibly be the point of planting a modern sculpture at an ancient temple site?

"Don't know."

"More worrisome, the sculpture seems to have everyone fooled. Or at least everyone working at the site. Even my former student."

P.P. looked surprised. "Student?"

I told him about Leap and his invitation to dinner.

"You me?"

"All of us, the group."

"Philen?"

"I'm afraid even Philen." I looked at P.P.'s watch as he sat back down. "We'd better get down to the bar."

He looked at the bottle of scotch.

"I suspect they have a single malt at the bar."

"Expensive."

"When did you become so thrifty?"

"For two." He smiled as he said it.

I laughed. "Yes, now you're in trouble. You've just converted me to single-malt scotch." We both took our last sips and headed for the bar. Peanuts, I thought as I wobbled down the stairs. I could do with some peanuts.

BEFORE we could even sit down, Martha said, "Arthur has been telling us the bad news."

"Bad news? What's wrong?" I asked, turning to Philen.

"I'll be leaving tomorrow. My wife isn't well, and she's been pressuring me to come home since we got here. I've finally given in."

"So sorry to hear that. Is it anything serious?" asked Mr. Jolly.

"We don't know. She's waiting for some test results."

Those results were awfully long in coming; he'd told me they were waiting before we left California. Arthur Philen is one of those people who always speaks in specifics and becomes irritated when others don't. The vagueness of his reply made me think, not for the first time, that he was a terrible liar.

"That's really a shame. There's so much still to see, and you'll miss Phnom Penh. The National Museum and the palace," I said. I noticed that no one had encouraged Philen to stay. In fact, I thought that I had seen relief on more than one face, further confirmation that these were not the backers to support his coup to overthrow Caleb New.

"And the Foreign Correspondents Club," said Barker, legs extended, upper body curved around his drink.

For some reason he'd gotten it into his head that the Foreign Correspondents Club, a restaurant in Phnom Penh, would be the culinary highlight of our trip. Maybe he was right, but his mentioning it made me think of a category of traveler that I didn't much like. As if travel were a list of "must dos," ticking off this restaurant, that hotel, tallying up the museums, the ancient buildings. "You know, of course, that there's an FCC here in Siem Reap."

This brought him upright. "Nearby?" He turned to Courtney, "Darling, let's go there tonight."

"Of course, if you like."

"We have dinner here this evening," said Philen, recrossing his legs. "You could go another night."

"I believe they intend to go on their own. We'll wait for them to report back to us about it," said Mr. Jolly placidly.

"Yes, yes, of course," said Philen, flustered. "I wasn't thinking."

Barker and Courtney gave a little wave as they set off.

I watched them go, then said, "I'll be right back." I went to the reception desk.

"Excuse me. The couple who just walked out."

"Yes."

"They're in my group."

"Yes."

"And the gentleman was sick the other day and didn't join us when we went out on the helicopter."

"He became sick in Thailand?"

I was startled at receiving this revelation so quickly. "Thailand?"

"Yes, he hired the plane to Bangkok. He was gone such a short time. If he ate his lunch at the airport, their food is not good food." He waited expectantly for my question, unaware that he'd answered it already.

"Um. Do you know where they went this evening?"

"The Foreign Correspondents Club." He looked puzzled.

"Oh, that's right. I couldn't remember what he told me."

Following the others into the dining room, I thought of Barker in Bangkok. Barker in Bangkok when Grey was murdered. Barker taking a very short trip to Bangkok and rushing back to Siem Reap.

So that no one would know where he'd gone.

27

"I enjoyed those temples this morning," said Martha.

"I did, too," said Mrs. Jolly. "But I have to say I'm happy we're going to see sculptors this afternoon. The temples are beginning to merge into one enormous edifice."

"Yes," said Barker, raising his hands over his head and shimmying. "With lots of towers and more *apsaras* than one would ever want to see."

Everyone laughed, and Mrs. Jolly added, "Jenna, I read in my guidebook that it's also possible to see silk weaving and the preparation of the silk threads. Can we do that?"

"Yes, definitely. After the sculpture studio. Then, for anyone who wants to, we can do some damage in the market." A few had already visited the market briefly, but one visit hadn't been enough time to get through the dozens of stalls. "And I was thinking we might just stay in town and have dinner after the market."

"Go to a bar," said Barker. "To celebrate."

I must have looked puzzled.

"To celebrate our depleted numbers."

"He doesn't mean P.P.," said Courtney, squeezing my arm.

More laughter. The mood had shifted without Philen there. The wet blanket was gone. I'd been unaware of the extent of the effect he had on one and all.

P.P. and Philen had ended up on the same flight to Bangkok, Philen on his way home and P.P. headed back to buy his modern sculpture. When I last saw P.P., he was trying to bump himself up to first class to avoid being anywhere near Philen during the hour-long flight. Even though a week hadn't yet passed, he was anxious that someone else might buy the piece, or so he said. I suspected he just needed to get away.

"Ah, well. I'm not going to engage in this conversation. He is my boss, after all," I said primly, evoking more laughter.

"Poor you," someone muttered.

I smiled. "I made a reservation at one of the best restaurants. Or so the reviews say. I haven't been there."

"I think Barker is right," said Mr. Jolly. "A bar before the restaurant. Not so much for the alcohol, but to get the benefit of seeing as many establishments as possible. For our next trip." He raised his glass.

"Hear, hear," said Courtney, who drank very little, but who enjoyed beautiful surroundings. There were a few new, very fancy hotels.

"Sounds like a plan to me," I said. "After dinner, anyone who wants to go to the night market can, but the van can take back those who aren't interested in more shopping."

"After dinner sounds like the perfect time to take a walk," said Mr. Jolly. "You're pampering us by driving us everywhere."

I raised both hands in mock self-defense. "As you like."

"Is it far?" Barker asked as we stood to go in to lunch, our usual beer after temples having been downed quickly by one and all.

"No, it's right in town, very close."

WE piled out of the van into a large courtyard strewn with sculptures in styles dating from the sixth to the thirteenth century. I hoped the group wouldn't be disappointed. For years a single sculpture center had catered to tourists here in Siem Reap, where one could see young art students being taught sculpting, painting, and weaving. Now there were multiple artisan studios, and Vuthuy was insistent on our visiting this particular one, where he said the best sculptors worked.

"I think you're right," I said to him as I surveyed the sculptures placed around the garden.

"Yes, very good, these sculptors. Their teacher is the best sculptor in Siem Reap. In Southeast Asia."

I wandered around the courtyard, and he followed. "They used to carve the same sculpture over and over at the other studio." I rubbed a Buddha's curls.

"Yes. Here the artists are encouraged to do their own work." He thought for a moment. "Some popular images they repeat."

A man came out of one of the buildings that edged the courtyard, distractedly wiping his hands on a towel. He stopped short when he saw me. I did the same, for it was our Bangkok sculptor. He took a step back, and I took one forward, then he resigned himself to my presence and came over to greet me.

"Hello. Your friend is not coming? The round man?"

"He went to Bangkok today to see you."

"Ah," he said, seemingly unperturbed that he would miss P.P. in Bangkok. He turned and handed the towel to one of his underlings, who was blocking out a seated Buddha from an enormous piece of sandstone, too large to get inside. "I will give you our tour. Then my assistant will give your group a lesson in stone carving. He will show you how difficult is this work, and every person can carve one small stone. It is soapstone, which is soft, but a lesson in the work."

"Thank you. Someone will want to try. I certainly would." We had stopped in front of the finest sculpture, an *apsara*. Not a freestanding piece, she was carved out of three blocks of stone just as the celestial females are on the temples. Her head and headdress filled the upper stone, then her torso, and lowest, her legs. I looked at the details and saw what I expected. "You're a master."

Surprised, he said, "You recognize this as my sculpture?"

"Yes, isn't it?"

"How do you know that it is mine?" He looked disconcerted, though I wasn't sure why, as I knew he could distinguish each of his students' carvings.

"I doubt any of your students could match your abilities. Also, I'm beginning to recognize your style. Your treatment of the ear is exquisite."

"Thank you." Then, still looking unnerved, he turned to the group and began to describe the process of carving stone.

I wandered the courtyard as he spoke, looking to see if there were any freestanding sculptures that I might ascribe to him. As he began to move us into the first of three workshops—the sounds of tools against stone came from all three buildings—I asked, "Do you have any more of your work here?"

"No."

"You must sell your sculptures quickly."

"Yes." He turned his attention back to the group, pointing out the next stage in the carving.

Barker, overhearing our conversation, had hung back as the others entered. Pointing to the *apsara*, he said to the sculptor, "I'm interested in buying that sculpture over there."

"Thank you. We will discuss it after the tour. I would be honored." He led the others into the building.

It was the first time Barker and I had been alone since Grey's murder. Before he could wander off, I said, "Where were you the other day?"

"The other day?"

"When you didn't go with us to the temples."

He said truculently, "In my bathroom mostly."

"Oh, of course, they do have bathrooms on private jets. I almost forgot."

He paled. "How did you know?"

"Siem Reap is a small town. Someone rushing off on a private jet for the day becomes a topic of conversation."

"I didn't kill him. Honestly. I didn't even see him. I got to his apartment, and I pounded on the door. I thought for sure I heard someone inside when I arrived, so I kept pounding. But he didn't answer."

I have no training to identify a liar. Nor do I have my father's ability to spot a lie. But he sounded convincing. "Or the killer didn't answer."

"Yes, I thought of that." He looked toward the building where the others had gone, seeking escape. "And I tried to break down the door."

"You're joking."

"No, I'm not. It's harder to break down a door than it looks in the movies. Thank God. Because if it was the murderer that I heard—" He looked rather green.

"You might be lying there with Grey."

"Cutting someone's head off. I mean, how does someone even think of doing that? Yes, well, you told us that the Khmer Rouge cut off all those heads that were in the tower at the Bakong, but . . . I don't know, I can't imagine it."

His pallor suggested he could imagine it. Still, I didn't think he'd done it.

"But you knew he was coming here. Why didn't you wait for him?"

"I did. I met the morning plane and when he wasn't on it, I got angry. Angrier. I decided to go to him. I hadn't planned it."

"Seems extreme."

"Yes, well, I'd been brooding, then when P.P. said Grey was coming, I fumed all night. I couldn't sleep. I was imagining my conversation with him. It was a stupid, impulsive thing to do."

Martha's voice rose above the chiseling. "Where do you quarry your stone?"

I didn't hear the sculptor's answer.

"I brood," Barker said, raising his hands, then dropping them at his sides in defeat. "I get myself worked up. I was so furious at him, I did feel as if I could kill him. But, well, I couldn't have. I just couldn't."

I didn't know what brought someone to murder. All sorts of motives, emotions. It was ironic that we stood in this courtyard where he had just said he wanted to buy a fake sculpture. He intended to buy a fake sculpture, while the thought of someone having tricked him positively infuriated him. "You might want to work on that temper," I said.

He nodded, and I stepped aside to let him head to the studio. Though I didn't think he'd killed Grey, I wouldn't follow him down a dark alley.

The space was clean and bright, a bank of industrial sashes filling the wall opposite the door. Five young sculptors were seated on the floor, a block of stone on a small pedestal before each of them. They chiseled away, their work in various stages of completion. I squatted down in front of the student with the most complete carved head. He swiveled it so that I could better see Radha's face—one more version of the head that was giving P.P. and me so much grief. That had given others even more.

Each of the students, I saw, was working on the same head. And all the heads arrayed along the shelf that filled the far wall were the same. So much for everyone following his own muse. "Radha," I said.

The boy nodded.

I stood, and as if to confirm for myself what I already knew, I said to no one in particular, "These are all Radha."

The sculptor stopped the speech he'd been making. "Yes. I was commissioned to make the replacement head for the ancient sculpture at the museum. As I was carving it, a tourist group came to watch us work, and everyone in the group wanted to buy this head. So it seemed a good one for the students to carve, as we should be able to sell these heads.

"We have sold many already. You may have seen them in the museum shop. By selling the heads and other sculpture, the students are able to pay for their food and small needs. The work prepares them for restoration work on the temples. That is difficult work. Sometimes, if they are very talented, they are able to make a good living selling sculptures they create especially for tourists, rather than doing the hard work of restoring temples. They work as artists rather than workmen."

"How many of these heads have you made?"

"Many. There are many students."

"No, I mean, how many have you yourself made?"

"Oh, I see. Three. Only one was correct for the replacement. The other did not turn out correct. Not the correct angle; she leaned forward." He tilted his head to demonstrate. "Also I made one smaller practice one before the replacement."

Well, that confirmed what we'd come to believe. P.P. had bought a fake, this other head that he had made. The flawed head that tilted slightly down. I hadn't thought about the angle of the head until he mentioned it, but I thought if we tried to put P.P.'s head on the sculpture, it would tilt. And the collector we'd visited in Bangkok had the smaller head.

"When did you sell the small head?"

"The day that you came to visit. I took it to a collector who had been trying to buy it from me."

I thought back on our visit to the second collector in Bangkok and remembered him saying that he had recently purchased it. "What did you use as a model? Since the head had been stolen when you created its substitute, you must have had a model."

He answered without looking at me, and I couldn't see his face. "I had many photographs. It is not so difficult to work from a photograph."

"Do you know where that head is?"

"No. I sold it."

"To the museum."

He looked confused. "The museum did not want that head. It was at the wrong angle."

"Yes. Sorry to interrupt. You sold it to?" No one seemed to mind the interruption. They were either listening to our conversation or watching the young men work.

He went back to speaking to the group, pointedly not answering my question.

"THIS isn't my key," Barker said to the receptionist who was handing us our keys. "Who is in room 218?"

"That's mine," I said. "Goodnight, everyone. I need to buy some stamps to put on all these postcards I bought in the market. I'll see you in the morning." I was speaking to the group in general, but Alam in particular. He hesitated, then turned with the rest and said goodnight as they moved toward their rooms.

I didn't know why Alam was the only one of the group who had chosen not to stay in the old building. But then, there were lots of things I didn't know when it came to Alam. I didn't know how to walk down the corridor to our rooms together, because I didn't want the awkwardness of him going into his room and me into mine. Or worse, the awkwardness of him wanting me to go into his room or to come into mine. Or the very worst, him not wanting to come in and me wanting him to.

It was one of the above, but I was too confused to sort it out, which was why I was stepping up to the concierge's desk to buy stamps. Hoping Alam would walk quickly to his room. Planning to walk slowly myself. Or I could stop in the bar and have a nightcap, so that he wouldn't hear me go into my room. So that he wouldn't pop his head out to say, want a nightcap? Or some such.

As usual, I was avoiding a decision, a discussion, an uncomfortable moment. I was avoiding any form of commitment as if it were the plague.

"Can I help you?"

"Oh, sorry." I'd been standing before the concierge, looking blank. "I need some stamps."

He riffled through a drawer. "I will have to get them from the shop. I do not have any here. How many do you need?"

I tallied the cards I needed to write: one to each member of my family, a few to friends at the museum, one to my landlady, Rita. I followed him toward the small shop that fronted the restaurant. "Ten should do it."

"For the letter or the postcard?"

"Postcard, please."

As he sorted through an enormous ring of keys that he pulled from his pocket, I perused the stand of books in the tiny shop. Mass-market mysteries, coffee-table books on Angkor, guidebooks, and a scholarly work on Sambor Prei Kuk, the early temple that we had visited on our first helicopter trip. I pulled it off the rack, only to discover that there was a second volume behind it.

I had to have them. I always had to have those scholarly books published by small local presses that you know will go out of print before you return. You can never find them in the West. "I'd like to buy this."

"I am sorry, miss, I am unable to sell the items in the shop when the shop is closed. It is possible for you to buy it tomorrow."

"Can I help?" asked the assistant manager who had been so kind to Martha after she fell.

"I'd like to buy this. Could you just put the sale on my room bill? Or could I pay for it first thing in the morning? I'd very much like to read it tonight." That wasn't entirely true. I was dead on my feet. But it seemed to be the only copy they had, and I was afraid someone else might buy it. I might not be a collector, but I am a bibliophile.

"Yes, certainly. I will arrange to put it on your room bill. You are buying stamps also? We can put those on your room bill as well. If you could just come to the front desk and sign the receipt."

"Thanks," I said to the concierge as I followed the assistant manager toward the desk. "By the way, have you had any luck figuring out how the snake got into my room?"

"I am sorry, miss. I feel certain that the staff is not responsible. It must have come into the room when the sliding door was open to air the room. Sometimes when our visitors leave and no one is coming to the room that day, we will leave the doors open for airing."

"So you're saying that the snake was in the room with me for a few days before we discovered it?" I shivered.

"Possibly, miss."

"You're sure that no one could have come in, someone not staff?"

"One staff saw a man who he did not recognize, but he was an old man and I do not think he would have been able to get in the room."

"An old man?"

"Yes. He was confused and had wandered onto the hotel property. The room boy made him leave."

"What did he look like?" The only old man I could think of was Mr. Cha's servant. And there was Mr. Cha, who admitted to being old but didn't look it.

"Old, miss, gray and bent. Walking with a stick."

That didn't sound like his servant. If it had been him, the room boy probably would have mentioned how evil he looked. Or would he? I wondered if he looked evil to the locals, or only to Westerners. I picked up my books and stamps. "Thank you. To bed. Tomorrow is another day."

"Where do you go tomorrow, miss?"

"The old palace foundations, Phimenakas, and Preah Palilay, the small Buddhist temple."

"Mrs. Martha too? I do not think she can do so much walking."

"She's in better shape than the rest of us. Don't underestimate Martha."

"Her injury. Is it better?" He looked sincerely concerned.

"She doesn't complain, and when we ask, she deflects our questions. She's been insisting on going everywhere."

"Yes, I see. Very stubborn, I think. Like my grandmother. I think sometimes when a person gets old, they get very stubborn about what they want. About what they can do. They feel they can do anything and should be allowed to do what they want."

"Yes. Tenacious, like a dog with a bone." I thought of her and Mr. Cha the other evening. By the time she had finished with him, he was looking quite irritated. "Goodnight. Oh, wait, I've been meaning to ask you. Do you have bicycles for rent?"

"I'm afraid not. But if you would like to borrow my bicycle while I am working, you are most welcome."

"That's very kind of you. If you're willing, I'd love to borrow it in the morning for an early ride. What time do you arrive?"

"I am here at five."

"My goodness, what a long day. I'm happy to pay to rent the bicycle."

"Not to worry, miss."

Which wasn't a no. I had to remember to bring some money down with me in the morning. I hoped he wouldn't mind if I took a long ride. My bicycle muscles were itching for exercise, and the thought of riding out to the temples by myself was like the promise of water on a desert island.

28

It was dawn, a risky time on the road, because the traffic was already heavy and the visibility wasn't good. Luckily I'd brought a flasher, which I'd adjusted on the back of the seat and promised to leave with him went I left, payment for the use of the bike.

Our hotel sits on the main road leading to the ancient temple precinct. Bicyclists vied with tuk-tuks carrying goods and, in one at least, six young women. But the worst threat were the tourist buses that streamed toward Angkor Wat for the sunrise. All in a hurry to get their people to that causeway on time. All bigger than me and seemingly unconcerned about the little people, the pedestrians and bicyclists.

I stopped at the kiosk that allowed entry into the four-hundred-square-kilometer Angkor Archaeological Park, showed my pass that I'd purchased the first day, and continued on. The road was wider at this point, and the buses flew by me. There was an occasional close call with the people walking toward town for work, but negotiating traffic would be easier once I reached Angkor Wat, the first temple one encountered. The bus traffic would diminish after that, though it wouldn't stop altogether, as some would continue on to the Bayon so the tourists could photograph the towers in raking light to better capture the details of those eerie faces.

I veered around a herd of Japanese tourists crossing toward Angkor Wat, all carrying flashlights in the dim dawn, all oblivious to everything but their feet or the guide holding a white flag at their fore.

Picking up speed, I continued my journey north toward Neak Pean. Adjacent to the late twelfth-century Preah Khan, the small temple sits on an island in the middle of a tank. A good distance to ride, and a jewel of a temple. My lungs filled, my legs pumped. I was in my element. To avoid the tourists, I flew past the west side of the Bayon, the faces on the tower only hinted at in the pale light, then on past the palace, its walls merely dark masses.

The road became more deserted, except for occasional motorbikes bearing entire families heading away from their homes, to work or school. I heard one behind me, maybe a guard headed toward a temple or returning home after depositing someone in town.

The entrance to Preah Khan loomed to my right, but I continued until I was past its outer precincts, where I turned toward the east. Not too much farther to go now. The trees thinned, and the landscape filled with scrub. The air was crisp after the night's rain. I turned down the dirt road toward Neak Pean. The sound of the motorbike behind me cut off somewhere nearby, and I was engulfed in silence.

There was no guard in sight, so I could ride all the way up the dirt track to the northern spout that emptied the tank during the rainy season. I'd been here in the dry season, when no water surrounded the tiny temple island, but even then, tourists were confined to the stone walkway around the tank and weren't allowed to approach the temple on the island at its center. I didn't mind that; it added to the mystique of the place.

I hoped the motorbike behind me wasn't the guard, who would probably throw me out at this early hour. I propped my bike against a tree, walked the short path to the edge of the pond, and began to make my way around, looking at the building, the carvings of Lokeshvara on the exterior walls, the serpent that coiled at the base of the circular foundation supporting the small, elegant tower. This was the temple I'd mentioned to the group when we were looking at the Lokeshvara images at Banteay Chhmar. The rising sun made the pond water glisten, and I threw a stone in to watch the colorful ripples.

When I came to the eastern side, I stopped and looked toward my bike and the dirt path, expecting to see a guard, or another tourist seeking an early morning moment of silence at this isolated site. No one came. In front of me stood the huge stone Balaha, the horse incarnation of Lokeshvara who saved a group of shipwrecked sailors from ogresses on an island. The sailors clung to the massive horse to keep from falling into the sea. Nice to have a savior, I thought.

I heard movement in the brush and trees behind me. When I looked around, it stopped, and when I turned back toward the temple, I heard leaves rustling, branches swishing. Someone was trying to be quiet. I thought of the motorbike I'd heard and my bicycle, not so far away. I continued walking in that direction as nonchalantly as I could but slowly picking up speed. Leaves rustled; twigs snapped. It was all I could do to keep from looking in the direction of the noises, but if someone was following me, I didn't want him to know I heard him.

The sound increased. I redoubled my pace, mentally assessing the distance between my bike and me. I couldn't outrace a motorbike, but if I rode west through the fields toward Preah Khan, I might be able to evade one. The field, inundated during high rainy season, would be bumpy and difficult to ride, as would the temple compound, strewn with fallen stones. I just hoped the field had drained enough to allow a bicycle, but not a motorbike. I broke into a run and heard the person behind me pick up speed.

"Hey," a voice yelled from the dirt path up ahead. "No open. No open."

A man materialized. Disheveled and wearing only a *lungi*, he gesticulated at me, at the bike. He must have been sleeping nearby and been woken by the motorbike or the sound of me—us—walking around. The footsteps behind me retreated.

"No open," he repeated, coming up to me.

"Sorry," I said, looking back for a glimpse of whoever had been hunting me, but there was no one in sight. Had I imagined it?

The guard—I supposed he was the guard—pointed at my bike. "No open."

"Okay, I'm going." I handed him a dollar, which seemed to appease him.

As I picked up my bike, he was looking over his shoulder. He must have seen both the bike and, further down the path, the motorbike. Then I realized that even if I cut through the field and Preah Khan the stalker could easily catch up to me on the road into town. I'd be even more vulnerable on my bike then I was here. I rode my bike the first fifty feet.

The motorbike was parked at the edge of the path. The guard was between the stalker and me, unknowingly holding him at bay. I got off my bike, pulled my pocketknife from my fanny pack, and stuck it into the front tire. That should slow him down, I thought. But for good measure, I stuck my knife into the rear tire as well.

The guard yelled something, and I jumped back on my bike. Hurrying down the dirt path, I saw that the field was still inundated with water. Luckily his flat tires meant I didn't need to go that way.

I heard the engine start up behind me and then the motorbike begin to move.

I turned left onto the main road, listening to the motor's sound, louder, faster, moving closer. I shifted into a higher gear and pedaled with all my strength. The motorbike turned onto the road and traveled a short distance before the engine cut off.

I didn't let up until I came abreast of Angkor Wat, where the buses were reloading, the crowds a fog of safety. I downshifted, but didn't slow. I'd wanted an aerobic workout, but fleeing from a predator wasn't what I'd had in mind.

ODD, I thought, sipping my espresso, fingering the page. I recalled a sculpture in that niche. I turned back a few pages in the Sambor Prei Kuk monograph I'd purchased at the gift shop, looking for a photo of the standing male deity that had enthralled me on our visit to that site on the first helicopter trip, but I couldn't find one. Perhaps the sites were merging together for me, as they seemed to be for everyone else. I'd have to look at the photos I'd downloaded onto my computer.

"You look wide awake." Alam pulled out the other chair at my breakfast table. "May I join you?"

"Yes, of course." I closed the book and set it on the floor next to my purse. "I went on a bike ride."

"Already? No wonder you look so perky. Where did you ride?"

"Out to Neak Pean and back."

"And you're perky, not exhausted? That's quite a ride to have taken before eight in the morning."

"Exhilarating." I thought of my pursuer. "But I didn't have time for a shower, so don't get too near me." No sooner were the words out of my mouth than I regretted them. The last thing I wanted was for him to think about getting near me.

"Okay, I'll take that advice." He looked around the room for others in the group. We were the first. "So today we have a morning excursion to some minor temples, then the afternoon free?"

"Yes. Everyone needs some down time. Myself included."

"Would you be interested in a visit to a spa? The reviews say it's Siem Reap's best. And a few margaritas at the Mexican restaurant?"

"Mexican?" I laughed. "Sounds tempting. But I thought I might visit a few more sculpture studios."

"Does that count as down time?"

The waiter arrived, and I was saved from answering. "Would you care for coffee, sir?"

"Yes, please. And a cheese omelet."

"I will prepare that for you now, sir. There is a buffet, as you see."

"Yes, thank you." He folded his napkin onto his lap. "Will P.P. return today?"

"I don't know. He hasn't contacted me." I appreciated that he wasn't pushing me about the spa and the margaritas. I wasn't sure if that meant he understood my answer as a no, or if he knew me well enough to recognize that if he pushed at all, I'd only step back.

"May I ask you a question?"

I hesitated. "Yes."

"Yesterday, when we were at the sculpture studio, you had a look on your face."

"A look?"

"Yes, as if something had dawned on you, as if you had come to some sort of realization."

I was surprised that he could read me so easily. "I think what I realized was how distinctive his style is and that I was becoming familiar with it."

"I don't understand. Had you seen his work before?"

"Oh, I guess I didn't say yesterday that P.P. and I had met the sculptor in Bangkok. A dealer took us to see him. He was in the middle of working and not too happy to have us there. About all he said was that P.P. could purchase the sculpture he was completing for $35,000."

"That much? For a copy of an ancient Khmer-style sculpture?" He refolded the napkin he had in his hand.

"No. It was modern and gorgeous. He's extremely talented. You have to feel sad for him that he probably makes most of his money sculpting copies of old works when he should be given an opportunity to express his artistic abilities." I looked at my empty plate. "I'm going up to the buffet."

We both stood. "Is P.P. going to buy the sculpture?"

"Yes. That's why he went back to Bangkok. Of course, he didn't know that the sculptor was here. That was a surprise, a Thai sculptor working in Siem Reap. I wonder how the locals feel about it."

"Indeed." As we arrived at the buffet, the waiter came up with Alam's omelet. Alam took it and added a roll and a few pieces of ham to his plate.

The ham surprised me. "Go ahead. I'll be right back to the table." I'd picked up a roll and was eyeing the lovely French cheeses.

"The Camembert is particularly good," Alam said "Would you cut me a little, too?"

Oh, dear, I thought. I'm having breakfast with this man. A dangerous step for me. It seemed he was ignoring my assertions that nothing more could happen between us.

Back at our table, I pushed half of the Camembert onto his plate before sitting down. He snitched a piece of the goat cheese I'd taken.

"Hey," I said, putting a hand over the plate to protect my territory.

He smiled as he put it in his mouth.

I studied my cheese. "I went back to the sculptor's studio after the dealer left."

"What dealer was that?"

I swallowed hard. "The one who was decapitated."

His hand stopped halfway to his mouth, and he put his fork on his plate. "Decapitated. Right after taking you to the sculptor. Like the man in Atherton who owned the Radha head?"

"Yes. But it has to be a coincidence."

"Do you honestly believe that?"

"No. Not for a minute." I rubbed the back of my neck.

"Are you worried about P.P. in Bangkok?"

"I've been trying not to be." I spread some Camembert on the perfect little round roll. I wasn't following my morning diet, but I had burned a lot of calories during my ride. Guilt assuaged, I took a bite. I considered telling him about Neak Pean, the motorbike, the person following me. But with the bright sun flooding the room, this man seated opposite me, I felt safer now and had almost convinced myself that I'd imagined it.

"Are you afraid for yourself? This does give entirely new meaning to that snake."

"A snake? Not another snake?" asked Martha, who had snuck up on us.

"The *nagas* on the causeway to the Bakong. Alam likes those snakes."

"How's that cheese?"

"Sublime. I've been avoiding it all week, Alam sits down to join me, and what do I do but let him talk me into ignoring my diet?"

"You don't need to be on a diet. Not with that figure."

A flicker of a smile and a raised eyebrow on Alam's face.

"I'm going to get some of that cheese. And an omelet." She set off.

"Why are you smiling?"

"The way you let her know that we didn't come to breakfast together."

"Well, I don't want them to get any ideas."

He ignored me. "But it does make that snake more worrisome. You shouldn't ride off by yourself in the dark early in the morning."

"Why? Do you want to come with me?" I challenged him.

"Where can I get a bike?"

"Good morning," said the Jollys in unison.

"Morning." I didn't answer Alam's question.

"That omelet looks yummy," said Mrs. Jolly, peering down at Alam's plate.

"I thought you were only eating fruit," said Mr. Jolly as they headed to the buffet table.

"Let's not talk about it here," I said. I wanted to get up and get another roll, but controlled myself.

"About the bike?"

"No, the snake."

"Did you see another snake?" asked Courtney, her voice rising.

"No, no more snakes."

"C'mon, c'mon. Good morning," Barker said automatically, not stopping to sit, and moving her toward the buffet.

"I feel as if I'm in a situation comedy," I said to Alam.

"Except nobody is laughing," he said under his breath.

Mrs. Jolly sat at a nearby table. She placed her napkin on her lap as she surveyed her very full plate. "I feel much more relaxed now that Arthur is gone," she said. "He's a horrid man. I think the group will be ever so jolly now."

One and all laughed and exchanged glances. Mr. and Mrs. Jolly were the only ones who didn't know that "Jolly" was their nickname.

She looked up, but only for an instant before returning to her omelet. "Not just my husband and me."

Up to that moment, she had seemed so docile, so cheery and spacy and out of touch with all that was happening around her. Before I could assure her that we didn't call them the Jollys in mockery, but in admiration, Barker sat down a few tables away, a pile of pastries on his plate, and asked, "We have the afternoon free, right?"

"Yes."

"I've been thinking about that *apsara* I bought from the sculptor."

Uh-oh, I thought. I hope he isn't going to back out.

"I told him to send it to our Napa address, but I've decided I want to install it in the city, out on the patio. It doesn't seem right putting the fake with the real, do you think?"

"No, not really. I hope they haven't already packed it up and shipped it."

"Me, too. I'll go by this afternoon and change the address."

"Good idea."

"I've been studying this morning's temples," said Courtney, holding up her guidebook. After taking a long time at the buffet, she had arrived back at their table with a few pieces of fruit and a small bowl of muesli.

"Good for you. And with that as my cue, I am going to go gather my thoughts. I want to be as prepared as you all are. Enjoy your breakfast." As I stood, Alam grabbed the last bite of cheese from my plate. I was about to tell him he shouldn't do that or people would get the wrong idea, but then it occurred to me that that was exactly what he wanted. For the first few days, he had been the last one down for breakfast.

29

"Girls," P.P. said as he poured me a small scotch, having dragged me to his room upon his arrival from Bangkok.

I hoped he wasn't getting stingy. It wasn't that I wanted to drink. I just liked the taste of this stuff. I took the glass as he handed it to me, pushing thoughts of my brother and father from my mind. I set it down, watching the amber liquid quiver as the glass touched the table. It was early in the day to be drinking. Still, I had eaten lunch and didn't have any plans for the afternoon except a possible trip to a spa. I wondered how single-malt scotch mixed with margaritas.

"You're pacing," I said.

"Girls," he said again.

I extended the arms of the chair and put a leg up on one of them. It wasn't so comfortable, so I put my leg back down, and picked up my glass. Surely he could understand that just the word "girls" conjured an endless list of interpretations. I thought first of the Bangkok entertainment district Patpong. Maybe he had gone to Patpong while he was in Bangkok, and . . . But I didn't want to know, and would he really announce his hanky-panky to me? After all, I knew his wife.

I gave up. "Girls what?"

"Kidnapping."

"In Patpong? Yes, I suppose—"

He scowled. "Are you daft? No. Mr. Cha."

That brought me up. "What are you talking about?"

"His house. Girls. Thai, Khmer, Indian, a Balinese. Others? Maybe."

"How did you discover that? I thought you went to Bangkok to see about your sculpture. You didn't tell me you were going to see Cha."

"No. Yes." He took a sip; his glass was much fuller than mine. P.P. rarely drank in the daytime, but it seemed to have become a habit for all of us since our arrival in Siem Reap. Usually beer.

"You have to explain, P.P. I don't want to play twenty questions."

While P.P. paced, I brought the scotch to my lips, felt the liquid on them, and didn't swallow. Drinking before going on a date with Alam was a bad idea. It wasn't a date, really, just a visit to a spa, shopping for a present for his mother, cocktails, then dinner. I swirled the whisky in my glass.

When I itemized our plans, it certainly sounded like a date, especially when you added in the fact that we'd had breakfast together, the most intimate meal one can share with another person.

"Cha invited me. Wasn't there. A girl answered the door. Cook. Indian. She asked me to help her."

That woke me up. "I don't understand."

"One of his goons was there. Didn't speak Hindi. She asked in Hindi."

"What can we do?"

"Done." He smiled complacently.

"What do you mean, done?"

"I called the police."

"And they came? While you were there?"

"No. I'm not an idiot." He sipped his scotch.

"You don't think that Mr. Cha will figure out that you were the one who called?"

He stopped his pacing. "How?"

"Deduction. You went to the house, spoke Hindi to one of his girls, then the police came. What did the police do?"

"Took the girls."

"Including his cook?"

That stopped him short. "He won't like that. Can always find new girls, but a great cook." He shook his head and began pacing again, this time a little faster.

"This is not going to stand you in good stead with Mr. Cha. You didn't end up seeing him, I assume." I thought for a moment. "What does this mean?"

P.P. sat. "What?"

"What does this mean about Mr. Cha? What kind of person is he?"

"Logging." He nodded to himself as if he'd answered the question.

"Well, that isn't good, but it isn't kidnapping. Kidnapping suggests a whole other level of deceit, of criminality. A complete disregard for other people."

"Entitlement."

"Yes, that." I swished the scotch around in the glass. "A devaluation of human life."

P.P. bounced in place.

I looked at him, his roundness. I thought of Mr. Cha and how different they were, but how similar they looked, and I choked on the sip of scotch I'd just taken.

"What?"

"Do you remember when we went to the sculptor's house?"

He waited, the bouncing increasing.

"And his wife looked startled when she opened the door?"

"Yes."

"Then the sculptor pulled away from you when you walked up to him?"

"No."

"He did. And I believe they thought you were someone else."

He got where I was going. "Ah. Cha."

If I hadn't known better, I would have thought he was speaking Hindi, saying *acha*, yes. Which he was, in a way.

"So they know he's a scary person."

P.P. nodded.

"But then why were they afraid of him? What does Cha hold over them?"

He was thoughtful, then said, "Thai."

I waited, then held my palms up to ask him for more.

"There were Thai girls. He kidnapped his daughter?"

"Could be. Could well be. And if he's holding his daughter, the sculptor would do his bidding."

P.P. sat, and we both contemplated the amber liquid in our glasses. I put mine down. It really was too early. P.P. took a sip of his.

"Is it possible that he's also dealing fake sculpture? I don't quite see it. The money he makes from logging, from his companies in Thailand, must far exceed what he can make selling Khmer sculpture in Bangkok."

P.P. shrugged, finished his scotch, and poured more.

I sat up. "Unless he has a way to sell directly to collectors in the West, where values are so much higher." I picked my glass up again. "And he has control over a sculptor capable of carving the highest-quality fakes around."

P.P. nodded.

"He could just be taking advantage of that situation. Maybe it wasn't something he planned, he just fell into it. Cha went to see the sculptor, saw his daughter, kidnapped her then or later, then forced the sculptor to work for him."

"Could be."

I continued. "Planting the sculptures at temples seems difficult to us, but if Cha has people working for him here in Cambodia—which he does if he's doing logging—"

"A network of people."

"Exactly—an army of people for all we know—then it wouldn't be so difficult for him to arrange." I stood and walked to the window, wondering at degrees of criminality, whether kidnapping and murder were on par. "It just doesn't make sense. He's a wealthy man who doesn't need to kidnap girls. He could pay them a high salary and they'd work for him. He doesn't need to sell sculptures—imagine how much he's making from his logging."

"His houses," said P.P.

"Exactly. He can afford to hire the best architects, to find the best building materials. He doesn't seem to have a family."

P.P. said, "We're wrong."

"We must be wrong." I took another swig. "Except that those girls were in his house."

He nodded.

"He's going to be very pissed at you. Very pissed."

P.P. took a swig of his drink.

"Why did you go to his house? Did he have art he wanted to show you?"

"Sell."

"He has art that he wants to sell you? When did he tell you this?" Before he could speak, I answered my question. "When you were canoodling over in the corner the other night, I suppose."

"Yes."

"Stone or bronze?"

"Stone."

"Strange that he told you to come to see him and then he wasn't there."

"No set date. Wasted trip. Sculptor not there either. I have to go back."

"P.P., you can't go back there. As far as I'm concerned, you've cut any ties with Mr. Cha. And the sculptor, he's here. Remember we were going to a sculptor's studio? Well, it turned out to be his."

"Here in Siem Reap?"

"Yes. It's a school, and they were all making your head."

I could see he didn't like that, and I realized, or rather I knew with more certainty, that his unhappiness over the head had to do with his pride more than anything else. He'd chosen a modern work. He'd made a mistake. An understandable mistake—I'd thought the head was real when I first saw it, too. "Your head was carved by the master sculptor, not one of his students. There's no comparison."

"Let's go." He put down his glass, stood, and shut the window. "Maybe we can't go to Cha, but we can go to the sculptor."

"I can't. I have other plans." I turned back to the window, the view, but when he didn't say anything, I looked back at him.

He was squinting at me. "A man."

"Why do you always assume a man?"

"Usually a man. Any man. Different man."

I harrumphed and took a last look out the window at the hotel grounds. "We can go there at some point. The group has revolted and opted for a morning off, not just the afternoon. Our only plan for tomorrow is in the late afternoon. We'll go first to Preah Khan and Neak Pean, then to the Bakheng to watch the sunset. Vuthuy has arranged for us to ride elephants to the top of the hill. You remember, we've driven by that temple on the hill half a dozen times."

He sat back down.

"You'll wait for tomorrow, won't you?" I walked back and set my glass on the table. The kidnapping had me worried. Helping those girls get away wasn't going to ingratiate him with Mr. Cha. I still wasn't sure about the sculpture. I just couldn't imagine it was enough of a money-maker to warrant this much drama. Of course, maybe it wasn't just about money, but was instead about power, if Cha was responsible. Or glory, if the sculptor was.

He stood and opened the window as if that was an adequate answer.

30

Men. My downfall. We tuk-tukked down the road toward town. The sticky monsoon heat that lay like a blanket over Siem Reap drained away any desire to walk.

"This place must have gone through some changes these past twenty years," Alam said, nodding toward the restaurants and hotels that lined the opposite side of the canal that bordered the main road. "I wish I'd come here then."

"Yes. I have a friend who was here in the early nineties. He said that when they went to see the sunrise over Angkor Wat, there were only a handful of people."

"Now the masses." A tourist bus swooped past us just as we turned down a side street. They seemed to have taken over the city, huge buses disgorging Chinese and Korean tourists who rushed en masse into the temples, then out again to visit the next. We bounced from one pothole to another, and I was uncomfortably aware of my shoulder rubbing up and down on Alam's arm as we did. On one particularly big bounce, he protectively put his hand on my knee. "Here's the spa."

"How'd you find out about this place?" I asked as I climbed out and he reached over to pay the driver.

"Online, then I double-checked with the assistant manager."

"After that ride, I feel like I need a massage." I rubbed my lower back.

"Then you've come to the right place." We climbed the few steps to the open veranda. It looked like a 1950s stage set for a bungalow in a tropical paradise. Bamboo ceiling fans moved lazily above us, potted plants surrounded clusters of rattan chairs. Two young women in sarongs and modest white shirts with cap sleeves smiled as we entered. Traditional music flowed around us.

"Good afternoon, sir. Good afternoon, madame." Three attractive women about my age stood at reception. "Can I help you?"

"We'd like to get massages," said Alam. "Can we see what you have available?"

She passed us a brochure and we pored over it. They had couple's massages, and I suddenly saw the pitfalls of this particular activity.

"Just a traditional massage for me," I said, putting down the brochure like it was a hot potato.

"No manicure, pedicure, facial?" Alam asked.

"No, no, that's okay."

He shrugged. "Two traditional massages."

"I'm sorry, sir, but we are booked now."

"Oh. What time can you take us?"

"We cannot today. Will you be in Siem Reap more days that you can return? Tomorrow we have time in the late afternoon."

"Yes, we're here a few more days. Anything available tomorrow morning?

"No, sir."

"Then we'll have to get back to you about a time. May I have one of your cards, please?" He turned to me. "Sorry, it should have occurred to me they'd be booked, given the great reviews they get. We'll have to figure out another time."

"Yes." I asked, "The market is just a few blocks, isn't it?"

"Yes, just a short walk." She pointed out the direction.

"Thank you. You don't mind walking, do you?" I asked Alam.

"We could try a different spa."

"No, no, that's okay. We'll come back another day." I hoped the relief didn't sound in my voice. "Now we can get your mother those cushion covers."

"Sounds good. A few gifts for other family members wouldn't be a bad idea either. Any thoughts for my sister and her family? She has two children, eight and ten."

"I'm sure we can find something." We fell silent as we came to the corner of the main road. Buses and cars and tuk-tuks kicked up more dust on this paved road than one would think possible during the rainy season. The dust did at least give one the feel of a provincial capital, of a time in the past, before tourism had taken over this sleepy town.

"There's another spa." He pointed.

"No, shopping is our mission now."

"You're relieved that we aren't having a massage."

I stopped, the pros and cons of answering truthfully coursing through my brain. "Yes. I think that I am. I don't want . . . I mean, I like you and all."

"I hope so."

"I like you, but I don't want to be with you."

He moved directly in front of me. "I get that intimacy terrifies you."

I took a step back, illustrating my terror. "I just really . . . "

"Let me finish. I think there is something here and I'd like to find out what it is. We may end up best friends. We may end up together. We may never speak to each other in a year's time."

I nodded.

"I'd prefer that you didn't nod at that last." He smiled. "Can we be open? Are you willing to try that?"

He must have seen the confusion on my face and wisely said, "Just give it some thought. We aren't jumping into anything. There's no pressure."

"Okay," I said, though I thought the conversation felt like pressure. At the same time, it was the least amount of pressure such a conversation might exert.

"Now to the task at hand. I'm thrilled to have someone help me with shopping. I always seem to overthink it." He lightly touched my elbow to steer me forward.

"I'm a pro. And I definitely don't overthink it." We arrived at the enclosed market. "Let's walk along the stalls open to the road first and go in from the far end. You can get a sense of what's here before we begin our hardcore shopping. We can wend our way to the stall where I got a good price for silk cushion covers the other day."

The roadside stalls were dominated by the worst of the tourist wares: postcards, appallingly bad bronzes, T-shirts. Alam stopped at one stall that seemed to have older things, but we quickly realized the goods weren't old, they were just terribly dusty. We were about to move on when I glanced in a glass case. "May I see those?" I asked the shopkeeper.

He reached in and began to pull out a tray of American lighters, a favorite sale item.

"No, not those, next to them. The coins."

He grabbed the small dish of tiny coins.

"Where do these come from?" I asked.

"Around the temples. The children find them. They are very old."

Alam looked over my shoulder at the bronze coins. Each coin bore the imprint of a bird and was about the size of a tiny fingernail. I picked up one after another, lining them up, looking for the clearest stampings. The man was correct that they were old. They were from the period following the Khmer Empire, sixteenth to seventeenth century at the earliest. "How much are they? They're very cute." A good idea not to let on I knew exactly what they were.

"Five dollars for one," he said.

"I'll give you a dollar for one, but I'll buy ten of them." I could give them to friends at the museum. They were easy to transport, and would be appreciated because they were old.

"And I'll buy ten as well," said Alam. "So you'll be making a small fortune."

"No, no. I cannot. Three dollars each."

I shook my head as I continued picking through the coins. "Two is our last price. That's forty dollars, if we can find twenty coins that we like. You're doing very well, my friend."

He didn't respond, which I took for a yes, and Alam and I continued picking the best out of the dish. Some were so worn as to be totally worthless, while a few were wonderfully clear. We'd gathered ten between us when he pulled another bowl filled with coins from below the counter. When we walked away from the stall, we were both satisfied.

"Well, that was great," he said, smiling.

What a smile, I thought. Tall, dark, handsome, with a winning smile. Couldn't go wrong with that. Attentive, possibly too attentive. Kind. What was I doing? I wondered if he was itemizing me the same way.

"Now what?" he said.

"That may be the high point of our shopping spree. Let's see. We should watch for more of those coins. Talk about an easy gift," I said. "The eight- and ten-year-olds. Nephews? Nieces?"

"One of each." He slid his bag of coins into his pocket. "I'm not sure if that's what the nurses have in mind for me to bring back, but I might get away with it."

I felt a pang of jealousy. "Do you have many nurses to please?"

He looked embarrassed. "In my office and at the hospital. Quite a few."

"You'd better figure out how many. Don't want to forget anyone."

"No, definitely not. Those are nice." He pointed at the first display of cushion covers that we came to as we entered the main market hall.

The woman stallkeeper saw his gesture, "Sir, silk, silk cushion covers. All colors, sir."

"How much?" I asked.

"Ten dollars only."

"Ay!" I shook my head and we entered the warren of shops, the shopkeeper calling after us. "Eight dollars. For you."

"How much do we pay?" he said quietly.

"Seven, lady. Seven dollars."

I ignored the calls behind me. "I paid four."

"That's much better."

"I wouldn't say that they're the highest quality, but they're all cheaply made here. In the market, at least. They were better quality at the silk-weaving shop."

"But they were charging Western prices at that shop, and I couldn't make up my mind. I'll buy my mother a few extras. Then if they rip, it won't matter."

"Good idea." We wandered, fingering goods, listening to the prices, which ranged from seven to fifteen, until we came to the stall where I had bought cushion covers a few days before.

"You come back," said the elderly shopkeeper. Her face was a wondrous maze of wrinkles. I had gravitated to her because of her traditional dress and because she hadn't tried to drag me to her stall.

"Yes. And I have brought a friend who will pay the same price that I paid."

She hesitated for a moment, then nodded. "Of course, mademoiselle." She looked at Alam. "He is a handsome friend from another country."

"Yes, a tall, dark, and handsome foreigner." I laughed. He looked startled and pleased, and though my first instinct was to cover for my comment, I smiled instead. "A foreigner to you, but from the U.S. like me."

She nodded and asked, "The same colors?"

"Blues and greens are what my mother would like," he said.

She pointed to a pile of covers, then went to the back of her stall to get more.

"How many will you get?" I asked.

"Maybe eight? Ten? They aren't so large. Do you have any larger?" he asked her.

I sat on a stool that the old woman kept in front of the stall and watched the activity of the market. I thought about what Alam had said. It would be nice to have him as a friend. It would be nice to have him as a lover. If only I didn't balk. I watched him pick up one cushion cover after another, arrange the various colors together, joke with the old woman, who instantly warmed to him.

It's hard work being a shopkeeper. So much competition, so little variety in the surrounding goods. I looked past the clothing to the food stalls on the far side of the market. Noodles and seafood, sweets. The place was bustling. Perhaps we should eat here, forget the margaritas and have a more local experience.

At one of the stalls, a man with his head down was eating intently. He looked up and I saw it was the old man who worked for Mr. Cha. The stall owner watched him, an expression of distaste on his face. I thought of Mrs. Jolly and Martha saying he was evil.

Another man walked up, greeted the stall owner, and prepared to sit down, but when he saw the old man he raised a hand and moved away. Two little kids, who had been running around their mother as she sat in a nearby stall, ran in the direction of the old man, but their mother, who hadn't been paying them any mind, suddenly shouted at them, leapt up, and dragged them back.

The food stalls overflowed with people, but the stall where the old man sat, and those around him, were quiet.

"What do you think of this one?" Alam said. "I'm inclined to get plain ones, but this one is quite nice."

"Yes, good, but then get more than one with a design. Any ikat design?" I asked the old woman. Then I turned my attention back to the old man. He pushed his bowl away and stood. I stood, too, wanting to see where he went, how people reacted as he walked through the market. "Be right back."

He cut back toward the fabric section, silence following him like the wake of a ship. Some inched away from him, others diverted their faces. No one wanted to have anything to do with him. He saw me and, without any hesitation, veered in my direction.

He nodded as he brushed past me, those empty eyes not so empty. Filled with threat. Threat and distaste. And then he was gone.

When I returned to the stall, I saw the old woman watching him. "Who is that man?" I asked, breathless, as if he'd sucked all the life out of me.

"Very bad," she said, dragging her finger across her neck. "Very bad. The Ghost."

"I'll take these," Alam said, intent on his purchase and unaware of what had just transpired.

I wasn't sure what had just transpired either.

He handed her the dollars. "Well, that was perfect," he said as she put his textiles in a bag. Then he saw my face. "Are you all right?"

"No, not really. I need to go back to the hotel and lie down."

"What's the matter?"

"Nothing. Just suddenly tired. Nothing."

I felt the old woman's eyes on us as we left. She'd seen me pale. She hadn't seen the suspicious thoughts that were forming in my head.

31

"A little postprandial exercise?" Alam asked as we headed out of the dining room. "Did your nap revive you?"

"Yes, it did. A walk sounds good. Anyone want to join us?" I asked the group.

Over the various no's and no thank you's, Courtney's groan was the loudest voice. Time off from the temples seemed to have worn everyone out. Even Martha, who I was sure would want to come, was nowhere in sight. So I wouldn't have a buffer between Alam and me.

He'd made it clear that we could be just friends. I really didn't know why I felt I had to push him away. Clearly I was drawn to the man, and the time we'd spent together had been pleasant.

He seemed to sense my vacillation. "Not a long walk."

"No, not a long walk."

"Around the square?"

"Sounds good. We can take a peek at the tourist performance across the way. See if it's worth attending."

"Great."

We hadn't walked far when it became apparent that I was the big attraction for the evening. "They're swarming." I swatted at a particularly large mosquito on my arm.

"They do seem to find you tasty. Let's go back. We don't want you eaten alive."

As we headed back toward the hotel, Alam and I and the dozen buzzing creatures needling me, I realized that by walking out alone with Alam I had created the situation I'd been trying to avoid—how I was going to get into my room alone. Not into his room. Not the two of us into my room.

As we climbed the steps and entered the front door, the doorman looked in horror at me and the swarm I'd acquired. They didn't seem to be bothering Alam at all. "Why are you looking so amused?" I asked grumpily.

"You're a mosquito magnet. Never seen anything quite like it. Maybe some vitamin B1 would help."

"How?"

"Changes your flavor."

"You think I'm too tasty?" I groaned. Why do I say the things I say?

Before I could extricate my foot from my mouth, he said, "Yes."

We passed through the exterior corridor that joined the main older building to the new building and climbed the stairs. When we got to the second floor, the lights were out in the corridor and the sound of thrashing was coming from farther down the hall.

"What's that?" I looked at Alam before shouting, "Hey, what's going on down there?"

The thrashing stopped, and I heard feet running down the hall away from us. I was fumbling in my purse for a flashlight when Alam switched on his phone. We could just make out someone lying on the floor halfway down the corridor.

"Find the light. Get help," Alam said, and dashed toward the figure. I ran my hands over the wall, but I couldn't find the light switch and didn't want to leave Alam, so I began yelling for help.

Doors opened along the corridor. Light from the rooms illuminated Alam and the person on the floor, and I found the light switch. Staff came running from behind me.

"We need an ambulance," Alam called.

The doorman reached me first, a waiter and the manager close on his heels. "We need an ambulance," I repeated, and the waiter turned to run back to the front desk. "And the first aid kit," I called after him.

I ran down the hall to Alam, and stopped, stunned to see P.P. lying on the floor. "Oh, my God," I said. "P.P., what are you doing here?"

"You," P.P. said.

Alam began to pull off his shirt.

"What are you doing?" I said.

"I'm going to make a tourniquet."

"No, take this." I pulled off the shawl I had bought at the market that day. "Is he okay?"

P.P. was struggling to get up. An enormous gash in his upper arm spewed blood as he pressed his hand to the floor.

"Stay down. Elevate your arm," Alam ordered. Much to my surprise, P.P. complied.

"We need to get this man to the hospital as quickly as possible," Alam told the receptionist. "Call ahead. Do you know your blood type?" he asked P.P.

"O."

"Tell them we're bringing in a man who will need blood and that he's type O."

A siren wailed in the distance. I knelt on the floor and grabbed P.P.'s hand.

"Did you see him? Who was he?"

P.P. shook his head. "Small. Wiry. Strong."

"Why—"

"You. He wanted you." He looked up at my door.

Of course he was right. In the dark, the attacker would have attacked the person coming to my door. He wouldn't have anticipated that it was someone other than me. He must have been watching the dining room. Seen when we left, rushed up here, turned off the light. Small, wiry. I thought of the sculptor. I thought of the Ghost, and the way he'd looked at me in the market. I thought of illegal logging, kidnapping, and the money to be made from fake sculpture. I thought of decapitation.

I wanted to ask P.P. more, but the concern on Alam's face prevented me. The tourniquet had stopped most of the blood flow from P.P.'s arm, but he'd lost a great deal already. His arm began to drop, and his eyes were closing. The siren came closer. Luckily, the French hospital was nearby, so the ambulance hadn't had far to come.

"Stay awake," Alam said.

I thought they only said that in movies.

P.P. was having difficulty holding his arm up so I stood, took his hand, and held it up in the air. Alam nodded.

Two men with a gurney rushed down the hall from the stairs. Alam was yelling to them, "Type O! IV!"

I felt faint. I don't have a problem with the sight of blood, but I do have a problem with someone trying to kill one of my friends. Not to mention trying to kill me.

"Put your head down," Alam said. He briefly touched my back before taking P.P.'s arm. "He's going to be okay."

The men piled him onto the gurney and began wheeling him down the corridor.

"What happened? Did he have a heart attack?" a woman asked from her doorway. I didn't answer. My eyes were on P.P.'s chest and the way it rose and fell, very slowly.

Alam said, "I'm a doctor. I'll ride in the ambulance with him."

One of the ambulance attendants started to object, but the manager said something in Khmer and he shut up.

"Me, too," I said.

"Not enough room," said Alam, and to the manager he said, "Arrange for her to come to the hospital immediately."

"Did you see the attacker?" I asked Alam.

"No."

"Me neither, just a movement down the hall. He ran quietly, as if he was barefoot."

Alam was pensive as they loaded P.P. into the ambulance. "Maybe. It's difficult to sort out."

As the ambulance drove off, a hotel car pulled up. The manager opened the door for me, then climbed in the front with the driver.

"You don't need to come," I said to him. "I'll be okay."

"No. Yes, I am sure you will be, but I want to make certain your friend will be fine. And you may need a translator."

"I speak French."

"Yes, but the police will come, and they may not speak English or French."

I hadn't thought of that. The hospital was less than a mile, and we pulled in as the doors closed behind Alam and P.P.

"HE'S going to be fine," said Alam, joining me in the waiting room. "He'll need some physical therapy for his arm. Might have damaged a tendon, but they had the blood ready. What blood type are you? They'd like us to replace the amount they used."

"A, I think."

"Not to worry. I'm O, and someone else in the group will be, too." He put his arm around my shoulder. As if he had turned on a faucet, the tears began to stream down my face. He pulled me in close and kissed my forehead. "Our timing was impeccable."

"Not really. If only we'd been a few minutes earlier."

"Then he might have tried to kill you." He squeezed more tightly.

"Not with both you and P.P. there."

"Why was he trying to kill you, Jenna?"

I blew my nose. "Fakes."

"Fakes?"

"Or kidnapping."

That befuddled him. "I get fakes; I don't get kidnapping. Have you kidnapped someone?" he asked, trying to lighten the moment.

"Although if it was about kidnapping, they would have been after P.P. Not me."

"Can you explain?"

I did.

"Before I fall completely in love with you," he said when I was finished, "could you tell me if you're always riding the edge?"

"Not usually, but it does seem to be my modus operandi of late. I guess it's just the life of a curator. People seem to think it's an exotic profession, and maybe they're right."

He looked thoughtful.

I looked thoughtful. Before he fell completely in love with me. Is that what he'd said?

32

"The Khmer gentleman was here to see you," said the doorman as we entered the hotel, exuberant and dripping wet. The sunset had been perfect, the pink sky reflecting the length of the enormous tank, which extended four and a half miles west from the top of the single hill that rose in the midst of the Angkor-period temples. Alone on the hill, in the center of the archaeological park, sat the Bakheng.

Picture perfect one moment, weighted down with clouds the next. The delicately painted cirrus clouds had suddenly massed to dark cumulus clouds and moved our way.

The crowd—for there is always a crowd at the Bakheng for sunset—watched the clouds gather and then, as one, began dashing down the hill as the first rain hit the far end of the enormous reservoir. But there was no outracing the wall of water that moved with surprising speed toward us. Gigantic drops hammered down for the last half of our plummet down the hill. I was glad we had only hired the elephants for the journey up to the temple, as the path turned slippery, and even a surefooted elephant would have had difficulty making it down. As it was, we clung to each other.

Our group was in great spirits, laughing as we made our way through the deluge to the van, hysterical with laughter when the first of us set foot on the bottom step of the minibus and the rain abruptly stopped. Martha had even forgotten the pain in her foot and rushed down the hill with us. The plan had been to go from the sunset excursion directly to a restaurant in town, but we were so wet that we had decided to come back to the hotel to change. I wanted to call the hospital to check on P.P., even though he'd said no more calls or visits today.

"He left a message at the desk, miss," the doorman said, eyeing my wet T-shirt. Or rather, what my wet T-shirt contained.

Khmer gentleman? I thought. I don't know any Khmer gentleman, other than our guide, Vuthuy, who was with us at the sunset. Or Leap, the conservator. "I'm sorry, who left this for me?" I asked as I took the note from the receptionist.

"The gentleman whose house you had dinner at the other night. You and your group."

"But he's Thai."

"No, miss. He lives in Thailand, but he is Khmer." His expression was impassive, but the woman behind the desk pinched her mouth tightly shut in distaste. They were both about my age, dressed in somber black suits and starched white shirts.

"Oh, I misunderstood." I started to leave, then turned back. "Do you know this man?"

"Yes, miss. Everyone in town knows this man."

"How's that?"

He looked at the woman, but she turned and walked to the bank of telephones behind the desk. "He is a very wealthy . . . I mean, he comes here frequently to dine."

"I see. Is he not well liked?"

The woman finally spoke. "I do not know who likes or dislikes him. He is a customer here."

Her message reached the man, who looked flustered and embarrassed.

"Thank you," I said. "And the Ghost. Is he Khmer, too?"

Both paled. "Yes, miss," they said in unison.

"Why is he called the Ghost?"

They looked at each other. "From the Pol Pot time," she said. "He looks like a man from that time who is dead. A man who killed many people."

I nodded. Not so dead, I thought. And not unused to killing people.

I walked slowly toward my room, reading as I went. The note was directed more to P.P. than to me. It was from Mr. Cha, telling P.P. that he was awaiting him in Bangkok, if P.P. would like to come to see him. He explained that he hadn't remembered P.P.'s last name. And that he was sorry to have missed him when he was in Thailand the other day. He regretted that he wouldn't be able to invite him for dinner while in town, as his cook had been detained.

I tapped the paper on my hand. Was there threat in the note? Certainly. I wasn't sure that I should show it to P.P. I didn't want it to inspire him to go to Bangkok. This man. I stopped. I'd misjudged him. He was generous with his collection and his food, friendly, warm, and I'd thought him a good person. I looked at the note again.

The female receptionist clearly didn't approve of the man. Because he was wealthy? Because of his businesses, his logging? For some other reason? Recent Cambodian history could make a person disliked for many more frightening and dangerous reasons than their wealth or their present business.

I tried to sort out whether the man's being Cambodian made a difference in anything that I thought about him. Was he more dangerous because he wasn't Thai? Yes, I thought. As an elderly Cambodian, he was of the generation who had been young during the Pol Pot era. Even so, my thoughts about him might be interpreted as racist, and I balked.

There had been murders and there had been attempted murders, and maybe they led back to him. Grey had said the head came from a collector. Had he meant Mr. Cha? He'd also said he needed to get the head back. I stopped walking. But the head was fake, probably made by the sculptor Grey had taken us to see. If Mr. Cha had commissioned the head . . . I searched in my pocket for my key.

Maybe Grey had thought the head was authentic and discovered it was a fake. Was that why he was murdered? I backtracked. When had Mr. Cha learned how good the sculptor was? When he made the replacement head for Radha? Of course, that didn't explain anything I suspected about the other fakes he'd made and that had been planted at temples.

I opened my door, looking back at the spot where P.P. had lain on the floor as I closed it. I wanted to know if Mr. Cha was responsible for my friend's pain. I wanted to know if he was a murderer.

I shivered. He was dangerous, and his servant seemed worse.

33

I walked past the luxury hotels toward the museum. No group, congenial as they all were, no telephone, no injured P.P.

The temperature approached 95 degrees, and with the humidity it probably broke 100. I flapped the hem of my loose shirt, thankful I'd gotten out of my pants and T-shirt. Traffic was minimal, as all tourists took a few hours after lunch to revive themselves before the late afternoon surge to Angkor Wat, the Bayon, or the Bakheng to watch the sunset.

I was going to look at Buddhas. We had a single Khmer Buddha sculpture at the Searles, a lovely twelfth-century seated Buddha protected by multiple *naga* heads. It had been George Searles's most treasured sculpture. He hadn't given it to the museum in his original endowment, which paid for the building and included over three thousand objects. It came to us at the time of his death, a donation from Mrs. Searles in his memory. It now stood at the entrance to the museum.

The theme was a favorite of the Khmer sculptor: the snakes' hoods spread to protect the meditating Shakyamuni Buddha from a downpour. I was curious to look at comparable examples and to study more closely the stylistic evolution of this image.

When P.P. and I went to the museum our first day in town, I'd noticed one work that was particularly close in style to the Searles sculpture. I hadn't had time to study it when I toured the museum with the group.

"HELLO. I didn't expect to find you at the museum. I thought you'd be sequestered in your room, trying to unwind after days of answering endless questions."

I jumped. "You startled me." I turned back to the Buddhas. Alam stepped closer, where he fit comfortably in the space beside me. As if I had reserved it for him. "My room doesn't hold as much attraction for me as it did before the snake."

"You can always find shelter in mine."

"That was a mistake." Yet I didn't move away.

"A rather pleasant mistake," he said evenly. "But really, what I'm offering is a safe place whenever you need one."

A safe place. A difficult concept for me. Safety sounded foreign. Boring. "Thank you. That's kind." The Buddha before me was a cousin to the example at the Searles. The tall, pointed headdress, the rather flat face, the fine details of his jewelry could have been carved in the same studio, though the position of the legs and tension in the body were different enough that the same sculptor could not have carved both. "This is close in style to the Searles's Buddha."

He nodded. "I still can't get used to the jewels and headdress the Buddha wears. If you hadn't told us about the Vajrayana ceremony, the crowning of the initiate, and how it might explain this iconography, I would have thought these were all fakes." He swept his arm in a wide arc, encompassing the room full of Buddha.

I felt him drawing me in and turned to move on to the next sculpture. He followed, moving closer as he did. "Yes, that ceremony and, of course, the historical Buddha's association with royalty are strong." I turned toward him, almost bumping noses. "Why are you here?"

"I needed to walk, so I started toward town and the market-place. But it was so terribly humid, I decided I'd do better to walk here and get the remainder of my exercise somewhere relatively cool."

"Ah." We were as close as we'd been. I didn't move away, nor did he. I felt as if I couldn't breathe. I felt as if I could breathe more easily than I had ever been able to breathe.

"I didn't mean to interrupt you. I'm going to go look at the Hindu sculpture. My father asked me to send him some photos, and I saw a few pieces the other day that I think he would like." He hesitated, raising one hand as if to touch me, then stepped back.

"They've got you working," I laughed as I steadied myself. "First your mother and her cushions, now your father."

"Yes, I suppose they have. They actually toyed with the idea of joining this little expedition, but I discouraged them." He dug his hands into his pockets.

"Too elderly?"

"No. They're both in good shape, and I'm very close to them. But two weeks together 24/7 might put something of a strain on our relationship."

"That's sensible of you." I walked a few steps to another Buddha Muchilinda, and the spell was broken. "Why does he want you to look at Hindu sculpture?" Alam's family was Muslim, and depiction of the human figure is of course prohibited in Islam.

"Our town had an important Hindu temple, and one of the priests befriended him. An unlikely pair in this day and age, the Muslim doctor and the Hindu priest, but it wouldn't have been a century ago. Or even when my father was a young man. Because of the priest, my father became interested in the art."

"Ah." I looked up at the Buddha, the hands, the jewelry, the upturned lips. He looked down on me. "I'm going to do a little serious looking here."

"See you later," he said as he walked away.

I watched him, both relieved and disappointed, but decided relief was the best, most appropriate emotion. Maybe he felt as I did and wanted to put that night out of his mind. Stupid thought. It didn't seem that even I wanted to put that night out of my mind.

An hour later, I was pleased to find him still in the museum, sitting on a bench in front of the Radha and Krishna. His hand glided over the small notebook he held, and I could see him vary his pressure as he drew.

"You're an artist," I said, surprised.

Embarrassed, he began to tuck the notebook into his pocket. I said, "May I see?" and sat down next to him.

He turned the page for me. "I had aspirations when I was younger, but my family wasn't happy with that particular vocation for me, so I went to medical school instead."

I took the notebook out of his hand. He hadn't really offered it and seemed reluctant to let it go. "That's a leap, art school to medical school. You are an obedient son."

"I'm sensible enough to realize that one can be a doctor with an avocation as artist, but the reverse isn't true. So it's my weekend pleasure."

He'd been drawing the Radha and Krishna. He was good. He'd captured their postures perfectly, the details of their clothing and jewels, and the charged emotion that flashed between them. This last thought startled me. "Charged emotion" isn't the sort of phrase that one usually associates with Khmer sculpture. I shut my eyes and tried to think of other Khmer sculptures that could be described that way.

Well, tenth-century Koh Ker sculptures could be dynamic in a weighty kind of way, alive, even touching. Elegant, refined, ethereal—these were the adjectives used to describe eleventh-century sculptures like the Radha and Krishna. But charged with emotion, no, never.

"Is it that bad?" he joked.

"No, quite the reverse. May I look at more of what you've drawn?"

He hesitated. "Yes."

I began to flip through the notebook. The most recent pages were filled with temples, temple details, niche carvings, huge trees sprouting from walls. "I didn't see you drawing these."

"I didn't actually draw them at the temples. I took photos and drew from those. We haven't been in one place long enough for me to complete a drawing. I did a couple of sketches on-site, but . . ."

"You were embarrassed?"

He gave that some thought. "More self-conscious. To stop and begin to draw attracts attention. People start to ask to see what you're doing, talking to you as if you're an artist. I'm not an artist. I happen to be someone who likes to draw."

I came to a page with a sketch of Courtney. A good sketch.

"I did that on the bus, when she wasn't aware and no one else was looking."

There were sketches of a few others, including me. I looked poised for something. On the next page there was another, of me looking sad. I wondered if I often looked sad. "You really are very good. You catch people's emotions." I turned back to the drawing of Courtney. "I suspect she wasn't very happy in this one."

"No, she was tired and wanted to get into the pool, not visit another temple."

I flipped to the drawing of me. "What was I?"

"Ready to go, fidgety."

I laughed. "Yes, I look it. And I'm beginning to get fidgety here." I started to shut the notebook, but he reached over and turned the page.

"And here you looked sad." I shrugged, and he flipped back to the fidgety page. "Do you ever stop?"

"Never." I turned toward the sculpture.

He continued sitting, though I could see he was gathering his strength. I'd seen it before, in friends, colleagues, the revving up to keep up with me.

"What about that Mexican restaurant? The description I read particularly mentioned their margaritas."

"Ah," I said.

"The review said the place is especially good on the second try. Sometimes, I guess, one just needs a fresh start." He took the notebook back from me and flipped through the pages, not really looking.

I looked at him, then at the Radha and Krishna. Was it possible we'd fallen under the spell of those two lovers? Maybe he was right. "A fresh start. You're a very persuasive man."

"It's one of my strengths."

"And your other strengths?"

"Persistence. Persistence is at the top of the list." He looked up from his notebook with that direct gaze of his.

Uh-oh, I thought. I'm in trouble. "Okay, margaritas. Speaking of persistence, I need one more look at this lovely couple. I want to imprint them on my brain." I stood and approached the Radha and Krishna, circling them. She leaned into him as lovers do, and though he didn't lean toward her, he did accept her. The balance of revealed flesh with drapery was perfect.

Their sarongs curved high in the back, then swooped down in the front, as the Baphuon-period sarong tends to do. On each of them, the sarong's tie flopped over a jeweled belt that was matched by the necklace that Radha wore. A simple band of jeweled cloth held her braided chignon in place, while his fat curls were tucked behind his ears and hung down to his shoulders.

I stopped my circling and leaned in closer.

"No touching," the guard called from the entrance to the next gallery.

I nodded, then walked around to Radha's other side and looked at her ear. "What is he playing at?" I murmured.

"What?" Alam asked.

"The ears."

He stood and joined me. "Lovely, aren't they? I've drawn a detail here." He flipped through his notebook to a Leonardo page filled with ears and pointed at one.

"This is hers, and this is his." He pointed at another.

"And this one?"

"That's from the Lokeshvara at Banteay Chhmar. I photographed it from all sides. The style seemed rather awkward and clunky to me, but some of the details were quite fine. Especially the ears."

"Yes, the legs are always like tree trunks on thirteenth-century sculpture, as if the artists were afraid of their works falling over or breaking at the knees," I said absently. I was standing very still, my hands on my hips, wanting fragments of thought to coalesce into something I could understand. Into an idea worth thinking.

He looked more closely at his drawings. "They're very similar, aren't they? Is that what you're looking at? If I didn't know better, I would almost think the same artist carved these ears."

"I would think the same."

He walked around to get a better look at Radha's ear. "The sculptor who made the copy of this head has captured Krishna's ear perfectly. Copied it exactly. And Lokeshvara's ear is the same. I'd say both Radha and Krishna rely on that sculpture—or rather, the sculptor relied on it as his model."

"No," I said slowly. "That's not it. The Lokeshvara is from a later period."

"So?" he asked tentatively.

"He carved all three figures. The Radha, the Lokeshvara, and the Krishna. He's fooled everyone into thinking that this sculpture is old and only the Radha head is new. Not an iota of it is old. It's entirely new."

Alam didn't say anything. He just walked around and around the sculpture.

"So they're all fakes? Even this one?" He pointed at Krishna. "Astonishing. But why?"

"I'm not sure. It can't be only for the money. Pride? Revenge?"

"We'll have a lot to talk about over dinner. Shall we go now? You're looking a little pale. I want to get some sugar into you." He took my arm and led me out of the galleries, then called a tuk-tuk over to drive us into town.

"We need to drive by the sculptor's studio first."

"Is that wise?" he asked as he waited for me to climb in.

I shrugged.

"I FEEL disoriented," I said as I lifted the frosty margarita glass to my mouth. The restaurant was painted turquoise and yellow, the chairs and tables red and green. Above, paper garlands extended from the piñatas hung in the corners. Mexican music played low on the sound system, and, disconcertingly, the Khmer bartender was speaking Spanish to a couple of customers.

"You think this is disorienting. We could have gone to the German restaurant a few streets over and eaten wurst and schnitzel. At least this feels tropical." With his feet up on the rung of the chair opposite him, he looked fully relaxed.

I laughed. "No, thanks. German food is a little heavy for this heat. You'd have to be desperately homesick."

"Yes, or feel a craving."

Was his desire to come here a craving? I looked at the brightly colored walls, the bar that at this early hour had filled with youthful travelers, the tostadas that the waitress was carrying to the next table. Ah, the downfall of travelers—if the setting is Western, you think you can eat a salad. "What did the reviews recommend in the way of food, or did they only focus on the margaritas? Which are delicious, by the way."

"Enchiladas, I think. I'll admit that the margaritas were the draw."

"Enchiladas sound a little heavy. How about guacamole and chips? Or maybe nachos?"

"Nachos sound like a good start." He signaled to the waitress.

As we waited for our food, we sank into a companionable silence, each of us content to people watch, to enjoy our margaritas, to think our separate thoughts.

"I wish he'd been there, the sculptor."

"I feel ambivalent about his being there. I was afraid of what he would do when you accused him of carving the entire Radha and Krishna."

I said, "He doesn't seem like a dangerous man to me."

"Not always easy to tell." He poked at his margarita with the straw. "You've solved the puzzle. Now you can stop."

I looked at him incredulously.

He laughed. "I didn't think so."

"No." I thought about what I would do next. "I do think it's interesting that his students said he'd gone back to Bangkok to be with his family." I thought about P.P. freeing the women in Mr. Cha's house.

"Those look good," he said when the waitress set down the plate.

I reached for a chip slathered in cheese and balancing a jalapeño slice. "And they are," I said through a mouthful.

Alam didn't say anything more, just dug in.

"Why did you come on this trip?" It was a question that I wanted answered, but I shouldn't have voiced if I thought he'd come because of me. I mentally slapped my forehead. I kept asking him questions, making comments that suggested I was interested in him.

"A number of reasons." He thought for a moment, then said solemnly, "Further India."

I bristled until I realized he was teasing me. Scholars of Southeast Asia emphasize the uniqueness of the region, not the Chinese or Indian influences, and definitely not the idea of

Further India. We don't like the term "Indochina," as I had explained to the group on the first day of the trip when someone used it. "Very funny."

He grinned. "I've always been curious. I suppose it comes from hearing about the Vietnam war, the genocide in Cambodia. Seeing photos of the temples and the landscape, Bali with those rice fields, Angkor Wat with its towers. Southeast Asia has always drawn me. And, I have to admit, if I were to collect sculpture, I'd probably go in for Cambodian sculpture."

"Not Indian?" I asked, surprised, since he clearly knew a good deal about Indian temple art.

"No. The sculpture in India comes from the temples, and it feels like sacrilege to collect it. Of course, the same is true here."

I frowned.

"You might expect me to say that for religious reasons, having been raised as a Muslim, I don't want any art that depicts humans. But that's not it. I've bought Indian miniatures, though that's not my main interest. It has more to do with the fact the sculpture was initially intended as architectural, actually part of the fabric of the buildings. It was never meant to be portable."

"A moral stand."

"Yes, I suppose." He took another chip, spinning the string of cheese that was attached to it, and asked the waitress for more chips with guacamole and extra-spicy salsa. "And also, I picture my father and the Hindu priest. I only remember seeing them together a few times, but their friendship made an impression on me. As did my father's insistence—even in the light of today's events—that people of different religions can live side by side. That there's no need to fight. I feel that I need to honor my father's open-mindedness."

I thought of P.P. and Alam not getting along. I'd wondered if one being Hindu and the other Muslim had been a factor. Apparently not from Alam's perspective.

"Which isn't to say I would impose my morality on anyone else. Or that I don't like being able to visit museums in the West that have these sculptures. It's not something I've thought deeply about, it just doesn't feel like a good choice for me." He had veered back to the topic of his collecting.

I understood. There were sculptures in Western museums that gave me qualms and others that did not.

He dug into the guacamole, which had just arrived. "You have to try this. It's delicious."

He was right, though I felt a little reluctant about the uncooked tomatoes. One can't always be cautious, I thought, watching him.

"The sculptures," he said. "Can you explain to me what's going on? Why someone made those fakes?"

"I'm not really sure. It could have been for any of the reasons you mentioned."

"And who's responsible?"

"I don't know that for sure either, but I think it's Mr. Cha and the sculptor. Before today, I'd already noticed that the ear of the Lokeshvara, the ear of the replacement Radha—and P.P.'s Radha—and the ear of the *apsara* at his studio were all carved by the same person."

"You didn't notice Krishna's ear?"

"No, I just saw that today, and it has me completely be-fuddled. Though it shouldn't. Both the Radha-Krishna and the Lokeshvara were excavated at temple sites."

"Why? I mean, why would anyone go to the trouble to bury a new sculpture?"

"That's the question." I took another chip and dunked it in guacamole. "The only thing I can imagine is that they want pieces with good provenance."

We both thought.

"I suppose if he has some sculptures that he wants to sell in the West," I said, "he may want to have comparative pieces in place here in Cambodia. But it seems pretty extreme."

"It does. Does that mean the sculptor's the one who killed the collector and the dealer? And if he did, why?"

"No, no, not the sculptor. I think it's Mr. Cha and his minion, the old man." I thought for a moment. "And maybe other minions. I can't quite picture the old man in California, so maybe he sent someone else. I think Grey had figured out what was happening. Or maybe Grey was punished because he took us to the sculptor?"

Alam caught the waitress's eye and pointed at his glass. "The sculptor didn't seem such a bad sort."

"That's my impression too. I'd like to think he's gotten caught up in this against his will. Surely he's making the fakes, but the murders? Maybe he did something illegal and Cha has threatened him. I don't know, I'm just guessing." I twirled the ice in my glass.

Alam offered me a chip with melted cheese and guacamole and jalapeño. I opened my mouth.

I said, "There is another possibility. When P.P. went to Bangkok the other day, he went to see Mr. Cha, who wasn't home. The Indian cook answered the door and begged P.P. in Hindi to help her and some other women at the house to escape."

"You're kidding." He leaned forward in his chair.

"No. And P.P. called the police, who extracted the women. So that means Mr. Cha is involved in kidnapping and for all we know maybe even human trafficking. Which could mean that he has the sculptor's daughter or some member of his family captive."

"It's possible. And why has he tried to kill you and P.P.?"

"Well, we knew the sculptor, and we had the other head. I'm an art historian, and P.P. is knowledgeable about art. Maybe that was enough for them to try to kill me the other night when he injured P.P. instead. That and put the snake in my room, and have that person follow me."

"What person follow you?" This brought him up.

"On my bike ride the other morning."

He frowned. "You didn't say anything about that."

"No. I'm sorry."

"But you haven't gone riding again in the early morning, have you?"

"God, no. It seemed better to stick close to home."

He relaxed a little. "That does seem like a good idea. Do you think it's just money for both Mr. Cha and the sculptor?"

"That I don't know. I have the feeling it's more complex for Mr. Cha. The man clearly has plenty of money. Did I tell you that he's Khmer?"

"I thought he was Thai."

"So did I until the receptionist told me otherwise."

The waitress set down two more margaritas.

"Revenge. But what could the revenge be?" Alam asked.

"I don't know. Could he be mocking the Cambodians by having a Thai sculptor carve important and beautiful Cambodian sculptures? That they put in their museums."

"Do you think they're selling sculptures in the West?"

"Most likely. The thing that confuses me is that the man has money, and this is a pittance compared to what he makes from logging. Maybe some vendetta against a person in government? I doubt we'll ever know."

We watched a party of raucous backpackers cluster around tables on the patio.

"I didn't tell you that when we were in the market, I saw Mr. Cha's old servant."

"The old man?"

"Yes. He was eating over at one of the food stalls. Everyone was avoiding him. One man was about to sit down, but when he realized who the old man was, he left the stall."

He watched me intently.

"The old lady, the shopkeeper with the cushion covers, drew her finger across her throat when she saw him give me a look. And she called him the Ghost."

"What are you talking about? We weren't over by the food stalls. When did he give you a look?" He furrowed his brow.

"He saw me watching him when he was walking out of the market, and he turned and walked right by me. The guy gives me the creeps."

Alam took my hand and squeezed it. I didn't move it away.

34

"Jenna, we're very worried," said Martha. "We've been talking about it—the snake, someone trying to kill P.P. We need to put our heads together and figure out what is going on."

"Jenna," P.P. said. "He was trying to kill Jenna." The van hit a pothole, and we all rose in our seats a good foot. P.P. groaned and held his left arm gingerly.

Mrs. Jolly was patting her head, as if the bump in the road had caused her hair to horripilate. We were on our way to dinner at the young conservator, Leap's, home and she'd been worrying all day about what to wear. She had confided in me that she didn't want to overdress, but she didn't want to underdress. Courtney had arrived at the van bejeweled like an Angkor Wat–period *apsara*.

P.P. added, "He was startled."

"That you fought back? That you clearly weren't Jenna?" Alam volunteered.

"Yes." The car hit another bump and he groaned again. We probably should have put him in one of the hotel cars with its better shock absorbers.

"We're worried about you, Jenna. Someone seems to want to knock you off." Mr. Jolly broke into a smile. "I always wanted to say something like that, and I never thought I'd have the chance at my age."

"Dear, this is not the time to smile about such a thing," said Mrs. Jolly. "We need to discover who's trying to hurt our friends."

"A better starting point would be why," said Martha pragmatically.

Sitting midway in the van, I felt all eyes swivel toward me.

"I don't know," I said meekly.

"Jenna," Alam said firmly. "You owe it to everyone to explain. After all, it's possible, very slightly possible, that the group is in danger as well."

"Why would we be in danger?" Courtney asked, her voice shrill.

"By association," P.P. said.

"Yes," Martha said. "What if the killer has used up all his individual killing tricks and decides he has to, say, bomb the van, or machine-gun us all down?"

"Do you really think that's possible?" Courtney looked terrified.

"Don't be ridiculous," said Barker, scowling at his wife. "No one is going to kill us all. A group of tourists killed? The police would pull out all the stops."

"So fill us in," Martha said.

"Stop the van," Alam told the driver. "Before we get to Leap's, why don't we sit right here for just five minutes while you tell everyone what's happening."

I looked at P.P., then at Alam, who nodded encouragingly. "It all started with the head P.P. bought from Tom Sharpen's estate in Atherton." I gave them the briefest version of the story: our trying to track down whether the head was a fake or authentic, Grey's murder, the fake Lokeshvara. I stopped short of telling them that I thought the Radha and Krishna was a fake, though both Alam and P.P. looked at me expectantly. I also didn't mention, and still hadn't told anyone about, the sculpture I'd seen at Sambor Prei Kuk that wasn't in the older photographs in the book I'd purchased. Like the Lokeshvara at Banteay Chhmar, that sculpture must have been recently placed in the temple. Nor did I say anything about Mr. Cha.

"Right," said Martha matter-of-factly. "Driver, you can continue."

I hoped the driver hadn't understood half of what I'd said.

"Well, let's hope this fellow can help us out," said Barker. "This conservator. He lives here—and at Banteay Chhmar—and has a better shot at understanding what's going on than visitors like us do."

"That's true. But I'm not so sure about involving Leap." I wasn't so sure about having just involved all of them, though I felt a hundred percent safer now.

"I don't care about the fakes," said P.P. as the van pulled to a stop. Having his arm sliced open had been a sobering event. We all looked at him.

"Well, I care more now," said Mrs. Jolly indignantly. "It's uncalled for. Trying to kill someone just because they're trying to find out the truth."

As we climbed out of the van and were greeted by Leap and his wife at the door, I tried to think of a rejoinder to Mrs. Jolly. I couldn't.

"THIS has been a lovely dinner, dear," Mrs. Jolly said touching Leap's wife's hand.

"And such a beautiful hostess," Courtney said, somewhat in awe. Leap's wife, Srey, a dancer, was a great beauty, a celestial maiden from the walls of Angkor Wat. I wished I had the jewels and the silks to dress her accordingly.

I'd seen Courtney slide a couple of her bracelets into her purse when we first arrived at the house. A more sensitive action than I would have thought her capable of.

Leap looked googly-eyed at his wife. "Yes, isn't she?"

"We would love to see her dance."

"I'm sure her company can arrange a performance at Preah Khan for your group. For a fee, of course."

"You mean, inside that temple?" Martha turned to me. "Is that the one close by the temple in the middle of the pond?"

"Yes, that's the one." I thought about my last visit to that temple, the person lurking in the underbrush.

"That would be a fabulous finale to our trip," Mrs. Jolly said.

"I would be happy to foot the bill," said Mr. Jolly.

"No, no," said Barker. "I'd be happy to do it." The two of them put their heads together, arguing over who would pay.

"We leave in three days. Would the troupe be able to give a performance the afternoon before we leave?" Mr. Jolly asked from the huddle.

Leap consulted with Srey, who spoke little English. "Yes, they're free in the afternoon and early evening. They'd be very happy to perform. You won't regret it. The dance really gives the flavor of a performance of old. Especially in that setting."

"Yes," said Mr. Jolly. "We'll do it."

Mrs. Jolly clapped her hands together like a young girl.

"Shall we adjourn to the other room for dessert?" Leap asked.

"More food?" said Martha. "It's been delicious, but I don't know that I'm capable of eating any more."

"Thank you, thank you," Mrs. Jolly said to Leap's mother-in-law, who was refilling her teacup. Other family members were clearing the table. Srey's entire family appeared to live with them. Leap seemed quite content in their midst, and I wondered if his extended family in the States lived together, or if they had adopted the isolate, American way.

"Step up to the bat, Martha. I know you can do it." Mr. Jolly seemed as pleased as his wife by the prospect of the performance.

Martha rubbed her stomach as if trying to discover room.

"Are you all right, P.P.?" I asked as we rose. I'd noticed him gingerly touching his arm a few times, and he looked as if he were beginning to fade.

"Tired. Pain."

"Yes, I've been meaning to ask you all evening how you hurt yourself," Leap said.

"Attacked."

"You were attacked? A mugger? In the market?"

"Hotel. Murderer."

"He was almost killed," said Courtney. "They were after Jenna."

Leap stopped ushering us into the other room, looking from me to P.P. "That's terrible! Please tell me what happened."

"Yes, we were planning on doing that," I said. "We thought you might have some insights that would help us discover who did this to P.P."

"Me?"

"Yes, let's sit and I'll fill you in." In the other room his mother-in-law was placing a platter of sweets and fruits, and we crowded around it.

"SO I think that the only possible reason for someone trying to kill P.P. or me must have to do with the head that he bought at a garage sale."

"It does seem to look that way. But what could possibly be the connection?" Leap held the photo of P.P.'s head in his hand.

"Well, Grey's death ties in, since he's the one who sold the head."

"Yes."

I took a grape, which he had assured me had been well washed in distilled water. "I haven't given you the one part of the puzzle that connects to you. I'm sorry, not to you personally, but it connects to Banteay Chhmar."

"What on earth can that be?"

"The Lokeshvara."

"Ah." he smiled knowingly. "You doubt it, too."

I was surprised. "Do you question the sculpture?"

"Absolutely. I had planned to ask you about it. The surface is too perfect, the face, too. Too, well, modern somehow. I can't put it any more clearly than that. But . . ." He was thoughtful.

"The circumstances of its discovery," said P.P.

"Exactly. That's confusing. It was found, not just buried in dirt, but under at least a half a dozen stones from a crumbling wall. All overgrown with lichen, which makes one believe it had been under them for a long period. Of course that isn't logical when you think about it. Someone could have buried the piece, then thrown some old stones on top that had been lying there."

"Was the lichen where you would expect it? The stones where you would expect them?"

"I couldn't say. None of us could say. We had ordered the workers to clear and level the area by the entrance. And they were supposed to take care while they did it. You never know what you'll find. More tea?" he asked Martha.

"I shouldn't, but . . ."

"So when the workers called to us, saying they'd discovered the piece, any potential evidence—stratigraphy, you might say— suggesting it might have been recently buried had already been removed."

"I see." I thought for a moment. "Do you have any questions about the men who were working on the clearing? Any problem characters? Someone who has found an unlikely number of sculptures or fragments?"

"No, they were all men who've worked with us for a couple of years. You get to know them well and trust them. We've visited them in their homes and celebrated family events with them."

"Could one of them have betrayed you? Someone who needed money for a sick child, something like that?"

"No, I don't think so. Well, there was one, come to think of it. He hadn't been with us long when the statue was discovered.

An older man. The others didn't seem to like him very much. They steered clear of him. I think he may have been working in that area that day, though I don't believe he was the one who found the piece." He thought for a moment. "He came and went, which I assumed had to do with his age."

"When you get back, can you question him?"

"He's gone."

"Gone? Stopped working?"

"He vanished one day. As a matter of fact, I think he vanished the day you came out to the temple."

P.P. and I looked at each other. "Can you describe him?"

"He was older, as I said, but surprisingly strong. Dressed in traditional clothes, not Western trousers. Taciturn and a little crabby."

"One of the other workers must have known him."

"No, I don't think they did. I got the feeling he wasn't one of the locals, though I don't recall being told that. As I said, they avoided him."

"Is there some physical detail that might identify him?" Alam asked.

He thought for a moment. "A scar on his arm, a knife cut, it looked like. And I do recall that his feet were quite extraordinary. Very wizened, so much so that I wondered that he could walk, though he was quite nimble. They looked almost as if they had been bound. I doubt that he was able to wear shoes. But of course, in this weather all anyone usually wears are sandals."

The Ghost. "Well, when you get back, can you ask the workers about him? He may have something to do with all this."

"What time shall we have the performance?" Barker asked. His question came from nowhere, and we all looked at him.

Leap said, "Around four? Would that work?"

Barker was an odd one, seemingly engaged one minute, then changing the subject the next for no obvious reason. Socially awkward, but something else. For a moment I again wondered if he might have killed Sharpen and Grey. But I couldn't imagine how he could be involved with the fake sculpture, which eliminated him from suspicion. That is, if the sculptures had anything to do with the murders.

35

Vuthuy, the perfect guide, charged up the path, feeding us information all the while—the early history of Mount Kulen, the pottery kilns, the reclining Vishnu, the ancient capital that once stood on this mountain sixty-five kilometers from Siem Reap. We caught glimpses of flowing water as we walked, and I saw the others strain to search for the *lingas*, the dozens of phalluses carved into the riverbed, symbols of the Hindu god Shiva.

Vuthuy's ability to project his voice amazed me. He'd talked all the way through the long drive and hadn't let up yet. I would have lost mine by now. His information was good—he made my job easier—and he was cheerful, solicitous of the others, and courteous toward me. He'd asked if I had any books that I might want to leave with him, so he could learn more, and hadn't been shy about asking for information he didn't already have. He aspired to be an art historian—to work in the museum, or in the field at one of the temples where he now led tourists—but he hadn't yet saved the money to move to Phnom Penh to attend university. I wondered if I might be able to get the group to help fund his dream.

Only P.P., his bounce returning after his injury, could match Vuthuy's energy. He was close on his heels, but the rest of us could barely keep up. "Don't worry," Vuthuy laughed. "You're almost there. Not so far, and worth the journey. You have come across the world to see Angkor. Not so far to climb a mountain to see the capital from the time before kings reigned in Angkor." He was walking backwards up the narrow path as he spoke, so we saw the expression on his face when it happened, before it happened, as if he realized what he'd done. As if the trigger he'd stepped on told him an entire story before he'd begun to read it.

The explosion knocked P.P., who had slowed to tie his sneaker, off his feet, and behind him Martha, who was waiting impatiently for him to rise. The rest of us, farther down the slope, could only watch as Vuthuy flew into the air. Into the air without his leg, the blood shooting from his thigh as if it were the fuel propelling him upward, off into space. A downward swoop of blood from his neck, where a piece of metal was sticking out, joining the flow from his leg.

Maybe he really was headed into space, if that is where heaven is. "Don't move!" I yelled. "Don't anyone move. Not an inch."

"I need to help Vuthuy!" yelled Martha, struggling to her feet.

"Don't move," Alam said firmly, reaching forward to grasp her arm. "He's beyond help. And there might be more mines." She wrestled her arm loose. "P.P., block her."

"Stop!" P.P. shouted directly in her face, with such ferocity that it arrested her in her tracks.

I realized that she hadn't heard what Alam said, that P.P. had yelled so loudly because he, too, had been deafened by the explosion. My ears were ringing from the blast.

We waited. It seemed an eternity, but I knew they would come. The landmine team that we had seen at the bottom of the hill knew that sound, the sound any one of the four million landmines still in the ground in Cambodia would make. Alam had spun Martha around so that she couldn't see Vuthuy. Her sobs were heartrending. She'd enjoyed the young man, sitting across the aisle from him on the bus, next to him at lunch.

What the hell was that mine doing on this trail where dozens of people walked every day? A trail that had been cleared years before, where mishaps shouldn't happen as long as you stayed on the marked trail. I looked to either side of us, searching for the big red sign with the skull and crossbones and the word "Landmines," the sign that dotted the countryside, but it was nowhere in sight.

I heard them coming up the path.

"Do not move," the lead man said unnecessarily, then stopped when he saw us standing on the path and, up ahead of us, Vuthuy lying broken in the middle of it. "There?" he asked incredulously.

"Yes. In the middle of the path," said Barker angrily, his arm around Courtney, whose sobs had subsided to an occasional soft sputter. "I thought this area was safe. You don't even have any signs posted."

"No. Safe. For years safe." He turned and spoke to his men in Khmer, then turned back to us. "Please. Do not move."

"We aren't moving. We won't until you tell us," I said. It was as much an order to the group as reassurance to him.

The men went up ahead of us. As the last one passed, I handed him my scarf. He looked puzzled, and I pointed at Vuthuy. He nodded and, when he arrived at his body, spread it over him as best he could. I shivered in the hundred-degree heat.

After half an hour with the metal detectors and careful inspection by eye, the leader said to us, "I will take you down now." He told one of the men with the metal detectors to go ahead. Or that seemed to be what he was signaling.

"Surprising," the leader of the landmine team said as he herded us down the hill, two men taking the lead, checking for more mines along the path. "Not usual, this." He'd pointed at his neck.

WHEN we arrived at the parking lot, one of the members of the landmine team was arguing with a Western couple who were about to climb up the hill. The couple didn't stop insisting until they saw our faces, heard P.P.'s gruff "Blood everywhere," saw it dotting P.P. and Martha, who looked like they'd been painting a ceiling red.

Like us, they seemed to suddenly realize that those signs that one sees everywhere in Cambodia had as much meaning for the present as they did for the past. With that single explosion we weren't just on vacation, we were part of a history so recent, so loaded, so violent, that it had seeped into our lives. The lives of Westerners who had just come to look.

We didn't climb into the minibus right away. I think it was because we weren't all there. We were waiting for Vuthuy to hurry us along, to bring the stragglers to us. But there were no stragglers, and he would never herd another group of tourists.

When they stretched the tape across the entrance to the path and turned to look at us before climbing back to the scene of the disaster, we stepped up into the minibus and into our seats, where the driver had placed icy water bottles.

The ride back to Siem Reap was quiet, each of us absorbed in our own thoughts, until P.P. leaned over the back of my seat and said, "It was for you." Then he leaned back. It was the thought that had been pummeling my brain from the moment it happened. I was their lecturer, surely I would be the one to lead us up the path. The killer hadn't counted on our smart, enthusiastic guide.

A tear slid down my cheek, and I turned toward the window so that no one would see. Was it a tear for me, or for him?

"How did the mine get there?" Courtney asked, bringing me back to the present.

"I don't know. I don't know anything about landmines. Perhaps the trigger was buried deep and the heavy rain eroded the soil over it. I just don't know."

Alam watched me from the seat opposite. I wondered if he thought that I believed my words. Or if, like me, like P.P., he knew that the landmine had been placed there recently. That whoever placed it there must have been nearby, in the jungle, watching as we came closer and closer. Cursing the young Cambodian for being ambitious, for taking my place at the front of the line.

Any suspicion I had of anyone in the group had vaporized with the explosion of the mine.

But I didn't want to say any of this. I didn't want the group to worry. Only a few days left, and we should be able to get out of this country in one piece. Each and every one of us.

AS a single organism, we headed for the bar.

Our favorite cheerful young waiter greeted us. He had already pushed the low tables together and set out half a dozen bowls of nuts. He knew our appetites. "And what would you like today? A pitcher of beer?"

It was a fair assumption. We usually ordered a pitcher when we'd returned hot and sweaty. "A bottle of your best single-malt scotch," I said.

The waiter looked uncertainly at the men, who were lined on one side of the table. The women had the view out the windows.

"My bill," said P.P.

"The second one will be on mine," said Mr. Jolly.

"Oh, dear," said Mrs. Jolly. "I haven't had single-malt scotch for decades."

"Seems like a good time to start, dear," said Martha, gripping a fistful of cashews so tightly that there wouldn't be any salt on them by the time they reached her mouth. "They say it might take a hundred years to clear all the mines."

"Really? That's terrifying," said Courtney.

"There are at least forty thousand amputees in the country. Can you imagine what that means? It means that probably every Cambodian knows or is related to an amputee or someone killed by a mine."

"That sounds as if it may well be right," said Mrs. Jolly. "It's very sad."

The waiter returned with a pitcher of water and additional glasses. "I am very sorry for the trouble you have seen today," he said, averting his eyes from us.

"You don't need to apologize, young man," said Mrs. Jolly firmly. "This doesn't reflect on you."

"It is our burden. Even for the young like me, who were only babies or unborn when those bombs were placed." He held the drinks tray up against his chest, shielding his heart.

"Your burden, but not your doing. We're the ones who should apologize to you. For seeing only those wonderful temples rather than the pain and tragedy of your lives."

As he turned to walk away, Martha asked, "Did you know Vuthuy?"

"Yes. He was friend to my older brother."

"Do you know anyone who has been harmed by a land-mine?" Mr. Jolly asked. "Other than Vuthuy, I mean."

"Yes, we all do." But he left before we could ask him more.

Barker raised his glass. "To Vuthuy."

"Yes, to Vuthuy," I said along with the others.

The scotch hit me like a sledgehammer. It was going to be a long afternoon and night.

36

"Miss Jenna, the police." The fist pounding on the door pummeled my throbbing head.

"Yes, yes." I sat up, though my heavy head felt as if it were still on the pillow. Lovely flavor, that scotch, hideous aftereffect. I tried to recall if we'd eaten as we drank.

Well, at least I'd ended up in my own bed, not the one a few doors away. "I'll be there in five minutes. Nap," I said in explanation.

"Yes. I will tell them." Footsteps echoed down the hall.

I had to duck into the shower before meeting anyone. A minute of scalding water, then a clean shirt, a little eyeliner.

P. P. and a bulky man sat in the far corner of the bar. They rose as I walked toward them. His face was as smooth as a nursing baby's, his eyes bright above youthful cheeks, but his receding hair and slight paunch announced his age.

Without introducing himself, he said, "There were some problems with the landmine."

I thought, yes, it exploded and killed a man. "There were?"

"It was not the usual landmine. It was not an old landmine."

"It was planted. Recently," I said matter-of-factly.

He looked startled. "Yes, it was. How did you know that?"

"It was in the middle of a path where hundreds, thousands of people have walked in the past twenty years. It had to have been planted there."

"And do you know why?"

"To kill me."

The conversation was not going as he had planned, and his implacable face was looking unsure. "Why would someone want to kill you?"

I hesitated. "Because someone has been creating large numbers of fake sculptures and selling them to Western collectors as authentic. They're planting them in temples, to give their sculptors' work authenticity so they can sell other works by the same sculptor. With so-called authentic pieces they can say, "This is like this well-known excavated sculpture." They realize that we've figured this out, and they want to stop us from exposing them. So they've tried to kill me."

He waited.

I waited.

"And can you tell me who this person is?"

What would be the good of telling him? Bribery was rampant. No one with power was ever charged, let alone tried. For all I knew, he was Mr. Cha's ally and would also want to kill me. Of course, if he wasn't in on it, he might be able to help us to stop this man. "No," I said.

He was taken aback. Before he could answer, I said, "I don't know who it is. I have suspicions, but I don't have any proof."

He watched me silently, turned to look at P.P., and looked at me again. "I understand that you have gone to Mr. Cha's for dinner."

Word gets around. "Yes, that's right."

"So you met the Ghost?"

"Who?" P.P. asked.

"Yes," I said.

"So you know," the detective said.

I didn't answer.

P.P. opened his mouth, and I glared at him. The policeman turned to him, and he pretended to stifle a yawn. The man didn't wear a uniform. I wondered if he was a detective, or, because we were foreigners, the chief of police.

I tried to change the subject. "The landmine. How do you know that it was new?"

He waved his hand at my trifling question. "Metal. Numbers." He sat thinking for a minute, and I bit my tongue, because I knew from TV and mysteries I'd read that detectives keep quiet in order to get their suspects to talk. Their suspects, and their witnesses.

"How much longer are you here?"

"Just tomorrow."

"Stay in the hotel tomorrow."

"We can't," I said.

"Why?"

"First of all, because we're tourists. Secondly, we've arranged a performance out at Preah Khan. And it's our last day."

"I would prefer that you stay at the hotel, swim in the pool, have cocktails in the bar, go to the spa." He actually looked at my feet. To see if I'd had a pedicure?

"I'm sorry, but we aren't going to do that. At least I'm not. Maybe some of the others will. I can't believe that there will be another attempt on my life. On any of our lives."

He swiveled his head between us. "Have there been other attempts?"

I hesitated before saying, "Yes."

He sat up a little straighter. "What? Tell me."

"Someone put a snake in my room. A viper. Someone attacked P.P. when he came to my room to ask me a question. The man had turned off the hall lights, so he thought it was me. Someone followed me when I was riding my bike one morning."

"You didn't say," said P.P., looking at me with concern.

He looked at P.P. Trying to assess whether P.P. could be mistaken for me? No—trying to figure out if P.P. was my lover.

"It's not like that," I said.

P.P. frowned, uncertain what direction the conversation had taken.

He stood and we stood, assuming that he was about to leave. But he walked to the window instead. After a few moments, he turned back to us. "What time is the performance?"

"Four."

He nodded. "And earlier in the day? What then?"

"Our plans are still open."

"Let me know. Tell my officer half an hour before you go sightseeing. Not earlier, it is better that no one knows what temple you visit." He gestured toward the lobby, where a uniformed officer was standing. "Tell everyone you can about the performance that you will see at Preah Khan in the afternoon."

"I'm sorry?"

"Tell every employee here, tourists you meet in the dining room or at the temple you visit in the morning. Your pedicurist." He looked at my feet again.

"You want them to find out?" I was incredulous. "Are you using us as bait?"

His eyes had narrowed as he formed his plan. "Not really. I will see you tomorrow." He began to walk away.

"By the way."

He stopped, waiting for me to go on.

"He's killed two other people."

This opened his eyes.

"He decapitated a collector in California who had bought a head by the same sculptor. And he decapitated an art dealer in Bangkok."

He looked from me to P.P. "Who is the sculptor?" I told him the name of the studio, and he wrote it down. "As I said, let the officer know at the last minute."

"Okay."

"He is a very dangerous man. Do not underestimate him. Killing you is nothing to him."

"Who?" I asked. "Which one of them?"

But he walked away.

"He knows," P.P. said.

"Seems so. I wonder if everyone here knows." I looked at the waiter and bartender, who must have heard our entire exchange.

The waiter gave an almost imperceptible nod. Or so I imagined.

37

"We'll meet here in the lobby at three," I said as we slowly climbed the steps to the hotel entrance. Vuthuy's death and our last morning of temple viewing had left us all a little sad and deflated.

"I'm exhausted. That scotch yesterday did me in." Courtney held her head. She'd come down this morning dressed in a sloppy T-shirt and dirty shorts. I wondered where she'd found them in her pristine wardrobe. They certainly made a statement. One had the sense that Barker had heard the statement, as his usual quiet had fallen into silence. "It did me in, but it also made me feel like I was twenty."

"Right," I laughed, and we linked arms.

"We could have lunch in the room," Barker offered tentatively, as if trying to gauge her state of mind.

"Perfect." She gave me a smile, unhooked her arm, and they headed off.

"I'm going to have lunch by the pool," Martha said. "I haven't been in that lovely pool once, and this will be my last chance. Join me?" she asked Mrs. Jolly.

"For lunch, but not the pool. You, dear?" she asked Mr. Jolly.

"Sounds very decadent," he said. "We could get a bottle of single-malt scotch brought out there." Everyone groaned. He laughed.

"I didn't eat much breakfast," I said, "so I'm going to walk into that dining room, sweaty as I am, eat, then take a nap." The headache that had throbbed through the night and into the morning had finally dissipated, and I felt my appetite returning. Thankfully, as I didn't want to miss out on the buffet.

"I'll join you," said Alam and P.P. in unison.

Oh dear, I thought. Though they did seem to have called a truce in the midst of all the drama. Maybe Alam coming to P.P.'s rescue had created a bond that I hadn't noticed. "Well, let's to it."

I SAT, my plate overburdened but not as full as P.P.'s. Alam was still at the buffet.

"What to do?" P.P. asked quietly.

"About what?"

"Mr. Cha."

"I don't know that there's anything that we can do. The detective seemed to know all about him. As does everyone else in town. We've been the only ones in the dark."

"Suppose so," he said.

"You know how difficult it is to prosecute a powerful man in Southeast Asia. Even those responsible for the genocide here in Cambodia have gone unpunished."

"Mr. Cha?" Alam asked, sliding into his chair. His plate looked as if he was eating in a fine French restaurant: a little of this, a bit of that, all carefully arranged. I was surprised not to see a sprig of parsley or a tiny flower floating in a little sauce.

"Are you one of those people who can't stand if a pea rolls over to the mashed potatoes?" I asked apprehensively. I'd been around men who were like that.

"No," he said. "Don't worry. This is just my first course. I need to ponder my main."

I looked at my plate, on which appetizers mingled with the fish main course, a slice of fruit acted as a barrier between vegetable and bread. A waiter set down a bowl of soup in front of me.

Alam cut into a neat row of hearts of palm. "I don't see that there's anything we can do about him. He's been terribly devious."

"Killed three people," said P.P.

"Three that we know of. Who knows how many more?" Alam put the hearts in his mouth.

"Kidnapped some," P.P. said.

"Yes, I wonder how the Thai police are handling that."

"Well, I think Barker and Jolly's idea of harming his business might be the way to go." I should have gotten the soup first and eaten that, then gone and piled up my plate, so that everything didn't get cold. Now I was torn.

"Illegal," said P.P. Neither Alam nor I said a word. He added, "Illegal to kill, too,"

"We'll have to talk with them."

"With Mr. Cha and the Ghost?" P.P. said in alarm.

"No, Barker and Jolly."

"Or not," said Alam.

"What do you mean?" I asked.

"Just what I said. Let Barker and Jolly do what they're going to do. Let Martha contact her environmental groups. See what they can do about his logging. No doubt some aspect of it is illegal."

"But then if they get caught—"

"Their decision." P.P. was making short work of his pile of food.

"Yes, just as P.P. helped the young women Cha held captive at his house. That was his decision."

"I see what you mean."

"Don't have to be involved," P.P. said before taking two enormous bites in a row, so that his round face grew rounder.

"Well, I am involved, you know. He's been trying to kill me. And you too, P.P."

"Right, but you don't have to be part of the solution," said Alam.

I finished my soup, leaving me with the rest of the food on my plate to get through. Luckily, I have multiple stomachs, like a cow, and there would still be room in my dessert stomach. As I was scanning the desserts table, I realized Alam was watching me. "What?"

"For someone so small, you can really put it away."

"I'm an active person."

"Not," said P.P., standing.

I began to object.

"I think he may have been speaking about himself," said Alam, translating for him. P.P. bounced his way toward the buffet.

"God, how can he eat more than what he already had?" I said.

"You're stopping?"

"No way. Did you see those desserts?"

Alam laughed as he rose. "I'm going to get my main course."

38

I looked at myself in the mirror. I was still myself. The crazies hadn't killed me. I could have been dead by now. If I were dead, my parents would mourn. My brothers would mourn. Dead, and for what? Some fake art?

I looked at myself in profile, untucked my loose shirt where it had gotten caught in the back of my pants. I pulled at the purple streak of hair, tucked it behind my ear. I'd change that color when I got home. Maybe pink. It hadn't been pink in years.

What did I want from life? Martha wanted to save the world. Alam wanted to save people's hearts from giving out. P.P. wanted *things*. Other people seemed less clear, and I supposed that I was more like them.

We weren't meeting for another half an hour. Clarity wasn't going to come to me looking in the mirror. All I saw was a short young woman who looked to be at a loss. That wasn't helpful. I reached for my backpack.

I'd given everyone the option not to go to Preah Khan for the performance that afternoon, just as I'd told them they shouldn't feel obligated to go back to the Bakong in the morning. But they were all game. Only Barker seemed hesitant. At first I thought he was afraid, but I quickly realized it was his concern for Courtney.

Quite sweet, really, though a bit overprotective. I would suffocate with that kind of attention.

When I went downstairs, none of the rest had left their rooms yet, and the bar hadn't acquired the lively look of a five o'clock bar, or even a noontime bar. I smiled at the bartender and waiter.

"Scotch, miss?" the waiter asked as he set down a bowl of nuts.

"Never again. Iced tea, please. But first I have a question for you."

"Yes, miss." He stood at attention, and I noticed, for the first time, that his pants were a bit too big, his sleeves a bit too long. Perhaps he hadn't had this job long and still wore the last waiter's clothes.

"Does everyone in Siem Reap know Mr. Cha?"

He frowned, then answered diplomatically. "It is a small town, miss. It looks large, but it is small."

It looked pretty small to me. "Is he a bad man?"

He looked uncomfortable.

"I'm asking for myself, out of curiosity, not for the police or anyone else. Let me rephrase that. I think he's a bad man. I think he's responsible for the attempts on my life. Is that in line with what local people think about him?"

He was really frowning now.

"Would most people agree with me?"

"Yes, miss," he lowered his voice to a whisper. "And the Ghost. He is a very, very bad man. Maybe more bad."

"Tell me." Of course he seemed worse—he carried out the killings, he was the weapon. But was the weapon more lethal than the one giving the order to wield it? I wasn't sure.

He leaned toward me. "He killed many people during the killing."

"Why has he not been tried?" I whispered. I knew that was a stupid question as soon as it was out of my mouth. "I'm sorry," I said. "Hardly anyone was tried, and then only recently."

"That is right, miss. He went to Thailand with Mr. Cha, where they found new names. So that when they came back here to do business after the war, people could only say that they were the same men who had killed many, but they could not prove this."

"I see. Thank you for being honest with me."

Pretending to wipe something from the low table in front of me, he lowered his voice even further. "One person who went to the police to complain about him died. A machete." He stood up and said more loudly, "Yes, miss. I will get your iced tea."

The bartender had heard the beginnings of our conversation, so the iced tea was already on the bar waiting for him. I had spent time in Vietnam. I had spent time in Myanmar. In both places, people lowered their voices when they gave you information that might be incriminating in some way. Even when no police were around. Even when speaking to friends or around friends. This young waiter and the bartender seemed to be friends, but he'd still whispered.

Fear, real fear. Not surprising in a country where thousands had died for nothing more than wearing glasses, for being literate.

When he returned, I asked, "Have you heard that Mr. Cha kidnaps women?" Out of the corner of my eye I saw that the bartender was nodding.

"Yes, miss. Women do not want to go to his house to work because they may not come out of the house."

"And the families of these women who don't come out. Do they do anything?"

"They complain to the police."

"The man who was here yesterday?"

"No, to the head police."

"So he wasn't the police chief?"

"No. He is a detective. He is a good man." He hesitated. "His daughter has disappeared."

"Oh, that's terrible. Do you think that Mr. Cha took her?"

He shrugged. Speaking in general was one thing, I supposed; the specifics were way too scary.

I reached for my iced tea and he walked away. Had I made a mistake by not telling the detective everything? I could still contact him, but he hadn't given us a card or even identified himself. To me, at least. I'd have to ask P.P. if he'd given him one. No, I would see the policeman soon enough at Preah Khan.

"That's a big scotch," said Mr. Jolly.

"Iced tea."

"My idea exactly." He signaled the waiter and pointed at my drink. "Let's get a couple of pitchers."

"When we get back after the performance. Do you have all your cameras?" Mr. Jolly's assortment of cameras had become a joke within the group.

"Absolutely," he said complacently, and flashed me the inside of his vest, with its many pockets for cameras. He was at ease with my teasing. "I've been lying on my bed conniving."

"Oh, dear. And what have you been conniving?"

The waiter set down his iced tea.

"A downfall."

He didn't need to say more. I didn't want to hear more. "Sounds very naughty."

"Yes, very."

I thought for a moment. "We hear a lot, especially on TV shows, that big business is a nest of vipers—stealing company secrets from each other, hacking, theft of all sorts—is any of that true?"

"In some cases yes. Not in all," he said seriously. "I can tell you in all honesty that I have never sunk to those lows. Fortunately, the nature of my businesses doesn't really require me to. But I have discovered that one needs to keep some hackers on one's payroll. To keep people off one's turf, you understand."

"Self-defense, so to speak." I smiled.

"Yes. I have some very talented young people in my IT department." He leaned forward confidentially. "Some of them have spent time in the clink."

I laughed, both at the antiquated term and at his pride in hiring ex-cons.

"They're very appreciative that I've given them jobs with pay commensurate with their talents. They're also very appreciative of having the opportunity to flex their muscles. Their minds, those busy fingers on the keyboard. I sometimes call them into my office to regale me with their past feats. The ones that landed them in the clink. Public record, you know, so they aren't telling me anything new." He looked off dreamily. "Well, occasionally."

"You needn't say more."

"About what?" Barker asked, sitting down. He motioned to the waiter, who brought him an iced tea.

"About our little escapade. Where's Courtney?"

"She's coming. Takes her longer to get ready."

I heard laughing on the stairs, and Courtney, Martha, and Mrs. Jolly entered the bar.

One of the receptionists came in. "Your bus is here, miss."

"Thank you. We'll be out in just a moment."

Barker took a few quick sips of his iced tea, and Courtney walked up, wrested it from his hand, and gulped a few herself. She was looking a little more put together than in the morning. We were going to go into town after the performance, first for a last jaunt through the marketplace, then for dinner at another posh restaurant.

"You're sure you want to go?" Barker looked up at Courtney, who was standing next to his chair.

She tousled his hair. "Worrywart. I'll be fine."

As the group headed toward the entrance, I trailed behind them, thinking about our first meeting. They'd been a little wary of each other, but now P.P. listened intently to Martha, nodding, saying a word or two, then taking her arm to steer her up onto the bus. Barker and Mr. Jolly had their heads together, laughing like old friends at something one of them had said. Courtney spoke earnestly to Alam, probably about the new life she was planning.

Mrs. Jolly seemed to be thinking along the same lines. Slowing to wait for me, she said, "Isn't it wonderful, dear, how we've all become friends? I wouldn't have thought it that first night. I said to Mr. Jolly, it's such a disparate group, I'm not sure about traveling together for such a long time."

"Yes, yes it is." I flushed to hear her call her husband Mr. Jolly.

"Ready?" the driver asked when we'd taken our seats. It was one of his few English words. Martha had tried to teach him new words, but "ready" was the only one he had any use for.

The driver's voice was jarring to me, probably because he wasn't Vuthuy. More jarring was the empty seat at his side, where Vuthuy would have been cheerfully talking about Cambodian dance, the heat, the Bakong, where we'd gone this morning.

I looked out the window to shut out his absence and thought about the morning.

I was happy that the group had chosen the Bakong as the temple they wanted to visit again. It made the trip seem complete. Our first day and our last, not to mention the complex symbolism the temple brought to mind. The driver's brother was a monk at the monastery that lay within the grounds of the Bakong, and he had arranged for us to have a cup of tea with the abbot. It was a lovely visit.

"Are you okay?" Alam said from behind me.

"Yes. Fine."

"That empty seat."

"Actually, I was thinking about the abbot this morning. He was very kind. He seemed to know what we all needed."

"Yes, he understood."

"And he didn't smile when he talked of death."

"That's bothered you, too?"

I turned to look at him. "Everyone here seems to smile when they speak of the genocide. I know it's the awkwardness, the terror of it all, a way to try to overcome the reality, but I find it disconcerting. I think it distances us, the visitors, the foreigners, from what happened. Which may be the unconscious intent. I'm not so sure that it's healthy for the Cambodians."

"Hard to know. Cultural." The minibus stopped at the checkpoint for the archaeological complex. A guard came inside and walked down the aisle comparing the photos on the passes with the people.

"This is a first," I said. Usually they just tallied up the passes and the passengers.

"Yes. I wonder why."

Barker caught my eye as I was looking down the aisle. "It's been a great trip, Jenna," he said. "I just want you to know how much we've enjoyed it. We could have done without the murder and the murder attempts, but really, it's opened my eyes."

"It's not quite over. Tomorrow to Phnom Penh, the Silver Pagoda, the museum. The grand finale."

The driver took the passes back from the guard and handed them to Mr. Jolly behind him. He took his own out of the pile, then passed them back to the rest of us. We set off down the long approach that ended at the south side of Angkor Wat.

I pointed out some elephants working at the side of the road. One held a giant log in his trunk, while another was up-rooting a tree.

"Stop, stop!" cried Mrs. Jolly. She hadn't missed a photo op the entire week. "My grandchildren!" As she climbed off the bus, she instructed Mr. Jolly on the angle she wanted.

THE mahouts happy with their tips and the elephants having taken a bow, I moved back and sat next to P.P. When the bus reached the moat that surrounded Angkor Wat, the driver turned right.

No one else noticed, but I called out, "No, no, we're going to Preah Khan."

"Ta Prohm," he said. "Police, Ta Prohm."

"But our performance."

He shook his head, shrugged his shoulders, and kept on driving.

"Why are we going to a different temple?" Courtney asked fearfully, falling into her earlier role of vulnerable female.

"I don't know. He just said police. They must have moved the performance."

"Let's go back," Barker said, being protective again.

"No, we're going on," said Mrs. Jolly. "We promised that young woman we would see her dance. Her troupe is counting on our money. You two can stay on the bus if you like. I suspect the performance has been moved for our safety."

"We can give them the money." Barker had moved across the aisle to sit beside his wife. "We don't have to watch them dance to give them the money."

"I will not let a hoodlum dictate what I do," said Martha. "I want to see this performance. I think it will be a high point of our journey. Those modern dancers, just like the dancers of old. I already have the picture in my mind."

I looked out the window, the closest one could get to escape on a bus. I had to look across P.P. Thinking I was trying to catch his eye, he raised his eyebrows in anticipation, but I didn't have anything to say. The change in plans made me anxious as well. Was the police detective working with the Ghost? Had they contrived to get us in a spot where we would all be macheted to death, blown up by a bomb, machine-gunned down like criminals in front of a firing squad? The last seemed unlikely, but I could quite vividly imagine the rest.

But it wouldn't make sense, the detective getting us killed or kidnapped. Unless he planned to trade us for his daughter. That was a possibility.

I frowned, and P.P. asked, "Problem?"

"Don't know," I muttered.

Voices were rising. Something needed to be done.

"Please calm down," I said. "We're all on edge. Let's just wait until we get there. Someone will be able to explain. And if we still feel nervous, we don't have to go into the temple. We'll just go into town and get more single-malt scotch."

That got a few chuckles, but Barker couldn't let it go. "You may want—"

Alam said calmly, "She's right. Let's just see."

We passed the enormous pyramidal form of Pre Rup rising on our left. "Remind me which one is Ta Prohm," said Mrs. Jolly.

"It's the temple with all the trees growing from the walls. It was built the same time as Preah Khan, by Jayavarman VII."

"J7," someone said, and the group laughed.

"He was some developer," said Mr. Jolly. "You environmentalists would have had your hands full with him."

Martha laughed. "Yes, we would. Especially since he was building religious establishments. Some right-wing fundamentalist must have been supporting him."

More laughter, and everyone settled down for their last look at the tanks and temples that make up this enormous site.

39

"Here," said the driver emphatically, as if we wouldn't have known. Buses and vans, motorcycles and hawkers filled the large, sandy parking area. Women carrying scarves and all the other paraphernalia for sale descended on our bus, jockeying for the spots closest to the door.

"Well, we certainly aren't alone here."

"Safety in numbers," said Mrs. Jolly cheerfully, already headed out the door. She was fearless.

"I'm staying on the bus," said Barker.

Courtney kissed his cheek and said firmly, "I'm not."

Looking out the window, I said, "The detective is here. The one who came to talk to me after the landmine."

"He's probably in Cha's pocket," said Barker just loudly enough for me to hear.

"No, apparently not. His daughter is missing."

The detective was walking our way, a smile on that implacable face, if I wasn't mistaken.

"You are safe here," he said, shooing away the hawkers.

"And not at Preah Khan?"

"We don't know yet. We caught him there. The Ghost. He had a landmine of the kind that killed your guide."

"That's great! Can you prosecute him for having the landmine?"

"Yes, we can. The serial number on the mine was not far from the number on the mine that your guide stepped on."

"That sounds incriminating," I said.

"But there is more. We were able to get a fingerprint on the mine that exploded, and I feel certain it will match his."

"That certainly sounds cut and dry. And it's a huge relief. I'm surprised, though, that a fingerprint could survive an explosion like that."

"Yes, it is a surprise." The hint of a smile left his face.

"And . . ." I hesitated. "And his boss?"

"Once we found the landmine, we were forced to search his boss's house." He looked around him at our group. Everyone was listening intently. He nodded to P.P.

"We found another landmine and many weapons in the old man's room. Nothing in Cha's part of the house, except his servants. We brought them all in for questioning." The smile returned.

"And your daughter?"

"How did you know?"

"Siem Reap is a small town."

"Yes, my daughter. Others' daughters. Many people are happy tonight."

"And Mr. Cha?'

"He is not so happy. We have brought him in as well. But he will not stay long. His lawyer arrives shortly from Phnom Penh. The chief has given him some good food, a comfortable place to wait." He looked at me to see if I understood that Mr. Cha had the chief in his pocket.

"I understand. But isn't the kidnapping of the women enough to hold him?"

"He says he knows nothing. He blames all problems on his servant. If that does not work, he will threaten the families. He has threatened the families. They are not saying anything."

"Has he threatened you?"

"He does not need to say anything. He merely looks at me and I see the threat."

"And you're afraid."

He looked me in the eye. "I have just gotten my daughter back. I need to protect her and my other daughter, my wife. I understand the threat, and—" he shrugged.

I wanted him to take a stand, but I understood. "Well, as we say in English, there's more than one way to skin a cat."

He frowned.

"Kings have been brought low by more than the assassin's bullet," said Mr. Jolly, making the point more clearly than I.

"Did you know that P.P. got the women he held in Bangkok released? He will be charged with kidnapping there, I imagine."

A smile flitted across his face. "We are not in America. And he is a powerful man."

"No. No, it isn't America. It's hard for us to make the adjustment."

He began to walk away.

"Why did you move us here to Ta Prohm?" I pointed toward the walkway ahead of us, leading to the temple.

"We want to make certain that the Ghost hasn't already laid down any landmines at Preah Khan. I do not know how he thought he could single you out from the group. He may have intended to kill all of you."

"The cad!" Martha said. I could see the fire igniting her. If Barker and Mr. Jolly weren't able to bring down Mr. Cha financially, she would do it by making problems for his logging business. "You and I have to talk, young man. I need some information."

"The dancers are waiting for you," he said. "I am afraid there are many people who have gathered to watch."

"But that's wonderful," Martha said. "I just hope that there will be room for us."

"Don't worry," he smiled.

When one speaks of an ancient Khmer temple, one is really talking about an enormous compound, a city. One ancient stone inscription records details about life at Ta Prohm, where eighty thousand people maintained the temple—priests, cooks, laborers, dancers. The approach to the temple is long, and though the police try to keep out the hawkers, there are always musicians, often blind or legless, lining the walkway, playing traditional instruments.

As we drew near, I saw that there were dozens of people lining the path, some sitting, some standing, all looking our way. I hesitated.

"It is fine," said the detective, who was walking beside me.

"Who are they?"

"Local people who have come to pay their respects to the person who is responsible for the arrest of the Ghost."

We walked. People bowed. Some reached out to touch us in gratitude. Some offered gifts. "So many people," I said, emotion welling up.

"So many murdered by this man."

"But Mr. Cha?"

"His time will come. The Ghost was his good luck. We all hope his luck has run out."

An old woman stepped in front of me. I realized she was the shopkeeper who had sold Alam and me the cushion covers. She extended a bag to me and said something in Khmer.

"Her husband and all her children. He killed them during the genocide."

Tears filled my eyes. This is why she had let me know that the Ghost was evil. "*Aw khon*," I said. Thank you. I touched her hand.

"Look!" Martha cried out. "It's Vuthuy's wife." A tidy young woman was pressed between two young girls, each wrapping an arm around her. They stared at us, the two girls looking nervous,

Vuthuy's wife determined. "I told you about our conversation with her. She's a weaver. Vuthuy encouraged her and the weavers in their neighborhood to form a cooperative. He was a supportive husband."

The detective said something in Khmer to Vuthuy's wife, who nodded. She responded to the detective. He frowned a little, asked her a question, then translated. "She says her husband wanted them to form a cooperative and set up a stall in the market."

"Oh, dear," said Martha. "She didn't mention the stall in the market. I suspect it is expensive to rent one of those stalls. We'll have to help her with that, too. We've already agreed to help with the cooperative, and we should help her with the stall too. Please tell her that."

"Yes, yes," said Courtney, who had joined us in time to hear the conversation.

He translated, and a brief smile flitted over her plain features, turning her into someone lovely. She spoke again.

"She is asking if she might request another thing from you." The detective looked uncomfortable, apparently not happy with the job of translator, or with this woman's requests.

"Of course," I said.

She hesitated. The two girls nudged her, and the older one nodded encouragement. A string of sentences burst from her, so quickly that I wondered if she had rehearsed what she wanted to say.

"She asks for her daughters. Girls do not have the advantages of boys—school, the opportunity to leave the village, to go to university. She and Vuthuy do not have sons, and her husband wanted education for their daughters."

Martha nodded. I said, "That's wonderful."

"She asks if you would help with her daughters' educations. A sum of money each year to pay for books and uniforms. Not so much. Here in Cambodia," he explained, "parents must pay the teacher a small amount to add to the little salary the government gives him."

"We'd be happy to do that," I said. "And if they need a bicycle to get to school, we'll help pay for that too." To Martha, I said, "Few girls here go on to middle school because the schools are often farther away than the local elementary schools, and their parents are nervous about them walking long distances. There's a nonprofit here that supports young girls by giving them bicycles and their families a yearly stipend to pay their expenses. We can find out what they provide and give an equal amount."

"Perfect," Martha said.

"I want to pay for the girls," said Courtney from behind us. "It will give me an excuse to come back, so I can watch those two girls grow up and go to university."

"Yes, dear, that would be a very good thing for you to do," said Martha.

"We must go in," said the detective.

"We'll speak with you more after the dance," said Martha. "You must come watch, too. After all, it is your heritage." She took Vuthuy's wife's arm, and the younger girl reached for her other hand.

As we walked, I said looking around me, "I just hope that it all works out as these people hope. That the Ghost goes to trial. That he's convicted."

"He will never get to trial," said the detective as he nodded at someone, a friend, a relative.

"But you said all these people think it's over with him."

"It is over. He will be killed in the jail. He has so many enemies. It's not possible that he will be tried. There is nothing that we can do to protect him."

"Are you happy with that?" I asked, astonished.

"It is the only justice we will get."

A young woman reached out to me, and I stopped. With her lovely round face and full cheeks, she looked familiar. Then I realized. "Your daughter?"

"Yes, my daughter. Alive."

She handed me something small wrapped in cloth, but as I began to unwrap it, she took it back from me and dropped it into the bag the old woman had given me. "*Aw khon,*" she said. "*Aw khon.*"

THE detective was right. Dozens of people were crowded around the spot the dancers had chosen for their performance. A silk-cotton tree grew out of the wall and rose like an enormous banner above the temple, the audience, and the stage.

The detective parted the crowd and led us to chairs that had been set up for us.

"Why do they get to sit there?" yelled out a tourist who was squished between an overweight man and the wall.

"They're paying for the performance," said the detective.

"Shut up. They could make us leave," said another tourist to the first.

Alam sat next to me and draped his arm over the back of my chair. I looked at him, startled, but he didn't notice. He was watching for the performers.

Musicians sat to one side of the tamped-down area where the dancers would perform. One rose and approached Martha, the oldest of us, bowed, and said something. The detective replied. She looked at me, astonished, then came to me and thanked me as well.

"It was really all of us," I said to him as she walked away. "Martha and Mrs. Jolly were the first to talk about how evil he was."

"Would they have met him without you?"

"No, but—"

P.P. stood up. "I would like to say a few words—to my group, to the Cambodians gathered here." He nodded toward some of the tourists. "Please bear with me.

"I've learned a great deal during the week I've been in Siem Reap—about the past." He waved an arm toward the temple.

"Cambodian history, and, not least, the burden of the recent genocide. I owe a debt to Jenna, our lecturer, and to Vuthuy, our guide"—he nodded at Vuthuy's wife—"for sharing their knowledge.

"I also owe a debt to the Khmer people, who have welcomed us to their country and treated us with such generosity and kindness. Sadly, the person who made us most welcome is not with us today. I'd like to dedicate this performance to his memory, to Vuthuy. You are missed." He nodded abruptly, his eyes brimming with tears, and sat.

Our group clapped, and many joined in. Whispers sped through the crowd, and I suspected someone passed the word of how Vuthuy had died. The detective leaned toward Vuthuy's wife to translate. Martha wiped a tear and said to me, "Who knew?"

I knew. I smiled at my friend, who hadn't looked up since sitting down. I knew that P.P. was a sentimental soul who cried when he watched movies and who had armored himself in his telegraphic speech.

The music began: the steady thrum of the drums, the eerie stringed instrument, the wavering voice of the elderly woman who took up the song first, then was joined by two other singers.

The crowd gradually fell silent, and as the first of the dancers entered, oohs and ahs muttered through the throng. I felt goosebumps as Srey followed. She wore the headdress of an Angkor Wat *apsara*. The metallic threads and bright silks of her costume shimmered in the afternoon light, and as she raised her arms in a graceful gesture, I looked past her at the temple, testament to a bygone era. The singer's high, thin voice rose as the beat quickened ever so slightly and the other dancers joined Srey in gestures from the past.

Leap appeared and stood where the dancers had come in, his arms across his chest.

"Just look at him. He's so proud," said Martha.

"Lovely. Yes, he must love her very much." My chest felt tight, and I glanced over at Alam.

"Don't worry. You'll find someone. I'm sure of it." Martha patted my arm. She looked at Alam's arm and muttered, "Though maybe you have."

I flushed. Was I so transparent, so obviously in search of someone? I hadn't thought of my dash from one man to the next as a search, but rather as a movement from one potential set of problems to another.

Martha patted my arm again and turned back toward the dance. Looking from her to Mrs. Jolly, I was suddenly sure that they had talked about me. About why I was alone. About Alam and me. I would find someone, she said. Yes, I would, if I could only sit still for a moment.

Mr. Jolly handed a video camera to Mrs. Jolly and, patting his various pockets, settled on his panoramic digital, then stepped back to include the tree in the shot. It would take a wide-angle to catch all this: the sense of the place, of its history, the thousands it took to build a single temple of the dozens of temples. The mystery evoked in each and every one of the silk-cotton trees as they sprouted, tiny seedlings taking root in the inch of soil stranded between carved building blocks.

Mrs. Jolly raised the video cam and swung it slowly around to capture the audience, silent, attentive, in awe of this spectacle of another time.

"Wonderful," Alam said, his arm still over my chair, though not touching me.

"Yes, truly," I said, looking at his profile. I shook myself of the magic of the place. I needed to watch the performance.

Mrs. Jolly brought the camera back toward the musicians and settled it on the steady base of her hands. I was pleased to think that we would all be able to look again at this event.

"A balm," said Martha. "This performance is the balm we needed."

"Yes, it's the perfect way to end our time in Siem Reap." Barker had been right in feeling that today was the end of our trip. Phnom Penh would be anticlimactic after this.

40

"I don't know what it is about airports that exhausts one so," said Martha as we stood watching the doorman unload our suitcases from the back of the small bus.

"It's like some people," Mrs. Jolly said behind us. "The ones who drain the energy right out of you. Like Arthur Philen."

"Yes," I said. "It's exactly like that." The flight from Siem Reap to Phnom Penh is only a quick hop, but the trip had already taken hours: rising absurdly early, hurrying through a light breakfast, arriving at the airport, then waiting an extra hour for the plane, which was late for no apparent reason other than that we were in Cambodia.

"I'm going in to see how my husband is getting on," Mrs. Jolly said. He'd taken our passports and accompanied our Phnom Penh guide into reception to check us in. I was hoping he would come back soon with the room assignments, so we could tag the bags. We had a lot to do today, and I wanted to get going. First the Palace and the Silver Pagoda, then lunch, then the afternoon at the museum. One of the best in the world, as far as I was concerned.

"No, no," P.P. shouted as the doorman set his briefcase down as if he were flinging a bag of garbage.

I cringed and wondered, not for the first time, why P.P. didn't just carry it with him like any sensible person would.

"Here, I'll oversee this," said Mr. Jolly, waving at the suitcases as he hurried down the steps. "You go in and tell the group the schedule. I'll make sure the right bags go to the right rooms."

"Okay." I grabbed my suitcase to carry up myself. The fewer the staff had to deliver, the sooner we would get out of here. I needed to change our lunch reservation to a later time, wanted to use the bathroom, to change my shoes, hang up a dress for tonight's last dinner.

"Should we get our own suitcases?" Courtney asked anxiously.

"If you like, but they're putting the room numbers on them now and should have them up quickly.

"I'd rather not wait. Get mine, will you dear?" she said to Barker. He turned and headed out the door. The balance of power seemed to have shifted.

"Let's meet down here in fifteen minutes," I announced. "No need to change. You know we're running a little late."

"See you then," said Mrs. Jolly as she headed toward the rooms, key in hand.

"I think I'll grab mine, too," said Alam. "Want to get my camera."

"You put your camera in your suitcase?"

"Sure."

I watched him head out the door. Well, we were certain to get out in fifteen minutes if everyone carried up his own bag. I looked around the expansive, well-ferned lobby. The old building had been perfectly renovated. It was too bad we didn't have more time to enjoy it. Tomorrow we'd fly early to Bangkok, then home. I was ready.

"Miss, you have a message."

My heart double-thumped, as one's heart does when an unexpected message arrives in an unlikely spot. I thought of my brother Eric and kicked myself for not being in closer contact with my mother. I took the message and ripped open the envelope.

Don't forget to check in with me. Arthur Philen.

Honestly, trying to manage me from afar. I handed the envelope back to the receptionist. "You can throw this out." I'd check in when I walked in the door of the museum two days from now.

Mr. Jolly came in. "Well, that was easy. Everyone but Martha took their bags. How long do we have?"

"About ten minutes."

"See you shortly," he said.

The group hurried in silence, everyone thinking of how they'd fill the ten minutes.

"Looks like our rooms are next to each other," Alam said as he unlocked his door.

"Yes, it does." Down the hall, Mr. Jolly was looking our way. He was the one who had gotten the room keys from the receptionist for us. Was that a smug expression on his face? I would have to watch out for these people. It was bad enough having a mother who tried to fix me up, let alone an entire contingent of museum patrons.

"HERE we are at the museum," the guide said, pulling open the door of the bus. We'd been spoiled in Siem Reap by Vuthuy, who had been so charming, so knowledgeable, so easy in sharing stories, facts, insights. After about five minutes of listening to this fellow, the group had turned away en masse and questioned me instead. He wasn't happy about that. It occurred to me that I could help him out a little by giving him a guidebook before leaving. After all, I had planned on giving all my books to Vuthuy.

As I stood, my water bottle fell to the floor and rolled under the seats. I waited for the others to walk by before getting down on my knees to retrieve it. When I finally recovered it, three rows back, everyone else had left the bus, climbed the steps to the museum entrance, and was entering the building. I hurried to catch up, clambering off, taking the first step in a bound.

"You will not get away with this," Mr. Cha said, coming around the rear of the bus.

I turned quickly, expecting a gun to be aimed in my face.

Mr. Cha looked cool and calm in the blazing heat. "You cannot steal my servants from me," he said. "This does not make me happy."

"I haven't stolen any servants from you. I don't know what you're talking about." The lie came smoothly out of my mouth. Surprising what adrenaline allows one to do. It coursed through me, prickling my arms.

"He has been with me since I was a boy."

"Who?"

"You need to keep quiet. That is all I wanted to say. You need to keep quiet." He stretched his hand out in front of him, palm down.

I glanced up at the entrance to the museum, judging the distance I needed to run to get away from him. He was mad. No, not mad, but without humanity. Evil had become his way of living, and I doubted he even realized how far it had carried him from the rest of us. The others had turned and were coming back toward the steps, led by Mrs. Jolly. Oh, no, I thought. What is she going to do?

"Hello, Mr. Cha. How nice to see you. Are you visiting the museum today, too? You will join us, I hope."

He frowned.

She walked down the steps. "We so enjoyed our evening at your home. Jenna has spoken so highly of your collection and has been so appreciative of your kindness."

He looked uncertain.

I tried to look befuddled, which wasn't difficult. I was as confused as he was by Mrs. Jolly's friendliness. Then I realized what she was doing.

"No, thank you. I saw your group getting off the bus, and I thought—"

"Hello, hello," cried Alam, bounding cheerily down the steps. "It's so nice to see you. What brings you here to Phnom Penh? Are you joining us? Jenna, did you arrange this little surprise?"

"No, I—" I tried to maintain the veil of confusion. I didn't want this man, this murderer of thousands, to be angry with anyone in the group. Including me. Alam moved between us.

Cha's driver appeared behind him, glaring at us. Mr. Cha began to back away. The heat couldn't make him perspire, but this unexpected friendliness was giving him a little sweat mustache.

He looked at me for a long moment.

Then I saw it in his eyes. The instrument of his cruelty was gone, but his cruelty remained. His luck, his luck was gone, though he may have a dozen more to kill for him. But without his luck, he was afraid. We were arranged in front of him, and his driver was blocking his escape behind. Was the driver trustworthy? Mr. Cha must have wondered. Who could he trust? He had aged this past week, I saw. His body looked diminished. His angry eyes darted, no longer confident.

Then he saw that I saw. He pulled himself together. "I'll be off. Just saw you climbing off the bus and thought . . . Sorry. I have a meeting." And he turned on his heel, pushed the driver ahead of him, and left.

The others watched him leave, P.P. bouncing on his heels behind them, wise enough not to show himself, Courtney raising a hand to give Mr. Cha a little wave. All smiling as if the encounter were a pleasant one.

"We did it," Courtney said.

I didn't answer. I'd leave her with the fantasy that he'd been fooled. No need for all of us to be afraid. Hopefully he thought only P.P. and I knew his sins. As we climbed the steps, I let Alam take my arm. After all, he'd come to my rescue.

"Wonder if he's checked his finances today," I heard Mr. Jolly mutter to Barker.

"No, tomorrow. Remember? We decided to hold off until we were over the Pacific."

"Oh, that's right. I would like to see his face."

Martha had apparently overheard as well. "I told you that I spoke with my environmental group this morning. I'm meeting them at five. They're more than happy to try to thwart him. He's one of the worst offenders when it comes to logging. I learned that much from the detective."

"I'm going with you," Alam said.

Courtney fell back to walk by my side. "P.P. has put me in touch with the group taking care of the women Mr. Cha held captive in Bangkok. I'm helping them get home and begin new lives. And did I tell you one was the sculptor's daughter? He sent his thanks."

"That's wonderful." I was in a daze, with the fear that had pulsed through me, the adrenaline, the shift from what I thought was about to happen, to Mrs. Jolly's intervention. I gently detached myself from Alam and went to her. "That was brilliant."

"Yes, well. I wasn't exactly turning another cheek, merely presenting a different face. It's one of life's lessons. I learned it from my husband. Warmth and kindness will often achieve what confrontation never can." She stopped and took my hands.

"I'll remember that."

"I don't suppose that you will. Not right away. But it will come back to you. Hopefully the next time you get yourself in a fix. You seem to be quite good at getting yourself into fixes."

I laughed. "Yes, I suppose I am."

"It's all that energy that you have. And curiosity."

I nodded. I could see past her to the courtyard at the center of the museum and the many sculptures that filled it. In the gallery to the left the enormous bronze Vishnu that had been recovered from the western tank of Angkor was framed by the doorway. Vishnu lying on Anantasayin, the cosmic serpent.

Mrs. Jolly laughed as she watched my greedy eyes. "Get to your art, my dear. Get to it."